THE NUMEN OF BANDA

THE NUMEN OF BANDA

THE NUMEN OF BANDA FOLKLORE

About the book

The Numen of Banda follows Sosh, an iron-willed Kamba matriarch and Mau Mau war veteran from Kenya, who fiercely upholds traditional beliefs and customary laws. Her beloved grandson Benjo, a child prodigy, challenges these very traditions with his maverick views. Despite an inseparable bond between them and Sosh's vision of Benjo as her heir, their conflicting worldviews set them on a collision course. When tragedy shatters their fragile reality, Sosh reaches out for the mystical Numen of Banda, a legendary healer nested deep inside the Banda Salama Forest. In a quest to restore peace, ancestral spirits intervene, guiding Sosh and Benjo to navigate the delicate balance between honouring the past and embracing the future, weaving a tale of resilience, identity, and the enduring power of family.

Hillan Nzioka is a Kenyan-born literary enthusiast and natural storyteller who resides in Sydney, Australia. As a full-time career civil servant for the New South Wales Government, Hillan balances his professional life with his passion for writing. It is no wonder that no amount of bureaucratic engagement can erase his deep appreciation for the rich tapestry of his ancestral Kenyan culture. His observational humour and keen attention to the natural world distinctly influence his storytelling and infuse his narratives with vivid imagery and cultural depth.

To my family:

Pauline, my wife, Tina, my daughter, and Eric, my son.

You taunted, provoked, and occasionally wore me down, yet without you, this book would never have been finished.

Your relentless encouragement made all the difference.

The Numen of Banda is for you.

Contents

One

Chapter 1 – Sosh's Reign of Terror

The matriarch, perched on a rickety stool beneath a mango tree behind her dwelling house, shifted her haunches uncomfortably on the three-legged seat to reach for an earthen spittoon stowed beneath her perch. She lifted the lid and spat a mouthful of tobacco-contaminated spittle into the cuspidor before bellowing out the name of her twelve-year-old grandson, Benjo. In an instant, the poor boy burst out of a nearby hut and stood before his grandmother like an infantry soldier awaiting further instructions from a regimental drill sergeant.

"Go and tell your father to come and see me, now!" Grandma Sosh commanded without preamble or even lifting her eyes to meet Benjo's.

The boy stood still, listening carefully to his grandmother's diktats before quickly vanishing to carry out her wishes.

Benjamin Jogoo, affectionately known as Benjo, was a remarkable child whose decision-making skills were as sharp as those of an adult. His precocity was undeniable, and he had a natural talent for navigating complex situations with ease. Despite his exceptional abilities, Benjo's grandmother, Sosh, never openly expressed her fondness for him. However, she would occasionally let slip a Freudian comment, revealing her deep affection for her beloved grandson. Yet, she quickly brushed it aside to conceal her chronic atychiphobia.

Nonetheless, Benjo held a special place in Sosh's heart. She loved and cherished him deeply and, if given the opportunity, she would have mollycoddled him. Unfortunately, Sosh was too emotionally broken to provide the level of affection she desired for Benjo. Despite her disabilities, Sosh never missed a chance to offer him guidance and support in private. Sosh's advice to Benjo always concluded with a poignant reminder that a chameleon moves calculatedly, not to miss the footprint of its forefathers. She aimed to instil in Benjo a profound respect for the customs of his Aombe clan and the traditions of the Kamba people.

In return, Benjo absorbed Sosh's teachings in their entirety and kept them close to his heart as a token of gratitude. He understood the value of his grandmother's wisdom and cherished the unique privilege he had in receiving it. After all, when your grandmother tells you something, it is best not to run to your mother to find out if it is true.

Sosh's social and emotional struggles can be traced back decades, to the time of the Mau Mau war for independence against the British in colonial Kenya. The British had arrived in Kenya with the intention of imposing their will upon the people of this land, and many groups decided to fight back. One of the groups was known as the Mau Mau Rebellion, a violent protest movement against British rule in Kenya. The rebellion lasted from 1952 to 1960, and it had a profound impact on the people of Kenya. In retaliation, the British implemented ruthless tactics to quash any uprising, including the use of psychological warfare.

This British psychological warfare employed a variety of tactics, including false accusations, public humiliation, imprisonment and even torture to break the spirit of their victims. These practices had a devastating toll on the psychological well-being of those affected by them. Many Mau Mau fighters suffered from post-traumatic stress disorder depression and anxiety because of their experiences. Some were unable to cope with the psychological trauma they had endured and committed suicide as a result.

Tragically, this war had an irreversible psychological impact on Sosh's ability to express love and compassion towards others, including members of her own family. The savage suppression claimed the lives of an estimated eleven thousand innocent Kenyans, including Sosh's husband Jogoo. Mr Jogoo was captured on the outskirts of Nairobi while running errands for the Abardares Mau Mau command during Operation Anvil, which was conducted by the British security forces under General Erskine to flush out insurgents. The captors cut his tongue out before they strangled him and mutilated his body. Indeed, the psychological impact on Sosh and many other victims was so severe that it lasted for many years beyond the end of the Mau Mau rebellion and continues to affect many Kenyans today.

Unfortunately, due to complications arising from post-traumatic stress disorder caused by war-related experiences, Sosh's uncompromising demeanour was often misinterpreted as negative or hostile. And despite the end of the conflict, Sosh's inability to establish meaningful interpersonal relationships was palpable. Admittedly, since the end of the war, Sosh had not been observed publicly expressing compassion towards others, including members of her family, and even including her favourite grandson Benjo.

Sosh had served in the Kenya Land and Freedom Army (KLFA). Her confidential military discharge medical report noted that she exhibited significant symptoms of fear, anxiety, and anger, which resulted in emotional instability and unpredictability. Yet, despite her condition, Sosh was highly respected and feared in the community, thanks to her illustrious career in the KLFA. She remained one of only three female officers to ever attain the rank of field marshal. Her reputation in the south-eastern Yatta sub-county was unparalleled, earning her the admiration and respect of her peers. She was a trail-blazer, paving the way not only for other female officers but for her male counterparts as well.

Even as an octogenarian in her twilight years, Sosh's decisions remained resolute and decisive, and no one dared to challenge them. She superintended her family with an iron will, earning herself a formidable reputation among her peers for being as tough as reinforced concrete.

The KLFA was a formidable guerrilla force that fiercely resisted British colonial rule in Kenya between 1952 and 1960. Led by experienced ex-soldiers who had previously served in the African King's Rifles, a multi-battalion British colonial regiment that fought in both world wars, the KLFA bolstered their numbers by heavily recruiting and training hundreds of thousands of peasant farmers, many of whom were internally displaced natives alienated from their ancestral lands by British imperialism.

Sosh was a peasant recruit who rose through the ranks to become a field commander, graduating at the top of her class from the Wild School of Infantry (WSI) located deep within the Aberdare Forest. This school was renowned for its intense training, giving the KLFA a fearsome reputation and prompting one British journalist to dub the KLFA the "murderous Mau Mau rebellion". However, the Mau Mau moniker originated from the KLFA's secret codes, which were inadvertently picked up by the colonial press and popularized by right-wing British politicians in the 1950s. The phrase "Mau Mau" was a clever inversion of the Bantu words uma uma (get out, get out), which was a coded signal to alert fighters to evacuate quickly or take cover in anticipation of an imminent attack; when spoken quickly and repeatedly, it sounded like "Mau Mau" to British listeners.

If a person should be held accountable for all the good, he or she has not done, Sosh was guilty as charged. This was the reason she found herself sitting on a rickety stool beneath a mango tree behind her house, deep in thought and troubled. Due to her never-ending clan engagements, the matriarch had been putting off the decision to send her daughter-in-law, Minto, to consult with a medicine man. Those who were familiar with Sosh could confidently attest that it was uncharacteristic of her to procrastinate when it came to decision-making, no matter how simple or complex the situation was. Against this backdrop of frustrating delay, coupled with Minto's second miscarriage in as many years, the matriarch had had enough and resolved the night before to send her to consult with a witch doctor.

Sosh knew that she had to seek the intervention of Mesenet, the revered goddess of childbirth, to ensure safe and prosperous childbirth for her beloved daughter-in-law. She took the matter seriously and spent hours contemplating the best course of action. As she sat alone, lost in thought, time seemed to slip away from her. It wasn't until she felt drained, and so shifted her position, that she realized she had been lost in thought for over an hour, remaining in the same posture for that long. To make matters worse, she also realized that she had begun speaking to herself in a soliloquy, a behaviour that was both mortifying and frustrating. She scolded herself for losing focus and vowed to maintain her composure. With renewed determination, she continued her quest to ensure safe and successful childbirth for her daughter-in-law at any cost.

Sosh was known for her impulsive and spontaneous decision-making, which often led her to rely on her gut instincts for her final verdict. This trait was no surprise to those who knew her. However, when it came to Minto's medical attention, Sosh's indecision was a double-edged sword, much like the Kamba proverb states: do it and you will regret it; don't do it and you will regret it. No matter what decision she made, there would be consequences.

The situation was a contradiction in that any further delays in consulting a medicine man would worsen Minto's indisposition, while deciding to take Minto to a far-off land to seek medical attention would hurt Sosh's clan engagements. It was a difficult decision to make, and Sosh was feeling the weight of it.

Despite the conflicting priorities, Sosh boldly decided to send Minto to receive treatment from the revered Numen of Banda, who also served as the paramount chief of the Awe clan. When Sosh made decisions, they were unwavering and authoritative. She rarely sought out the counsel of third parties, except in extraordinary circumstances and in matters of life and death, such as when consulting the village oracle as the ultimate authority on a legal or metaphysical matter.

Due to her position of authority, Sosh's decisions were inevitably accepted as orders by her subordinates, including low-ranking foot soldiers, members of clan committees, family members and anyone else who was unfortunate enough to be captured by her decisions. The impact of Sosh's decisions was far reaching and profound, permeating down the ranks like dye bleeding into fabric. Her decisions set the tone for anyone who fell directly or indirectly under her authority.

Twenty minutes after being summoned by Benjo, Sosh's only son, Wasa, and daughter-in-law, Minto, arrived. They sat apprehensively before their mother, whom they secretly referred to as Hammurabi the Law-Giver. Hammurabi was a historical king of the Babylonian dynasty, notorious for his draconian laws and harsh punishments. The couple likened their mother to Hammurabi because of her quick temper and tendency to slap anyone who angered her. Fearing their fate, Wasa and Minto sat in silence, akin to cows resigned to their fate at a slaughterhouse.

About half an hour earlier, Benjo's frantic sprint had ended in a screeching halt outside Wasa's living quarters, whereupon he delivered to his parents the summons from Sosh to attend an imperative family gathering – much like a private detective serving a subpoena to a hapless recipient. As soon as Benjo informed his parents that Sosh wished to meet them urgently, Minto and Wasa exchanged a knowing glance. This was a common mannerism between the two, a reflexive response to the countless summons they had received from Sosh over the years. The couple was all too aware that their presence in such meetings was only to be seen, and not to be heard. Nonetheless, they had no choice but to comply with Sosh's irrevocable summons, whether they liked it or not. It was not going to be a comfortable affair anyway because Sosh was a patronizing old pain in the armchair.

Amid the tense silence, Minto's inquisitive mind began to wander, reflecting on ideas that seemed to come out of nowhere. As the more educated of the two, she was unencumbered by traditional folklore, a quality that was both a boon and a bane for her. Since her teenage years, Minto had always been opposed to the idea of consulting a traditional medicine man as an alternative to modern medical treatment. As an adult, Minto openly questioned how a man who had never stepped foot in a science classroom, who wore no underwear, and who walked with his genitals exposed could cure hormonal problems.

For this reason, Minto had personally decided that nothing short of the fear of Sosh's threat to strangle her would convince her to entrust her maternal health care to a dubious quack. Instead, she chose to boldly express her intention to visit a modern district hospital, consult a maternal health specialist, and undergo modern clinical laboratory tests.

Nevertheless, despite Sosh's disposition, Minto remained hopeful that her mother-in-law would view the situation from a rational perspective and choose to send her to a government hospital. Moreover, it was not lost on Minto that Sosh was eager to accept any solution that would bring an end to the series of stillbirths that had bedevilled her for years, provided that the solution did not damage Sosh's pride.

As the couple waited for Sosh to start the meeting, Minto found herself lost in thought once more. This time, she recalled a biology lesson from her favorite teacher, Lucy, during her Year 12 class. Teacher Lucy had explained that genetic abnormalities, not witchcraft, were the cause of spontaneous early pregnancy loss, also known as miscarriage. Minto remembered how Teacher Lucy emphasized that these genetic abnormalities could be caused by either an additional or missing chromosome in the nucleus of a pregnant woman's cells. In simpler terms, the teacher summarized the lesson by explaining that chromosomal aberration is a disruption in the formation of fetal genes, which can lead to stillbirth.

Teacher Lucy ensured that her students understood not only the senselessness of linking miscarriage to witchcraft but also the psychological harm that this falsehood causes to women who suffer from this unfortunate event. She also emphasized that those who miscarry are not at fault for their loss and that there is nothing they could have done to prevent it. Her lesson was in stark contrast to the Jungian archetypes of the Kamba traditional beliefs, which attributed all cases of miscarriage to witchcraft or infringement of taboo. Indeed, knowledge is not free; one must pay attention to acquire it, Minto concluded to herself.

Minto was reluctant to disclose her scientific explanation of miscarriage to her mother-in-law and husband. She recognized that their limited education may hinder their ability to understand the complexities of stillbirth, potentially leading to an unfortunate reaction, such as them accusing Minto of practising witchcraft. In such delicate situations, Minto needed to approach the matter with care and weigh the potential repercussions.

Moreover, Minto felt that she lacked the necessary language skills to translate complex scientific terminology from English syntax into the Kamba dialect, which made it challenging for her to convey the right information to them. After careful consideration, Minto ultimately decided not to share the scientific explanation of stillbirths with the duo, fearing she might be labelled a witch due to her infamous Aimu clan heritage.

The Aimu clan was a legendary and enigmatic group of individuals among the Kamba people that had existed for centuries. The clan was often associated with possessing potent witchcraft and magical powers, which had been passed down from generation to generation. Traditionally, their ancient knowledge of magic was shrouded in secrecy and only shared among their own. They utilized their mystical abilities to safeguard themselves and were renowned for their innate talent for detecting danger and repelling malevolent spirits.

A remarkable story of Aimu foresight is told about their successful prediction of the devastating famine of 1898, three years before it occurred. This prediction allowed them ample time to migrate temporarily to the neighbouring country of the Nyamwezi people in Tanganyika, where they remained until the famine had passed. The famine was catastrophic and pervasive throughout the entire Kamba land, killing nearly a quarter of the Kamba population, but the members of the Aimu clan were spared due to their mastery of interpreting omens.

Their magical prowess remained a source of awe and admiration, and their ability to protect themselves and others was unparalleled. Unquestionably the Aimu clan was a testament to the power of the ancient knowledge of the Kamba people and the importance of preserving it for future generations.

Eventually, Minto's inner conflict between modern medicine and traditional remedies was put to rest, as she chose to follow Sosh's decision irrespective of the consequences. Sosh's reputation for having a steadfast stance on matters made Minto hesitate to challenge her. Any attempt to challenge Sosh's decisions would have a snowball's chance in hell. It was like poking a hungry lion or, as Minto aptly thought of it, anger had become the dominant force in society, and people were akin to wounded lions, relentlessly seeking out vulnerable prey to devour. Minto, however, was determined not to become or willingly submit to being a prey anytime soon.

After what seemed like an eternity of silence, Sosh finally took a sip of water from a calabash and spat three times onto a nearby woolly caper bush before breaking the silence.

"Nga-Aimu," Sosh greeted her daughter-in-law with respect.

To which Minto submissively replied, "Woowi."

In Kamba culture, the term *nga-Aimu* referred to a woman belonging to the Aimu clan. It was considered a great honour to greet someone by acknowledging their clan origin, especially when greeting one's daughter-in-law. This tradition was deeply ingrained in the Kamba people's customs as a way of showing respect and appreciation for one's heritage.

During the traditional salutation between Minto and her mother-in-law, Minto's ululating response exemplified her humble submission to her superior mother-in-law's honourable greeting. This coded exchange was a customary way for a mother-in-law to greet her daughter-in-law in Kamba culture, signifying mutual respect and acknowledging the bond between the two families. Importantly, intra-clan marriage was taboo in Kamba culture, meaning that a daughter-in-law was always from a different clan than the family she married into.

The conversation between the two women was carefully crafted to avoid the use of each other's first names, as it was taboo in Kamba culture. It was considered disrespectful for a mother-in-law to address her daughter-in-law by her given or maiden name. Daughters are often named after their grandmothers or senior aunties and therefore calling them by their maiden names was deemed disrespectful to the senior family member after whom they are named.

To avoid any conflict, it was customary to refer to one's daughter-in-law by her clan's name. This practice prevented any accidental slip of the tongue that might lead to breaking the taboo. Violating this taboo could result in severe consequences, such as paying fines of up to seven goats or sometimes a bull to the daughter-in-law's kin.

Furthermore, the exchange of pleasantries before a meeting was a customary law that must be observed regardless of the meeting's intention. Even in acrimonious situations, such as mediating between two warring clans over disputes of murder or cattle rustling, exchanging pleasantries remained an essential aspect of communication in Kamba culture. This practice, believed to be dictated by ancestral spirits, was a way of showing respect and acknowledging the other person's presence and dignity.

"My daughter," Sosh began the family gathering with a commanding tone, "did you know that the umbilical cords of our ancestors are interred beneath the very earth on which we stand? And mine is among them."

Minto simply nodded in acknowledgment, fully aware that Sosh was not seeking a mere affirmation, but rather, creating an opportunity to share her reflections. Sosh's words conveyed a deep sense of reverence for their family heritage and the significance of their ancestral ties. She spoke with pride and respect for the traditions that had been passed down through generations.

Despite Sosh's captivating icebreaker, Minto couldn't help but feel that Sosh was preparing to deliver a truly impactful message. There was a sense of anticipation in the air, and Minto's attention was drawn to Sosh's every move.

Sosh was known for her relentless pursuit of perfection and her complete intolerance of any foolishness. Minto, keenly aware of this fact, recognised the shift in the air as Sosh began her pointed questioning. As Sosh's monologue unfolded, her facial expression hardened, and her voice dripped with fiery invective as she verbally lashed out at their neighbour. It was at this point that Minto understood Sosh was incensed by Kahab, suspecting the childless woman of being the witch responsible for Minto's heartbreaking stillbirths.

A descendant of the revered Aombe clan whose symbolic totem was the axe, Sosh's voice boomed through the room as she vehemently criticized Kahab, a childless woman from the less significant Asoka clan. Among the twenty-five Kamba clans, a fierce competition for supremacy thrived, with unofficial social hierarchy ranking the Aombe clan at the top, ahead of the other four in the big five clans.

Sosh could not fathom how a mere evil eye from Kahab could block her daughter-in-law's womb. Fury tightened her jaw as she glared around, determined to make her point. Unfortunately, in their Kamba community, barren women such as Kahab were often unfairly branded as witches, blamed for misfortunes like childhood illnesses and miscarriages. It was a misconception, a lingering echo of traditions that claimed to be right because it was always done that way in the past.

Nevertheless, although Sosh's words were blunt, they were not without reason. In Minto's era, the ability to conceive was highly esteemed, and those who were unable to do so, regardless of the cause, were frequently ostracized. Ms Kahab had been the subject of numerous rumours and allegations, and Sosh was merely the most recent in a lengthy line of individuals who had accused her of practicing black magic to harm others.

Despite Sosh's volatile temper, Minto was certain that she was mentally stable. Minto would often joke that Sosh wasn't insane, but rather had been in a perpetual bad mood for forty years. Nonetheless, Sosh's dedication to her clan heritage and her pursuit of perfection was boundless. Unfortunately, this often resulted in her becoming excessively emotional and irrational.

For starters, the Asoka clan boasted a rich and intriguing history, one that was steeped in tales of deceit and treachery. In the Kamba language, the name *Asoka* translates to "the sons and daughters of a snake" or simply "the descendants of a snake". This moniker earned the clan a reputation for being untrustworthy, a label that has persisted for generations.

Legend has it that the roots of the Asoka clan can be traced back to the twelfth century, when Mr Asoka and his wife were cast out from the mighty Aombe clan due to their cunning and duplicitous ways. Undaunted by this banishment, the Asoka family forged their own path, carving out a distinct identity as a separate Kamba clan through sheer determination and guile, defying the odds stacked against them.

Mr. Asoka, the revered and iron-fisted leader of the clan bearing his name, was consumed by a deep-seated paranoia, particularly regarding potential attack by the Aombe clan. This fear of real and imagined enemies grew so pervasive that whispers spread like wildfire of him decreeing the eradication of all snakes within sight – a drastic and uncompromising measure to quell the perceived threats, no matter how irrational, that plagued his mind. His fears were not without basis, however, given that the medicine men of the Aombe clan were reputed to wield power and command animals such as bees and snakes to attack the Maasai warriors during the fierce cattle rustling wars between them. Asoka's extreme precautions, though seemingly excessive, were rooted in the tales of the Aombe clan's formidable abilities, passed down through generations of the Kamba people.

Despite Asoka's deep-seated anxieties and the clan's turbulent beginnings, the Asoka clan persevered and flourished like a desert rose. They defied the odds, earning a reputation for their unparalleled shrewdness and ingenuity.

Their controversial roots, once a source of scorn, eventually gave way to grudging admiration and acceptance from other clans within the vast Kamba community. This shift was largely due to the Asoka's relentless determination and cunning in external trade with neighbouring tribes like the Kikuyu, Embu, and Mbeere. Their success greatly improved the overall economic status of the Kamba people.

As a result, the other clans turned a blind eye when occasional reports surfaced of economic frauds committed by Asoka clan members. In the Kamba's eyes, the Asoka's contributions simply outweighed their transgressions.

Armed with this hard-won acceptance, the clan thrived and gained notoriety for their cunning and guile, wielding these traits like finely honed blades. The Asoka members were characterized by a remarkable ability to deceive and manipulate those around them within the community, often utilizing their skills as deftly as a surgeon's scalpel to acquire power and wealth. Their ruthless pursuit of their objectives was widely recognized, and they were always willing to go to any lengths, no matter how unscrupulous, to achieve their goals. The Asoka clan's reputation for shrewdness and ambition preceded them, casting a long shadow that stretched far beyond the boundaries of the Kamba lands, etched into the records of the district commissioner in charge of economic crimes, marking them as a force to be reckoned with, feared and respected in equal measure, their exploits whispered in hushed tones even in the halls of colonial power.

The rumours surrounding Ms Kahab's alleged bewitching of Minto had cast her as the very embodiment of the Asoka stereotypes in the Yatta village. As a result, the villagers regarded Kahab as a notorious villain, a childless Circe, and an unrepentant troublemaker who brazenly defied societal norms, her very existence a thorn in the side of the community.

Interestingly, despite her status as a senior spinster, Ms Kahab had once been married to a wealthy local lapidary. However, the clan's council of elders had annulled the union on the murky ground of consanguinity, shrouding the decision in a veil of secrecy. Since then, she had remained unmarried, earning her the label of a professional spinster, a moniker that clung to her like a second skin. Nonetheless, her reputation had been further sullied by accusations of exploiting or meddling with the husbands and boyfriends of other women in the village, causing quite a stir in the community and cementing her as a pariah in their eyes.

Sosh's decision to verbally attack Ms Kahab was no mere whim; it was a calculated move born out of her legendary passion for battle and her reputation as a fierce warrior that preceded her. She was battle-hardened and always prepared to fight at the slightest provocation, her very presence commanding respect and fear in equal measure. No wonder, when whispers of rumours began to circulate that a woman from an insignificant clan had instigated her family's perils, Sosh's rage boiled over like molten lava. Incensed, Sosh remonstrated by lunging forward as if to grasp an imaginary Kahab, her fingers curling like talons, ready to strangle her with bare hands. Fortunately for Sosh, Kahab had already vanished from the village, seeking refuge far away after catching wind of the early warning about Sosh's intentions, leaving only the echoes of her infamy behind.

Frustrated by Kahab's sudden disappearance, Sosh erupted in a tirade of insults hurled into the air, directed at no one in particular. Her palpable arrogance was enough to make Minto tremble in her seat, the very ground beneath her seeming to quake with each venomous word. Unperturbed by the effect of her outburst, Sosh continued her berating unabated, her voice rising like a tempest: "I am *Katemi*, daughter of the mighty Aombe clan, a Mau Mau slasher who has never tasted defeat in battle, and a renowned gutsy swordswoman who has brought home a dozen human skulls from the bloody fields of Aberdare Forest!" Fortunately, Sosh's anger choked her before she could finish her rant, leaving her temporarily immobilized, a prisoner of her own rage. Despite her impressive reputation, Sosh's inability to control her emotions left her vulnerable and exposed, a chink in her otherwise impenetrable armour. Nonetheless, her choking anger did not prevent her from making her feelings about Ms Kahab known, her unspoken threats hanging heavy in the air and what else she intended to say was communicated by her non-verbal expressions.

Minto exhaled a deep breath of relief as the knot of anger in Sosh visibly loosened, the tension in the air dissipating like a fog under the morning sun. She knew from experience that Sosh's fury could quickly spiral out of control, escalating into a dangerous and potentially deadly situation, a storm that consumed all in its path. Sosh had a history of erupting into a homicidal rage when provoked, a reputation that had earned her the nickname *Katemi* among her peers, a moniker that struck fear into the hearts of all who heard it. This title had its origins in the Mau Mau war, where Sosh had carved her name into legend with each swing of her machete. In the Bantu languages, including Kamba, *katemi* translates to "one who cuts deeply," a fitting description for one of the war's most ruthless fighters, whose very presence on the battlefield was enough to turn the tide of conflict.

Having composed herself after the overwhelming anger, Sosh took a few measured steps towards the edge of the compound, her movements as calculated as those of a predator stalking its prey. Minto watched each step Sosh made closely. Sosh stopped near a thorn-apple bush, its gnarled branches reaching out like twisted fingers. Reaching for her snuff mull, she carefully scooped a pinch of tobacco onto her philtrum, the pungent aroma filling her nostrils and awakening her senses. Closing her eyes, she took a deep breath and inhaled a potent blend of formaldehyde granules that hit the perfect spot in her brain, igniting a violent sneeze that seemed to shake the very earth beneath her feet. The mollified expression on her face was a clear indication of immense satisfaction, a pleasure that only those initiated into the world of tobacco could understand. Minto, unfamiliar with the sensation, could only watch in fascination as Sosh savoured the moment, her anger momentarily forgotten in the rush of the tobacco's embrace.

After the powerful reflex, an involuntary reaction to nasal irritation, Sosh lifted her face upwards and inhaled deeply, filling her lungs with the fresh outdoor air. The air was imbued with petrichor, the golden fluid that flows through the veins of the immortals, a gift from the light showers of the previous night. The scent of the wet earth after the rain was invigorating, and Sosh felt a sense of renewal and rejuvenation wash over her. She took a moment to appreciate the beauty of nature and the simple pleasures in life, allowing the tranquillity to calm her frayed nerves.

Wasa and Minto did not take Sosh's berating lightly, for they were well acquainted with the devastating impact of her Intermittent Explosive Disorder. About a decade ago, Sosh had brutally attacked her neighbour, Mr Kiteme, with a machete, leaving him for dead following a dispute over Sosh's chicken that had wandered into and destroyed Kiteme's red haricot bean crop. When Mr Kiteme confronted Sosh at her home to voice his concerns, Sosh launched a vicious machete assault on him, inflicting life-threatening injuries upon the unsuspecting man.

Minto, the sole witness to the vicious assault, had been left with a lasting and profound impact, her nights haunted by recurring nightmares. Despite her best efforts, she had been unable to erase the traumatic memory of the attack from her mind. The sight of Mr Kiteme's injuries and the image of Sosh standing over him, wiping her bloodied machete on the victim's soiled pants, was enough to shatter Minto's resilience. However, what shocked her the most was the fact that Sosh was never held accountable for her heinous actions, a bitter pill that only added insult to injury.

If you were to ask Minto for her honest opinion, she would tell you that Sosh deserved to be locked away in solitary confinement for life. Unfortunately, to Minto's dismay, Sosh was released on a good-behaviour bond due to her impressive career as a freedom fighter. Minto strongly believed that the court's decision was a slap in the face to Kiteme's family and all those who had suffered at the hands of Sosh. Even to this day, Minto struggled to come to terms with how someone so dangerous could have been allowed to walk free in the community, a shadow of fear forever lurking in the corners of her mind. Nevertheless, the tragedy served as a stark reminder of the dangers of unchecked anger and highlighted the importance of holding individuals accountable for their actions, no matter their past deeds.

If truth be told, Sosh was a ticking time bomb, her rage simmering just beneath the surface, ready to explode at any moment, and everyone was aware of it. Her outbursts were merely the beginning, a prelude to the fury that would inevitably be unleashed once more. Minto had been left in a state of shock, the wounds inflicted upon her psyche so deep that they would undoubtedly take a lifetime to heal, if they ever truly could.

One week before the family gathering, Sosh had enlisted the assistance of a knowledgeable village factotum to embark on a crucial fact-finding mission. The objective was to gather information about a renowned medicine man who had been highly recommended to Sosh by the village headman. According to the headman's briefing, this medicine man was a distinguished healer whose services were in high demand, not only within the Yatta district but also beyond its borders. His reputation, spread by word of mouth, was unparalleled. He was a shaman of exceptional skill, known as the Numen of Banda, belonging to the esteemed Awe clan of priests.

For centuries, the Awe clan had made their home in the Banda Salama Forest, a vast tropical rainforest. This wise and revered group of elders dedicated their lives to the noble pursuit of healing and helping those in need. Their extraordinary ability to cure physical, magical, and spiritual ailments earned them a reputation as some of the most skilled healers in the land. The clan's healing practices, steeped in tradition, were passed down from generation to generation, their methods a blend of ancient wisdom and phytotherapy that had proven effective time and time again.

It was widely believed that the priests of the Awe clan possessed a unique power, one that could cure diseases and restore balance to the natural order of things. Their unparalleled knowledge of herbs and remedies, combined with their mystical abilities, made them highly sought after by those in need. Their services were often advertised through word of mouth by grateful patients who had benefited from their expertise.

Consulting with the Numen of Banda was undoubtedly the best course of action for Sosh. However, the task of safely transporting her family to the medicine man's abode, deep within the heart of the Banda Salama Forest, posed a monumental challenge. Information about the Numen's physical address was scarce, and details on how to contact or reach him were either incomplete or lacking. The only person who had a vague idea about the Numen's whereabouts was the village headman, who had gathered bits and pieces of information from third parties, suggesting that the shaman resided in a secluded village called Banda Salama, nestled within the lush tropical rainforest, directly across from the Banda Salama escarpment.

After carefully considering the limited information at hand, Sosh concluded that sending an advanced fact-finding emissary to Banda Salama was essential. Given the high stakes, this crucial step was necessary to ensure the safety of her family and the success of her mission. The emissary would face the daunting task of navigating the perilous terrain of the Banda Salama Forest and gathering as much intelligence as possible about the elusive Numen and his exact location.

Undoubtedly, Sosh was unwavering in her pursuit to find the enigmatic healer, regardless of the challenges she was resolute in securing his services. To achieve this goal, Sosh sought the assistance of a seasoned hunter, a terrestrial navigation specialist, and a fearless freelance emissary who had nothing to lose, even if it meant putting his life on the line for a fee. This intrepid and dauntless individual was none other than Mr Gaati, the village factotum, whose bravery and resourcefulness would be put to the ultimate test in the quest to find the Numen of Banda.

Mr Gaati was an enigmatic man, known for his unwavering resilience and resourcefulness. He made a living by taking on odd jobs that came his way, navigating the harsh and unforgiving environment of the village with patience and determination. Although his demeanour could be gruff and unyielding, his resolute spirit was a testament to his strength of character. Despite growing up in a broken family and facing numerous challenges throughout his life, he never succumbed to despair, always pressing forward with an indomitable will.

Mr Gaati's reputation as a reliable and trustworthy mediator preceded him, and he was often sought out by those in need of his services. His ability to remain calm and level-headed in the face of conflict was a rare and valuable trait, earning him the respect of all who knew him.

Admittedly, Mr Gaati was a dedicated community representative, always ready to serve with unwavering determination, albeit for a fee. He had been called upon many times before as an emissary in conflicts involving cattle rustling. In each of these instances, Mr Gaati fulfilled his duties honourably, returning to the village to continue with his odd jobs as if nothing had happened, his unflappable nature a source of both admiration and curiosity.

Interestingly, but not surprisingly, Mr Gaati was renowned for his sharp wit and insightful commentary on the true nature of money. Despite being looked down upon for doing odd jobs, he often quipped that money only exudes the glory of what it can buy, but not the sweat of whoever earned it. His humorous yet profound observations earned him a reputation as a wise and entertaining speaker, leaving an indelible impression on those who cared to listen.

Despite his humble beginnings, Mr Gaati had proven his diplomatic skills on numerous occasions. Two years prior, he successfully negotiated the release of twenty-two Aombe-clan herders kidnapped by the Aimu-clan cattle rustlers, along with the recovery of two hundred stolen cattle. This act cemented his esteemed place in the hearts of the villagers. Undoubtedly a gifted negotiator, Mr Gaati never shied away from the risks involved in brokering peace between warring clans and cattle-rustling gangs. He believed these perilous endeavours were necessary to achieve justice and restore order, his unwavering commitment to the greater good driving him forward.

Mr Gaati's negotiation prowess stemmed from carefully studying his opponents and their behaviour patterns, tactics, and strategies, allowing him to formulate effective negotiation plans accordingly. His ability to delve into the psyche of the kidnappers and persuade them to see reason was unparalleled. When questioned about his successful negotiation tactics, Mr Gaati explained that the objective was not simply to secure a "yes" from the opposing party, but rather to guide them towards acknowledging what was right. He humbly admitted that his greatest strength lay in his ability to empathise with the captors and treat them in a manner that aligned with their preferences, rather than his own. This was often accomplished by granting them a sense of control, albeit illusory, over the situation, a tactic that had proven invaluable in his many negotiations.

Mr Gaati's approach to negotiations was firmly rooted in the belief that understanding and respecting the other party's perspective was crucial to achieving a mutually beneficial outcome. He prioritized effective communication and building rapport, which had enabled him to navigate even the most challenging negotiations with grace and success. His unwavering commitment to finding common ground and fostering understanding had earned him a reputation as a skilled mediator, one whose services were highly sought after in times of crisis.

At Sosh's behest, Gaati embarked on a solitary mission to Banda Salama. For most, traversing the treacherous terrain and deciphering the subtleties of the wilderness would be a daunting task. But for Gaati, with his many years of honing his bushcraft skills, the journey seemed almost effortless. He returned successfully, bearing valuable insights about the Numen of Banda, including essential information such as the cost of treatment and the safest routes to navigate, as well as a brief but informative profile of the medicine man himself.

Gaati's unparalleled expertise and deep familiarity with the wilderness were instrumental in the success of his mission. He had traversed similar paths before, making him adept at handling the unpredictable challenges of such journeys. His ability to adapt to and anticipate the complexities of the natural world turned what would have been an arduous trek for most into a manageable expedition for him.

However, the same cannot be said of the task of escorting Sosh's family to the Numen's infirmary, which would present an entirely different challenge. In the absence of Gaati's mastery of bushcraft, the family would find the journey significantly more strenuous and perilous, a fact that weighed heavily on Sosh's mind as she contemplated the impending voyage.

In his debriefing with Sosh, Gaati shared the tale of his challenging journey to uncover the secrets of the legendary Numen of Banda. His adventure led him through a series of enlightening encounters with individuals who each held a fragment of the path toward the Numen. From a traveller who had only dared to skirt the edges of the Banda Salama Ranges, to a local who had reached the base of Mount Banda but ventured no further, and finally to a villager who knew someone from Banda Salama Village with directions to the Numen's domain yet had never personally encountered the Numen. These interactions collectively painted a picture of a figure endowed with immense wisdom and healing powers, rumoured to possess abilities like communicating with animals, making objects vanish, and summoning rain from the sky, each tale adding to the Numen's mystique.

Gaati's undeterred quest, assembled from snippets of lore, eventually led him to the Numen's chief steward, a figure as commanding as the myths surrounding his master. Emerging from the shadows of delicate silk mimosa trees, the steward's nearly six-foot-eleven stature, characterised by prominent ears, elongated arms, and a pronounced brow ridge, projected an aura of primal strength. His chest, as broad as a small table, and arms, reminiscent of the mechanical limbs of a robust machine, highlighted his extraordinary physique, a testament to the power that lay within the Numen's realm.

Ultimately, the Numen's formidable steward facilitated Gaati's audience with the legendary Numen of Banda. This circuitous journey culminated in a significant meeting, with the steward acting as the crucial link between the realms of myth and reality. The Numen's aura of mystery remained intact, his solitude only adding to the intrigue. This encounter significantly enriched Gaati's narrative, injecting it with a sense of awe and laying a solid foundation for Sosh's family's forthcoming journey, now charged with a heightened sense of wonder and eager anticipation.

Furthermore, Gaati recounted the fascinating fact that Banda Salama was the last human-inhabited village before the landscape plunges into a vast biome of dense equatorial rainforest. The area was notorious for its wild rivers and lush, verdant interlocking spurs, a natural labyrinth that promised both beauty and danger. The Numen of Banda's residence was nestled in the heart of Mount Banda, halfway up its tallest peak, a location that seemed to defy the very laws of nature. Indeed, the journey to Banda Salama Village from Yatta was not for the faint-hearted, requiring a level of courage and determination that few possessed.

Meanwhile, the pre-treatment diviner report, brought back by Mr Gaati and presented to Sosh, identified Wasa, Minto, and Benjo as the individuals who needed to travel to Banda Salama at the behest of the Numen of Banda for treatment. The revelation set the stage for a quest, fraught with danger and the promise of ancient wisdom, beckoning the chosen trio to venture into the unknown. This journey necessitated careful planning and preparation due to the treacherous terrain and unforeseen obstacles along the route. Navigating this journey would undoubtedly require a great deal of skill and perseverance, testing the limits of their physical and mental fortitude as they sought to unravel the mysteries that lay ahead.

To ensure the safety of her family during the journey, Sosh conducted a comprehensive half-day safety drill, aiming to instil essential survival tactics in them. She began by teaching them about shelter and protection from predators, her voice filled with a sense of urgency and purpose. Sosh demonstrated how to locate caves and hollowed-out logs, and taught them how to construct makeshift shelters using sticks and leaves, emphasizing the importance of these skills in protecting themselves from extreme weather conditions. The most intense moment came when Sosh took Wasa aside, drilling him on how to use a machete in close-quarters one-on-one combat. Minto, unable to bear the sight, had to close her eyes during this session, her heart pounding with a mixture of fear and hope that all goes well.

Additionally, Sosh taught them how to identify edible plants and animals that they could consume while in the wilderness, her knowledge a treasure trove of survival wisdom. She walked them through the process of identifying edible plants by examining their leaf veins, shapes, colours, textures, and sizes, her keen eyes picking out the subtle differences that could mean the difference between life and death. She also cautioned them about the dangers of confusing poisonous plants with edible ones, citing the example of the water hemlock, a deadly plant often mistaken for harmless ones like carrots, wild parsnips, and celery. Sosh emphasized the gravity of this mistake, recounting tragic stories of how such confusions have occasionally resulted in heartbreaking outcomes, particularly for young children. Her words, tinged with a mixture of concern and determination, underscored her desire for them to be well-prepared for any surprises the jungle might hold, arming them with the knowledge and skills they would need to overcome the challenges that lay ahead.

After the safety drill, Sosh made the big announcement that sent Benjo's heart racing with excitement: the departure was in just two days! The prospect of a wild adventure through the jungle was overwhelming. He could hardly wait to saddle up his horses and embark on the journey of his life. Banda Salama lay beyond the horizon, over two hundred miles away in Benjo's imagination. The mere thought of the journey sparked a sense of exhilaration, and he began to daydream about the potential landscape features they might encounter along the way: the dense foliage, the rushing rivers, and the towering mountains—all of it waiting for him to explore, beckoning him with the promise of untold wonders.

Unlike Benjo, who was completely oblivious to the inherent dangers, his parents were well-informed about the daunting obstacles that awaited them on their journey. To be honest, Benjo's excitement bordered on delirium, if not outright madness. He had no idea of the challenges they would face: circumnavigating the mystical Nzambani Rock outcrop, traversing the breathtaking Yatta Plateau, wandering through the land of the fearsome Akimi cannibals, and experiencing the heart-stopping act of crossing the tempestuous waters of the mighty Thika River. Despite the risks, his thrill for the upcoming adventure was undiminished, burning brightly within him like an unquenchable flame. The pinnacle of it all would be the spine-chilling encounter with the mystical priests of the Awe clan, a prospect that both terrified and enticed him.

Of all the prospects of the journey, Benjo was least enthusiastic about the idea of meeting the witch doctor or diviners. He shared his mother's scepticism about the ability of uneducated, malodorous individuals to access his personal file from the spiritual realm and predict his future. He wondered why such indigent men and women could not use their clairvoyance powers to improve their own livelihood, a question that gnawed at him relentlessly. In fact, he once confronted Sosh, demanding an explanation for why all diviners were dirty and unkempt. Sosh's cryptic response, "When God cooks, people don't see the smoke," failed to convince Benjo, but he wisely chose not to press the issue any further, sensing the depth of his mother's belief.

Not even the promise of the allure of witnessing the Awe clan's medicine men in action could quell the unease that crept into Benjo's heart; the mere thought of their mystical powers was enough to send shivers down anyone's spine. When Sosh mentioned the Awe medicine men while discussing the itinerary, it evoked memories of folklore that Uncle Kineene had once shared with Benjo, recounting a story of a rebellious clansman who had shown disrespect towards a visiting medicine man from the feared Awe clan, leaving a lasting impression on all who heard it, a tale that had been seared into Benjo's mind.

According to the story, a medicine man of the Awe clan ancestry had just completed a two-day journey to gather medicinal herbs when he passed through Yatta Village on his way home. Suddenly, a recalcitrant clansman insulted the medicine man by mocking his small stature and comparing him to a half-filled sack of potatoes. Feeling humiliated and angry, the medicine man decided to take revenge by casting a spell on the clansman, a curse that would forever change the man's life. The spell transposed the man's manhood from his crotch to his forehead, causing him immense embarrassment and shame. This incident was so bizarre that the local women and children couldn't help but follow the poor clansman around the village, laughing uncontrollably at his misfortune, their mirth only adding to his misery.

Amidst these unsettling events, the village elders were forced to hire a local medicine man in a valiant but ultimately futile effort to lift the curse. Tragically, the local wizard suffered an epileptic seizure upon arrival, his body convulsing violently as he attempted to break the spell. This unforeseen incident was misinterpreted by many by-standers as a deliberate act by the more potent visiting medicine man to undermine the local wizard's efforts, a display of his superior power. This misunderstanding further fuelled their confirmation bias, intensifying the existing fears and mistrust towards the Awe priests, their reputation growing with each passing moment.

It took the judicious wisdom of one local elder, Mr Musili, to navigate through a long and arduous process, his years of experience and keen intellect guiding him through the treacherous waters of negotiation. Mr Musili, renowned for his astuteness and negotiation prowess, played a pivotal role in persuading the medicine man to reverse the conjuration, his words carefully chosen to appease the offended party. With his expertise as one of the finest intertribal war negotiators, Mr Musili led the arbitration, which spanned five gruelling hours, each minute fraught with tension and uncertainty. Ultimately, a two-bull oblation and an additional payment of four billy-goats were required as compensation to the Awe talisman, a price that seemed steep but necessary to restore balance. When the price was right, the humble Nestor from Banda Salama agreed to reverse the spell, bringing profound relief to the victim and his family. However, not all were content with the resolution; the women and children, who had anticipated prolonged free entertainment, were left disappointed, their hopes of further spectacle dashed.

Benjo was thrilled by the folklore to the high heavens, his young mind captivated by the incredible tale. Without a doubt, Uncle Kineene was a masterful storyteller, and his abilities were no coincidence. During his prime, Kineene was a professional griot who served in the palace of Paramount Chief Savano of Kangundo Chiefdom, his words weaving magic and wonder for all who listened. Even in his retirement, Kineene's storytelling never failed to captivate his audience, his voice rich with emotion and his eyes sparkling with mischief. He concluded each tale by disclosing the moral of the story, which he cleverly referred to as "the third side of the coin," a phrase that stuck with Benjo long after the story had ended. His stories were designed to instil historical lessons or social norms in his listeners, making them both entertaining and educational, a testament to his skill as a master of the craft. As a result, Benjo never missed an opportunity to visit his favourite maternal uncle during school holidays to indulge in seamless sessions of storytelling entertainment, his mind transported to far-away lands and times long past.

In this instance, Kineene's third side of the coin concluded with a gripping tale of a disgraced clansman who was consumed by shame and humiliation after a paranormal experience, his life forever altered by the curse placed upon him. The weight of his experience was too much to bear, and he hastily gathered his belongings and exiled himself to a far-off Maasai tribe, never to return to the village again, his story becoming a cautionary tale for all who heard it. As Kineene concluded his captivating tale, Benjo found himself perched eagerly on the edge of his seat, brimming with excitement, his mind racing with the possibilities of what lay ahead on his journey, the unknown both thrilling and terrifying in equal measure.

The Kamba people have a fascinating saying that a child's true head shape is revealed after a haircut. This proverb seemed apt in describing young Benjo's excitement, which became vividly apparent after his grandmother announced their journey to Banda Salama. Indeed, on the eve of their departure, Benjo's excitement overwhelmed him, causing a momentary lapse in concentration that almost led him to forget a task assigned by Sosh the previous night. Known for her meticulous nature, Sosh habitually read aloud the next day's duty roster to family members before bedtime.

By a stroke of luck, Benjo stumbled upon the family granary while wandering absent-mindedly around the family compound. His curiosity led him to peer inside, noticing a dried goatskin still hanging from the roof thatch. Suddenly, the sight of the unattended goatskin brought him back to his senses and reminded him of the unfulfilled morning task. It turned out that Sosh had given Benjo precise instructions to deliver the goatskin to the local village knacker for sale, first thing in the morning. However, it was now well past midday, and the task was still undone. Benjo felt a wave of anxiety wash over him as he imagined Sosh's wrath.

Benjo found himself in a tight spot, urgently needing to think on his feet. As he pondered his next steps, he realised that his father had left the family bicycle at home that day. To swiftly complete his task and avoid facing Sosh's anger, he promptly decided to utilise the bicycle to expedite the delivery. Benjo felt fortunate as he counted his blessings. Indeed, good things come in pairs. Stumbling upon both the granary and discovering the availability of the family bicycle that day seemed too good to be true. Sometimes, there seems to be no substitute for luck, and for Benjo, this was one of those moments.

To prepare for his bicycle trip to the knackery, Benjo retreated to his room and slipped into his favourite Superman T-shirt and Calico shorts. The T-shirt wasn't just any ordinary shirt. It had undergone conspicuous modifications: the armholes were cut open and the sleeves were shortened for a look of stylish confidence. This wasn't the first time Benjo had chosen this magical shirt for a trip to the marketplace. Once, when his father had inquired about the deliberate alterations to the fabric, Benjo explained that he had modified the design to camouflage himself, making him appear tougher and ward off potential bullies in the village.

Without delay, Benjo hopped onto his family's sleek Black Mamba bicycle and raced down the loose gravel footpath towards the local knackery, as instructed by Sosh. He was determined to finish his assigned tasks before meeting with Sosh later that evening, to avoid Sosh's fury. With newfound confidence and energy, fuelled by the power of using the bicycle, Benjo zoomed down the hill with speed and determination. He was ready to confront any obstacles that came his way, as long as he kept making strides towards reaching the marketplace.

The knackery console was manned by a surly and unkempt individual, whose formidable presence made Benjo feel uneasy. The attendant's gruff voice and pungent body odour were so repulsive that Benjo wrinkled his nose in disgust. The man's uniform was in such a state of disrepair that its original colours were indistinguishable. Noticing this, Benjo couldn't help but concur that the uniform had undoubtedly seen better days.

The two strangers exchanged wary glances, each sizing up the other like one billy goat facing another in a standoff. From the moment they met, Benjo was put off by the attendant's cold demeanour and dismissive attitude. Despite his initial reservations, Benjo couldn't shake off the feeling that something was amiss about the knackery attendant. His intuition told him that his dislike wasn't just due to some superficial bias or horn effect, as the attendant's palpable lack of receptiveness left a sour taste in his mouth.

The good news was that, despite the chilly reception, Benjo was pleased to learn that Sosh had already secured the deal with the knacker, leaving Benjo with the straightforward task of delivering the goatskin to the attendant's counter and waiting for payment. With some free time on his hands, Benjo decided to explore the surrounding area, with no desire to interact with the cold-hearted recluse again unless it was unavoidable. As he surveyed the attendant's console, he couldn't help but notice an impressive array of tools scattered about, including a Brannock device, a Picard hammer, and an anvil. It became apparent to Benjo that the attendant was a true jack-of-all-trades, but he had no interest in getting to know him any further.

As soon as Benjo handed over the goatskin, the attendant quickly snatched it from his grasp and turned his attention solely to processing Sosh's transaction, as previously agreed. Despite his gruff demeanour towards Benjo, the attendant was cautious not to cross Sosh by messing up her transactions. It was not lost on him that his current role became available after the previous console operator was attacked and permanently disabled by Sosh for defrauding her of ten percent of a cowhide sale.

Benjo decided to stroll around the tannery to pass the time while he waited for the transaction to be finalized.

He walked the entire length of the dilapidated structure until he reached the backyard fence. In the far right-hand corner, next to some rusty metal drums, he noticed rows of ram skins that had been recently draped and stretched across wooden frames to dry using twine. As he approached one of the rows, he spotted a paralysis tick whose hypostome was still firmly embedded deep in the skin of the dead ram. Surprisingly, the bloodsucking vermin was still alive and thriving, completely oblivious to the fact that the ram was long dead and flayed.

As Benjo gazed upon the parasite clinging to the lifeless ram's skin, he couldn't help but feel a pang of empathy. He pondered why the parasite had chosen such a lethargic way of life when it could have pursued a more productive career, such as that of a plant pollinator. Nonetheless, the paralysis tick remained loyal to the common belief that parasites seldom abandon a monarch as long as the crown still glitters on their head. However, the irony of the situation was that the parasite had fed off the ram's success while it was alive but, in doing so, it had also contributed to the ram's downfall. Benjo's astute observation revealed a striking lack of foresight and planning on the part of the parasite. Its failure to detach from its host before the host's demise exposed it to the risk of starvation.

Suddenly, a deafening voice echoed from behind, causing Benjo to jump in surprise. He quickly turned around to find the knackery attendant standing there, holding out a wooden crib. Benjo's stomach churned with fear at being caught off guard. He realized that he had become so engrossed in the fate of a helpless parasite that he had lost all sense of his surroundings.

Benjo's peers had long recognised his unwavering focus on a single task as both a strength and a weakness. On the downside, this intense level of concentration sometimes left him exposed to attack via blind spots. Nonetheless, although the attendant's booming voice startled him, he was grateful for the reminder to stay alert. Benjo proceeded to collect the payment for the sale of the goatskin and walked away without saying goodbye.

The transaction at the knackery was a barter trade. Benjo brought a medium-sized goatskin and received back three chickens, each of a distinct colour – black, white, and red – in exchange for the goatskin. The birds were carefully placed in compartments inside a wooden crib, which resembled a miniature coop. Benjo swiftly grabbed the crib and secured it tightly on the bicycle pillion using a butyl rubber cord made from a discarded bicycle-tyre inner tube and disappeared in the same direction he had arrived from.

That evening, Benjo met with Sosh, who was pleased with him for completing the assigned task. This interaction was particularly significant as it was the last night before their journey to see the medicine man. To spice up the night, Benjo's grandma decided to share some folklore with him. Her stories were designed to captivate his imagination and alleviate his anxiety. She aimed not only to equip Benjo with the knowledge and wisdom necessary for the gruelling journey to Banda Salama but also to pass on her repository of folklore. In doing so, she hoped to preserve these tales for future generations.

Sosh began by recounting a captivating tale of two brothers assigned a treasure-hunt quest by their father. On their journey, the brothers faced untold difficulties: they navigated dangerous caves filled with mysterious creatures and encountered cannibals in the dense forest. Despite the daunting challenges, their unwavering determination propelled them forward. After a thrilling and suspenseful journey, they emerged triumphant, securing an enchanted feather known to bring luck and fortune. Sosh's story imparted to Benjo a valuable lesson on the importance of determination and resilience in overcoming adversity.

Next, Sosh shared another fascinating story, this time about an old woman living deep in the forest, endowed with powerful magic. Renowned throughout the woodland for her formidable abilities, she used her magic to protect vulnerable visitors from harm. Whenever visitors to the forest felt threatened and cried out, she would appear in a flash to shield them from the lurking perils. Regardless of their location in the forest, she was always within reach of any distressed caller. Her reputation for rescuing numerous forest sojourners from ogre attacks was well-known and widely respected. From this story, Benjo learned the value of respecting nature, and the profound impact of kindness and compassion.

Benjo cherished the priceless wisdom imparted by his beloved grandma through her enchanting stories. Yet, the anticipation of his epic journey to Banda Salama overshadowed everything else, filling him with a mix of excitement and nervousness. This whirlwind of emotions led him to politely excuse himself from Sosh's company. He retired for the night, mentally preparing himself for the adventures and challenges that awaited him.

The next day, at exactly four in next morning, the first rooster in the village let out a powerful crow that shattered the peacefulness of the dawn. It was a sound that Benjo had grown accustomed to hearing every morning, especially on school days. However, this time, the cock's crow seemed more intense than usual. Or was it just Benjo's imagination running wild with excitement?

At the third crow of the rooster, Benjo leaped out of bed with enthusiasm, eager to awaken his parents and commence their journey to Banda Salama. He was so elated that he stopped short of verbally expressing his gratitude to the rooster for officially signalling the start of the family adventure. To tell the truth, Benjo had barely slept a wink the night before, consumed with excitement and anticipation for the journey ahead. Throughout the night, he spent his time thinking about the new experiences and adventures that awaited him.

By contrast, Benjo's father was a heavy sleeper who struggled with chronic dysania, a condition that made it difficult for him to wake up in the morning, no matter how many hours he slept. Unlike his son, Wasa had no trouble falling asleep the night before. To put it simply, he could sleep through thunderstorms and even a massive earthquake.

To ensure a successful day, Benjo began with a short prayer, a ritual he had practiced since childhood, thanks to the Italian missionaries who ran the Yatta Catholic parish where he attended Sunday school. As he rose from his bed, he gently nudged the billy goat aside to make way for himself and opened the door to the outside. The goat bleated in protest, seemingly puzzled by Benjo's early morning briskness. However, Benjo remained indifferent to the goat. After all, the Kamba have a saying that no matter how nice you are to a goat, it will still eat your yam. Sharing living quarters with domestic animals was a widespread practice in Yatta Village, especially for young boys of Benjo age. In fact, Benjo had been sharing his grass-thatched abode with the family goats since he was just five years old. Despite the occasional push and shove, they had coexisted peacefully for many years.

The cohabitation arrangement quietly emerged as an unspoken pact between the humans and animals dwelling in every household. This symbiotic connection proved indispensable for survival since Benjo and his cloven-hoofed companions depended on one another. The ruminants contributed significantly to keeping the house warm during the unforgiving winter, while Benjo, in return, ensured their safety from nocturnal predators.

The unlikely partnership between Benjo and his goats was truly remarkable. To maintain warmth within the house, the goats would gather around Benjo's bed and huddle together, activating homeostatic heat transfer to regulate the temperature and keep each other cosy. In the process, the heat was also conventionally transferred around the hut, ensuring that Benjo remained warm as well. In exchange for their warmth, Benjo provided a sturdy roof over the goats' heads, shielding them from the harsh winds and rainwater.

Benjo's bond with his goats was nothing short of extraordinary. He'd often regale his classmates with tales about his air-conditioned mud hut, where he could regulate the temperature to his liking during the winter months. His friends found the joke particularly amusing because nearly all of them had either cohabited with domestic animals or knew someone who had.

Nevertheless, despite the unconventional living arrangement, it was evident that Benjo and his goats shared a profound bond that had been forged over many years of cohabitation.

At precisely ten minutes past four in the morning, Wasa summoned Minto and Benjo to the family shrine beneath the Natal fig tree, adjacent to the cattle kraal, for their final benediction from Sosh before embarking on their journey. The trio stood ready, eagerly awaiting the unique and strict bedaubing ritual that would accompany the blessings.

The Kamba community had a rich tradition of grandmothers blessing their families before they set out on a journey. This cherished practice had been passed down through generations and was deeply ingrained in the community's culture. Grandmothers were revered as symbols of love and protection, and their blessings were believed to bring wisdom, strength, and good fortune to their families during their travels.

To honour the Kamba customary laws, Sosh had implemented a series of regulations that each family member was obligated to adhere to prior to the bedaubing ceremony. These regulations included refraining from spitting, urinating, or defecating for a minimum of three hours before the ritual. Furthermore, Sosh expected all family members to maintain a respectful distance and remain silent while at the family shrine, unless spoken to directly. By following these guidelines, the family would ensure that the bedaubing ceremony was conducted in accordance with the requirement set by the clan council of elders.

It is worth noting that Sosh displayed remarkable leniency towards her family during the bedaubing ritual. The original rules established by the clan council of elders were much stricter and more severe. According to the clan's guidelines, participants were prohibited from excreting any bodily fluids, including urine, stool, saliva, or mucus, for four hours before the ritual. Additionally, they were forbidden from taking a bath or washing their faces for two days prior to the ceremony. It was believed that failing to adhere to these requirements would render the blessings ineffective.

However, Sosh, who sat in the clan council of elders, made an exception for her family. She exempted them from the bathing rule and reduced the abstinence time from four to three hours. This was a significant gesture of kindness and understanding, as it allowed her family to participate in the ritual without having to endure the full extent of the strictures.

Due to the strict rules of the ritual, Minto was forced to abstain from using the restroom, leading to an intense need to relieve herself. Despite the discomfort in her detrusor muscles, she persevered, understanding the importance of the bedaubing ritual in their departure. The blessings it promised made the temporary discomfort seem worthwhile. Even amidst excruciating pain, Minto's commitment to the ritual remained unshaken.

On that morning, the weather at the family shrine was bitterly cold, making it almost unbearable for the family members. The northeasterly winds were relentless, and, without any windbreakers, the family were left to endure the chill that seeped into their bones. The biting cold penetrated every inch of their bodies, leaving them feeling numb and vulnerable. However, the family's unwavering commitment to their course was palpable.

As the youngest member of the group, Benjo shivered uncontrollably as he looked haplessly at his family members, who stood together in solidarity. He couldn't help but wonder if the ceremony was a form of punishment in disguise.

Suddenly, two silhouettes appeared in the dark, approaching the shrine from the south end of the family compound. The faceless persons walked between the granary and a large Mauritius thorn tree. Benjo took a cursory glance at the shadows and noticed that the front silhouette walked with a limp on the right leg, reminiscent of his grandmother's walking style, but he restrained himself from making any conclusions.

As the shadows began to take shape, Sosh stood before the assembly, accompanied by a well-known village roustabout who was carrying a large calabash full of an unidentified liquid. Sosh murmured a few unintelligible words, an invocation of sorts, before commencing the ritual. Benjo, who had been anxiously waiting, could not have been more pleased to see the ceremony finally beginning.

The ceremony commenced in earnest as Sosh poured a libation from the calabash and offered a pinch of snuff on the ground to appease the family ancestors. She then dipped a bouquet of leaves into the calabash and sprinkled the unidentified liquid all over the participants' bodies. As the twigs brushed over their bodies, their carroty fragrance wafted in the air around them that was consistent with the fresh aroma of the wild sunflower twigs. The Kamba people have long believed in the power of wild sunflowers to bring good luck, making them a popular choice for blessing ceremonies.

Sosh carefully placed the wild sunflower twigs on the ground and retrieved a special cloth, along with burning incense sticks. As the sweet aroma of the incense filled the air, Sosh offered heartfelt prayers to the gods, seeking their protection for her family from any harm or danger. To conclude the rite, she poured fresh goat's milk from an ochre-coloured gourd and repeatedly spurted it over the bodies of her loved ones.

Benjo watched in amazement as Sosh took seven mouthfuls of the goat's milk and emptied them over their bodies, drenching them completely. By the end of the ceremony, Benjo was shivering and gnashing his teeth from the cold, but he knew that Sosh's love, and devotion had created a powerful shield of protection around them.

Meanwhile, Sosh's assistant carefully and precisely laid out two piles of wood in front of him – one larger than the other. Using black wattle, kindling and sprigs as faggots, he expertly crafted a large bonfire in the foreground of the shrine. The fire would serve as a source of warmth for Benjo and the other family members before they set off on their journey. As the fire crackled and popped, Benjo couldn't help but feel grateful for the warmth it provided. The frigid temperatures had been almost unbearable, and he was grateful to finally find some warmth. The family joined Benjo and huddled around the cosy bonfire, forming a tight semicircle. The flames provided a much-needed warmth, reviving their spirits. They started to share laughter and jokes, cherishing the moment before embarking on their journey. The family expressed their immense gratitude towards Sosh's assistant for igniting the fire on their behalf.

To wind up the ceremony Sosh spoke the final words with a gentle yet powerful tone: "May my blessings accompany you, dear children, as you embark on your journey. May your path be filled with joy, love, and peace." The family stood in silence, hanging on every word from Benjo's beloved grandmother. With a nod of her head, Sosh gave them permission to depart.

But before the family dispersed, Sosh called out to them once more. She pointed towards the loppy, who had been quietly assisting her in the ritual. "Oh, one more thing," Sosh said to them with a smile. "Mr Gaati here will be your chaperone on your journey to Banda Salama. Please pay attention to his guidance." Sosh spoke with authority and confidence, before strutting away like a fierce dog, leaving the family to digest the information.

In the Kamba language, the word *gaati* translates to "sour". When Sosh announced that Gaati would be leading their journey, Wasa and Minto exchanged a subtle yet significant glance. The couple had been together for quite some time, and their bond was so strong that they could finish each other's sentences. They communicated with each other in coded language to express their disapproval of Sosh's choice

of a team leader. As his name suggested, Mr Gaati had a sour demeanour that did not sit well with the couple. However, they knew
better than to openly challenge Sosh's decision.

Although Mr Gaati's background remained a mystery, his unexpected appearance at the bedaubing ceremony did little to dispel the
doubts that both Wasa and Minto had about him. For starters, he was
a homeless vagrant who roamed from village to village in search of odd
jobs, always wearing a permanent scowl on his face. He was also an
awkward vagabond who did not care where he spent the night. Despite these reservations, Mr Gaati's exceptional skills had earned him
a soft spot in the clan council of elders. They often relied on him to
solve some of the community's problems.

However, Wasa and Minto were not amused about having a total
stranger foisted on them, especially for such a long journey. Despite
their dissidence, Sosh was incorrigibly stubborn, and there was no
amount of bemoaning her choice that was going to change her mind.
The couple's best bet was to make the best of the situation and hope
that Mr Gaati would turn out to be an asset rather than a liability.

Two

Chapter 2 – The Two Rivers

As the sun began to rise, the family set out on their journey towards the Thika River. The sky was a beautiful blend of navy blue, soft pink, and vibrant streaks of orange and yellow. The morning dew on the grass sparkled in the light, creating a peaceful and serene atmosphere. The air was fresh and still, and the sweet melodies of the songbirds filled the air, adding to the tranquillity of the moment.

As they walked through the smoke-grey fog of the winter dawn, visibility was poor, but Benjo felt a sense of familiarity as he noticed the wintry morning dewdrops falling on his feet from the fingertips of leaves. The sunlight filtered through the trees, beckoning the team forwards as they departed.

However, Gaati knew that danger lurked in the jungle, and he took precautions to protect Sosh's family.

He organized them to walk in a single file, leading the way as years of navigating the bush and the local terrain as a seasoned hunter had honed his senses. The myriad experiences of living nomadically, outside the conventional confines of buildings, sharpened his situational awareness, allowing him to listen and scan the surroundings for any whisper of sound that might betray the presence of wild animals. Gaati knew the jungle intimately, as if it were an extension of himself. He was acutely aware of the dangers that lurked in the shadows, always prepared to confront them with the skill and readiness that came from a lifetime of adapting to the wilderness.

To ensure maximum safety, Gaati carried a large hunting bow made of tough African ironwood in his right hand. Across his left shoulder, he carried a quiver made of kudu-skin leather, filled with poisoned arrows, and a razor-sharp Somali sword was fastened parallel to his right thigh. He was prepared for any threat that might come their way.

Gaati was known far and wide for his exceptional hunting abilities. His reputation as a skilled hunter preceded him and for good reason. He had honed his skills under the tutelage of the finest hunters in the Yatta district, including his reputed paternal uncle, Mr Kilunda. Uncle Kilunda was a marksman par excellence, and Gaati was fortunate to learn from him.

During his pupillage, Gaati specialized in hunting big game, such as elephants, buffaloes, and rhinos. This specialization was reserved for only the most skilled sharpshooters among the hunters. His shooting accuracy was not just a result of his natural talent, but also his dedication and hard work and practice. He could hardly miss a hit from a hundred metres away!

The African-ironwood hunting bow was a lethal weapon, renowned among the Kamba people for its power and accuracy. Its missiles could reach speeds of up to three hundred kilometres per hour, delivering pinpoint accuracy, especially in still wind conditions. This bow is typically reserved for intertribal wars or professional hunting of large animals, making it a dangerous weapon in the hands of skilled hunters.

The arrowhead darts used with this bow were coated with a lethal cardiac glycoside sap extracted from the Dune poison bush. This potent poison can kill a large mammal within minutes, making it a frightening addition to the hunter's arsenal. Gaati's choice to use such lethal weapons demonstrated the seriousness with which he regarded his appointment to protect Sosh's family from any potential harm.

Unlike Gaati, who was armed to the teeth, Wasa Wasa bore no offensive weapons. His right hand was occupied with a secure crib holding three domestic fowls, a testament to the tasks and responsibilities he juggled amidst their arduous treks. Over his body was strapped a small leather bag, a personal trove containing essentials like the simi blade and snuff. The simi, a leaf-shaped double-edged blade ensconced in a wooden scabbard, was not a weapon per se but a versatile tool carried by men for general purposes, reflecting Wasa's readiness to lend additional muscle to Gaati when the situation demanded it.

As they navigated the treacherous paths and forded rivers, Wasa's attentiveness to the fowls' needs underscored the journey's complexities. He made sure they were fed and safe, often adjusting the crib to protect them from the elements and potential predators, a constant reminder of the additional layers of difficulty their quest entailed.

Minto's burden was a large sisal basket, a concealed trove of assorted items covered with goatskin and secured at the edges, items gathered for the Numen of Banda. The basket's contents, though hidden, were a silent declaration of the weight of their mission. Along the rugged terrains and through the dense foliage, Minto balanced the hefty basket, its contents a mystery to be safeguarded, illustrating the tangible and metaphorical loads they carried. Periodic checks to ensure the goatskin cover remained intact and the contents undisturbed became a ritual, highlighting the ongoing challenges and the significance of their quest.

As the team delved deeper into the jungle, the air grew thick with humidity and the scent of damp earth filled their nostrils. Suddenly, they started hearing a mysterious voice echoing through the foliage, consistent with someone singing. It sounded like a human voice, but there was something oddly ethereal about it. It seemed too early to have any form of human activity taking place deep inside the forest. The haunting melody grew louder and more beautiful with every step they took, prompting Gaati to veer off their intended course to investigate the source of the enchanting melody.

In the meantime, Gaati instructed the team to wait on the path while he ventured deeper into the bushland, determined to uncover secrets that had been hidden within these woods for centuries.

As Gaati disappeared into the dense foliage, the sound of a singer's voice grew louder and clearer. Drawing on his hunting experience, he estimated that the source of the noise was approximately two hundred metres north-west into the thicket. He navigated further, a dozen more metres inside the bushland, and reached a coppice, where he stopped to listen. The absence of tree canopies not only made it effortless for him to identify the source of the noise but also helped him to distinguish the singer's diction.

Suddenly, Gaati found himself standing in a small clearing, surrounded by lush foliage. In the centre of the clearing stood an elderly woman, her skin wrinkled with age, singing a hauntingly beautiful melody that echoed through the jungle. Her voice was angelic, and Gaati was mesmerized by her performance.

As Gaati listened to the sweet melody of the elderly woman's ballad, he was filled with a sense of wonder and awe. The repetitive lyrics were infused with raw emotion, and it felt as though the singer was telling a story.

The Abyssinian coral tree relieved me of the mumps,
The mumps belong to the wind and young cows,
The anthill of the savannah relieved me of the mumps,
The mumps belong to the wind and young cows.

As soon as Gaati recognized the lyrics of the song he stopped and stood transfixed, unable to move or speak. He knew that he was witnessing something truly extraordinary, a rare cultural practice that he hadn't seen for a long time. As per Kamba customary law, any clansman who witnessed the secret mumps dance had to swiftly retreat before the singer noticed them. And so, Gaati had retreated without delay.

In Kamba culture, there existed a fascinating and deeply rooted taboo that forbade any third party from infringing upon or witnessing someone infected by mumps while they were performing a self-healing exorcism rite known as the mumps dance. This taboo was particularly relevant during a mumps outbreak when victims performed a secret dance believed to cure the disease.

The Kamba people had a unique self-treatment ritual for curing mumps. It involved dancing to a ballad widely believed to have healing properties. According to their beliefs, singing this ballad on top of an anthill, especially one near an Abyssinian coral tree, could completely heal someone of the highly contagious viral disease. However, there were three mandatory conditions that had to be met for the treatment to be effective.

The first requirement was that the patient had to arrive at the designated anthill before the break of dawn. This was because the energy of the earth was at its most potent during this time, and it was believed that the anthill served as a conduit for this energy. By being present at this time, the patient was able to tap into this energy and use it to aid in their healing.

The second requirement was the wearing of a necklace crafted from clay-pottery shards and threaded through a cord of torpedo grass. This necklace served as a symbol of the patient's commitment to the process and was believed to provide protection from negative energy.

Finally, it was of utmost importance that the ritual dance remained a private affair, with no third-party witnesses present. The energy and focus of the dance had to be directed solely towards the patient, and any external interference could disrupt the process and potentially offend the healing spirit.

It was worth noting that the Kamba people placed great significance on the third condition of their ritual. Any interference from an
outsider had the potential to upset the delicate balance of the ceremony. This was precisely why Gaati, who stumbled upon the ritual,
quickly retreated to avoid jeopardizing the patient's recovery.

After what seemed like an interminable wait for the rest of the
team, Gaati finally emerged from the dense foliage, much to the relief of his comrades. With a casual demeanour, he informed them
that the mysterious human voice was emanating from a patient performing the self-exorcism mumps dance. He didn't delve into further details, but instead took his place at the front of the group and
resumed leading them through the jungle.

Despite the cursory explanation of the mysterious incident, the
team quickly understood Gaati's message regarding the mumps
dance. Unfortunately, Benjo missed out on the message, as he was
too busy enjoying the fruits of a snot-apple tree, playfully perched
atop its branches.

While Gaati was away investigating the mysterious noise, Benjo
saw a golden opportunity to indulge in the ripe fruits of a nearby
snot-apple tree. Gaati promptly commanded Benjo to descend from
the tree and resume his position in the file, so that the team could
continue their expedition towards the valley of a dry seasonal river.

Meanwhile, Minto saw an opportunity to educate Benjo about
the ancient custom of the mumps dance. Hitherto, Benjo had never
heard of this practice before, as it had become outdated with the
introduction of modern medical treatments provided by mandatory
government-sponsored community clinics and dispensaries. As
Minto explained the self-treatment dance, Benjo couldn't help but
burst into laughter and dismiss it as a mere myth.

The team walked at a leisurely pace under the beautiful tree
colonnades, enjoying the sweet melody of singing birds. Suddenly,
they stumbled upon a chaotic scene of potentially illegal land clearing – a coppice filled with dozens of freshly felled deciduous and

coniferous trees scattered about a carpet of fallen leaves and moss. Stacks upon stacks of firewood were haphazardly scattered on the ground, surrounded by withies of willow tree branches commonly used for thatching granaries in the region.

The team was drawn to the sudden shift in the landscape and the irresponsible destruction of native vegetation. The once lush and vibrant vegetation had been recklessly destroyed, leaving behind a barren wasteland. The team couldn't help but slow down and take in the extent of the land degradation before them. Their curiosity was piqued, and they felt compelled to find out who was responsible for such wasteful use of natural resources.

For this reason, they delved deeper into the issue and discovered that the damage was far worse than they had initially thought. The sight of countless mature hollow trees that had been callously cut down, along with the destruction of the undergrowth, left them feeling a deep sense of sadness.

During the unsolicited inspection, Minto came across a dozen or so male woodcutters in the thicket. Employing curved machetes, they were cutting down more withies progressively deeper into the woods. The presence of these loggers unequivocally confirmed Minto's suspicion that they had stumbled into a significant illegal land-clearing operation. The alarming quantity of trees that had been cut down and left to decompose was profoundly disheartening. Faced with this grim reality, the team found themselves deeply concerned about the long-term repercussions of such unlawful activities on the local ecosystem.

Despite their intense curiosity, the team decided to proceed with their journey, opting not to confront the woodcutters. They recognized that the responsibility of determining the legality of the woodcutters' actions was not within their powers. Moreover, the prospect of confronting a dozen armed able bodied men in the thick of the jungle was not prudent. Nonetheless, the encounter was deeply awakening, prompting serious reflection on the enduring effects such actions might have on the region's native flora and fauna. As they departed, the swish of cutting machetes and the clatter of falling trees echoed in their ears, a sad reminder of the devastating impact of human activity on the environment.

Disturbed by the wanton destruction of the pristine environment, Minto made a solemn vow to herself. Upon returning to their village, she would definitely report the matter to the Ministry of Environment and Natural Resources. She knew that the perpetrators of this heinous activity could cause irreparable damage to the environment if they were left unchecked, to the detriment of future generations.

The sun shone brightly as Minto's family and their guide made their way back into the dense woodland after a brief stop-over at the glade. They skilfully navigated their way through the sea of greenery. It was as if they had entered a different realm, one brimming with enchanting beauty and enigmatic allure.

The team trekked for four kilometres and reached a vast expanse of moorland. As they trudged through the low-lying shrubs, grasses, and forbs, Benjo's sharp eyes caught sight of a breathtaking spectacle. A flock of vulturine guinea fowls and francolins stood in perfect formation, foraging for food together. It was an unusual sight, as these two different species of birds would typically compete for food rather than share it.

Despite this confusion, the team couldn't help but marvel at the stunning contrast of colours displayed by the birds' resplendent plumage. Benjo was so captivated by the sight that he couldn't resist stopping to admire the rare sight. The vulturine guinea fowls' striking blue heads and necks, combined with their black-and-white striped bodies was a beauty to behold.

Benjo stood in awe, taking in the beauty of nature's creation. A reminder of the wonders that lay hidden in the world around them. However, Benjo's moment of awe was abruptly cut short when he realized that the rest of his team had already moved ahead, leaving him behind by about two hundred metres. Determined to catch up, he decided to take a short cut and walk the distance as the crow flies by circumventing a large bush willow. As he took the first turn, he found himself face to face with a troop of common dwarf mongooses skulking underneath a zombi pea shrub.

Watching the stealthy movements of the formidable carnivores, Benjo wondered over their intentions. He put one and one together and deduced that the unexpected alliance he had observed earlier between vulturine guinea fowls and francolins was indeed a form of symbiosis. A mutually inclusive partnership intended to safeguard the two species of birds from the encroachment of marauding predators. It was a fascinating discovery that added to Benjo's knowledge of the local food chain.

As an experienced herdsboy, Benjo was well versed in the natural law of mutual respect and recognition of each other's space in the jungle. He made a conscious decision to avoid crossing paths with the mongooses, preferring to observe them from a safe distance. It was not lost on him what the mongooses were capable of. He once witnessed the incredible power of a lone dwarf mongoose in the jungle taking down a giant king cobra, and he knew better than to underestimate their abilities. He kept a watchful eye to ensure that both he and the mongooses coexisted peacefully without infringing on each other's space.

After catching up with his team, Benjo followed Gaati's expert leadership down the Kwa Mulinga tributary. This seasonally dry riverbed drained stormwater into the Thika River, south of the team's desired crossing point, known locally as the Syukoni crossing point. Syukoni, in Kamba, refers to a natural watering hole along a watercourse, shared by both domestic and wild animals.

To navigate the wilderness without getting lost or being attacked by wild animals, the team relied on the expertise of their chaperone, Gaati, a bush tracker par excellence. Gaati was a skilled big-game hunter and a highly trained war scout whose skills came in handy for the mission at hand. Over the course of two decades, Gaati had honed his abilities to track spoors, the trails left by animals or humans, with an uncanny precision that allowed him to navigate even the most challenging of terrains.

Gaati's skills were invaluable as he guided the team through dense foliage, narrow pathways, and other treacherous landscapes that most people would struggle to navigate without getting lost or injured.

Gaati's decision to follow a meandering tributary rather than trek over bushland illustrated his bushcraft mastery. To a layperson, it did not make sense to follow a dry riverbed considering that walking over dry sand was physically more demanding than trekking over dry land due to a reduction in the friction that would be caused by shifting sand grains underfoot.

In contrast, Gaati knew that the riverbed was naturally devoid of vegetative cover, providing a safety buffer zone for his team. Although he was aware that the shifting-sand effect was a mechanical reality that made a person feel as if the ground was moving underneath their feet, draining energy from the calf muscles, nonetheless, he chose safety over labour. Moreover, given the prevailing circumstances, the safety benefits of his decision far outweighed the alternative considerations. He believed that it was better to be safe than sorry.

The team made steady progress without any hiccups until they arrived at the last meander of the tributary, which was notably larger than the other six. Benjo paused to pluck some bletting fruit from the wild medlar tree that hung invitingly over the riverbed. He quickly stuffed the fruit into the pockets of his shorts and caught up with the rest of the team. As they progressed further, the team found themselves in the lower course of the Kwa Mulinga tributary. This part of the tributary was characterized by a meandering course through flood plains and interlocking spurs, making it a challenging terrain to navigate. Despite the difficulties, the team remained steadyfast and more determined to reach the river crossing.

Benjo meticulously counted seven meanders that elegantly curved their way downstream towards the estuary, where the tributary disappeared into the mighty Thika River. The last meander took a sharp turn and then straightened out, revealing a breathtaking view of unnamed oxbow lake. This sharp bend of the tributary was caused by a colossal intrusive batholith that had lodged itself in the earth's crust and protruded into the river valley. The granitic dome was remarkably resilient, withstanding the relentless forces of erosion, including the powerful torrents of water, wind erosion, and the corrosive effects of chemicals over the years. Its sheer strength and durability were awe inspiring, a testament to the power of nature and the wonders of geology.

As the tributary flowed into the Thika River, Benjo paused to appreciate the stunning horseshoe lake on the resultant delta. The rest of the team followed suit, taking a moment to rest. The horseshoe lake added an extra layer of beauty to the already picturesque delta. Minto couldn't help but ponder the age-old adage that a river loses its name when it meets the ocean or, more precisely, a river's reputation fades away where the sea begins. In this instance, the tributary had lost its identity after merging with the powerful Thika River.

Benjo was overwhelmed with sadness and a sense of loss as he watched helplessly while his beloved Kwa Mulinga tributary was violently engulfed by the larger and more powerful Thika River. However, as the popular Kamba proverb warns, one should not challenge or stand in the way of the mighty. Nonetheless, the team persevered on their journey, eager to discover the wonders that lay ahead.

After taking a brief rest, the team resumed their journey towards the prodelta region of the river delta. As they approached the deltaic lobe, Benjo's sharp eyes caught sight of a large metal bollard with an inscription reading "Tana and Athi River Development Authority". Despite its intended significance, the team ignored the inscription and turned left, except for Benjo, who remained at the intersection of the two rivers to admire the beauty of the delta.

Benjo was captivated by the breathtaking beauty of the deltaic lobe, a fan-shaped sedimentary formation that emerged when the Kwa Mulinga tributary branched out into multiple streams to join the Thika River. As he ventured deeper into the lush greenery, he was awestruck by the currents that deposited sediments and silt, creating such picturesque views. Turning right, he continued his exploration of the silty alluvium deposits in the prodelta region downstream. The sheer power of nature and the stunning landscapes were out of this world.

The breathtaking scenery left such an impression on Benjo that he felt compelled to leave his mark on future explorers. He knelt and carefully etched his full name, Benjamin Jogoo, into the damp sand using a piece of debris he had collected from the alluvial deposits. It was a thrilling moment for him, knowing that he was leaving a legacy for future travellers to recognize that he had once reached the Thika delta.

After a brief but memorable excursion, Benjo reluctantly departed from the delta by walking backwards while keeping an eye on the pelicans feeding on a nearby isthmus. Eventually, he turned around and sped off to catch up with the rest of the team. Despite losing sight of the delta, Benjo's mind remained captivated by its beauty. He couldn't help but ponder the intricate processes that had formed such a stunning landscape.

The team continued their journey by walking upstream for another eight hundred metres, parallel to the river until they reached the Syukoni river-crossing point. Without any solicitation, Minto began to offer her ten-cent analysis of why Syukoni was chosen as the preferred crossing point for the Thika River. Her opinion was informed by the little knowledge of potamology she had studied in school many years ago.

"Did you know that it takes meticulous mathematical calculations to decide where to construct a bridge?" Minto had begun her unsolicited presentation to her companions with a captivating question to pique the interest of her audience. She explained that the ideal location for bridge construction was where the wavelength of a river meander is the shortest, ensuring safe passage for boats and swimmers.

Without pausing, she started explaining the sinuosity index, a method used by geologists to measure how much a river bends. But her audience was lost. It was as if she spoke an alien language. They tried to understand, but the more she talked, the less they grasped. It was like trying to catch smoke with their hands – impossible and confusing. It was for this reason that Gaati rudely interrupted her with a disrespectful comment during her explanation of the sinuosity method, asking, "Who asked you?" The aspersion abrupt silenced Minto and destroyed what otherwise could have been a captivating and informative presentation about the strategic choice of river crossings. Sensing the simmering irritation in Gaati's voice, Minto ended her explanation prematurely. She was all too aware of Gaati's fiery temper and what it could provoke. The last thing she wanted was to ignite a confrontation she knew they could both do without

At the river-crossing point, the only means of transportation available was an ancient dinghy moored fore and aft at the riverbank. Given the circuitous and dangerous nature of crossing the Thika River, the boat lacked a standard mode of propulsion. It could sometimes be propelled by pulling on a cable stretched across the river, punting with a pole from a standing position, rowing with oars, using sails, or utilising a small motor engine. According to local anecdotes, the dinghy had been operated by the same family for over five generations and had never been overhauled or replaced in the last half a century. Instead, any leaks on the boat were patched up using a traditional preservative extracted from local pinewood by burning the wood in a low-oxygen environment to produce a thick, dark, and viscous waterproofing adhesive: Stockholm tar.

Despite lacking proper maintenance, boat bravely moved through the Thika River's wild currents, carrying people from one side to the other every single day. Yet, the safety of its unsuspecting passengers was perpetually compromised, entrusted to a boat that was poorly prepared for such dangerous waters.

Minto confirmed that, indeed, the transport business was currently managed by two brothers, who were the fifth generation of the original family of mariners. Despite their youthful appearance, the brothers boasted twenty years of experience between them. The taller brother of the two was the pilot of the gaff-rigged sailboat. Despite his youthful looks, his appointment was not by mere chance, but rather by merit-based selection. As Minto's team would later find out, the pilot's commanding physical height and operational deftness saw him execute some of the most spectacular manoeuvres that left observers constantly on the edge of their seats.

The role of a pilot was not for the faint of heart. It required one to sit or stand at the stern of the boat all day, carefully manoeuvring the vessel to and fro across the river sometimes using a single large tiller mounted on the right-hand corner of the transom or any other mode of propulsion as the river conditions demanded. Meanwhile, his assistant, who happens to be the pilot's younger brother, was responsible for squatting in the middle of the boat to drain any uncontained water that leaked through the hull by scooping it with a plastic bucket to keep the boat afloat.

Together, these two brothers worked in tandem to not only steer the ship across the tempestuous waters of the Thika River but also to ensure their passengers and cargo arrived on shore safely.

The mere thought of crossing the river in a leaky boat sent shivers down Minto's spine. She felt nauseous and uneasy. Minto had been dreading this part of the journey from day one, when Sosh announced the journey to Banda Salama. Her heart was pounding with a mixture of fear and nervousness. Unfortunately for her, there was no other option but to cross the river in the dilapidated dinghy.

As the passengers began to board the vessel, they exchanged the customary pleasantries with the crew. However, Minto's exchange of greetings was merely a facade, as her mind was consumed by a deep-seated fear of water. The pilot's assistant noticed Minto's unease and attempted to soothe her nerves. Sensing the tension, the assistant leaned closer and shared a lighthearted joke about a duck teaching a frog to swim, hoping the humour would distract her from her fears and bring a moment of levity to the journey. Once everyone was seated, the pilot's assistant proceeded to guide them through the standard safety drills. He reassured them of their safety and attempted to maintain a friendly and calm demeanour, hoping to alleviate the tension. He even wished them good luck. Despite his best efforts, however, some things are easier said than done.

For Minto, the pre-departure safety drill was a disconcerting experience that left her more scared than equipped with survival skills. She took special exception to the instructor's iteration of how to activate a survival plan in the event of a capsized boat. The mere mention of the possibility of a capsized boat made Minto's heart skip a beat. Sometimes, when one is faced with extreme fear, he or she begins to question even the most basic of material facts. For this reason, Minto found herself questioning the difference between wishing someone luck and wishing them success. After pondering for a while, she concluded that success is measurable and predictable, while luck has everything to do with being at the mercy of fate.

However, healing is a process that takes time, and Minto eventually regained her senses. She realized that her premonitory thoughts were unfounded and blamed them on the devil and the village witch who had cast evil spells on her.

The pilot's assistant meticulously inspected the boat, ensuring that everything was in its proper place before distributing the luggage evenly to balance the vessel. Once the boat was balanced, the passengers were directed to sit on spots marked with white chalk on the bench seats. However, despite the best efforts of the pilot's assistant the boat was curiously tilted towards the stern, where Minto was seated. Minto, a daughter of the Aimu clan, was a robust woman with callipygian buttocks and weighed over hundred and twenty kilograms. Her weight was conspicuous, and it didn't take long for the pilot to realize that Minto's weight, rather than the positioning of passengers and luggage, was the reason for the boat's lopsidedness.

To rectify the situation, the pilot discreetly approached Minto and requested that she move to a more central location on the boat. Minto, who was initially taken aback by the request, quickly realized the logic behind it and obliged. With passengers' weight now evenly distributed, the boat was able to sail smoothly through the water, much to the relief of the pilot and passengers alike.

To prevent any potential instability during turbulent conditions, the pilot instructed his assistant to utilize the counterweight technique. This involved carefully measuring out a specific amount of ballast and placing it in a rusty metallic container, which was then strategically positioned at the bow of the boat, diagonally opposite Minto, as a safety measure.

To ensure the effectiveness of the counterweight, the pilot took five steps back and closed one eye to minimize the parallax effect. With a steady gaze, he observed the boat to measure the counterbalance. The results were impressive, as the boat's keel was balanced with pinpoint accuracy.

Finally, before embarking on the treacherous waters of the Thika River, there was a mandatory procedure that must be followed. The pilot, with a sense of duty, produced a worn-out notebook and a pen and requested each passenger to sign their name and date against a prewritten indemnity. This document read as follows:

I, the undersigned, hereby acknowledge that I am aware of the potential risks involved in navigating the Thika River. I understand that the river's currents can be unpredictable and that there may be hidden obstacles that could cause harm to myself or others. Despite these risks, I choose to embark on this journey voluntarily and assume full responsibility for any injuries or damages that may occur. I release the pilot and any other parties involved in this expedition from any liability and agree to hold them harmless in the event of any mishap.

I ———— of National Identity number ———— and date of birth ———— do solemnly indemnify Syukoni Ferries from any and all claims, lawsuits, demands, causes of action, liability, loss, damage and/or injury, of any kind whatsoever (including loss of life) whether caused by self, an individual or third-party entities. Signed on this —— Day of ———— Year ————.

As the pilot's assistant made his way around the small dinghy, notebook in hand, Minto couldn't help but feel a sense of unease. He was adamant that the boat could not depart until all passengers had signed the indemnity, a legal document designed to protect the company from financial loss in the event of an accident. The constant reminders of the danger of drowning only added to her anxiety.

Despite her reservations, Minto reluctantly signed the document, which she disapprovingly referred to as a death warrant. She was surprised by the level of sophistication in the company's business practices, especially given their remote location. In fact, the combination of remote operations and sophisticated legal documents only heightened her suspicion towards the two youthful brothers. If given the option, Minto would have abandoned the mission and returned home.

After cross-checking that every traveller was compliant, the pilot expertly launched the boat from the shore, using a technique that involved planting his right foot perpendicular to the levee. This created a fulcrum between his foot and the raised part of the riverbank, allowing him to summon all the power from his body weight and push-jolt the boat from the shore with a powerful thrust. The force was so great that he almost lost his balance, but he quickly regained his footing and jumped on board just in time to take his place in the driver's seat.

The travellers were mesmerized by the pilot's exceptional skill and agility as they watched him expertly navigate the boat into the deep waters of the river channel. It was becoming clear at this point that the pilot's job was incredibly demanding, requiring not only physical strength but also a deep understanding of the river's currents and conditions. It was not a role for the faint-hearted.

Despite Minto's initial fears, the other passengers on board were thoroughly enjoying the ride and taking in the breathtaking scenery, one moment at a time. The pilot's exceptional expertise and confidence put them at ease, and they began to feel safe and secure in his capable hands. As the boat gracefully glided through the water, they marvelled at the stunning beauty of the river and the surrounding landscape. Benjo was enthralled by the vibrant bird life in the wet meadow and shallow marshes, viewed from a perspective that was entirely new to him. The allure of the Syukoni Ferry as the preferred choice for crossing the Thika River became evident, boasting an appeal that drew travellers from far and wide.

Despite the charm, the team was also aware of the dangers lurking in the depths of the beautiful waters. The tranquil blue surface of the river was home to unpredictable currents, opportunistic predators, and other unforeseen obstacles.

Minto had a deep-seated fear of the Thika River, given her past traumatic experience. Three years back, while taking a leisurely stroll along the banks of the flooded Thika River, Minto witnessed a two-metres long crocodile viciously attack Tomi, the family dog, from the shore and drag him into the water. The gruesome sight of the dog's remains mixed with its raw offal and blood in the water was too much for her to bear. She became nauseous and vomited. The traumatic incident remained indelibly imprinted on her mind, triggering panic attacks whenever she neared the river. She was also occasionally haunted by recurring nightmares of Tomi's screams as the crocodile devoured him.

Despite the validity of Minto's trauma, it was unfortunate that her travel companions were either unaware or indifferent to the extent of her suffering. They immersed themselves fully in the novelty of crossing the river. Their spirits were high, basking in the excitement of the unfamiliar territory, utterly oblivious to the storm of anxiety and fear raging within Minto.

Interestingly, the Kamba people have a wise proverb that advises against insulting the crocodile's mouth while crossing a river. Minto found solace in this saying, choosing to shut out her haunting memories of past encounters with crocodiles in the Thika River. To calm her nerves, Minto cut two small twigs, placing one behind each ear, adhering to the Kamba belief that fresh twigs from certain plants can prevent vomiting. Whether the remedy was effective or not mattered little. Minto was too overwhelmed by nausea from an involuntary panic attack, and therefore willing to try anything to alleviate her symptoms.

As the boat glided downstream, Minto's keen eye caught something peculiar. The pilot seemed to be relying solely on the natural water currents instead of steering the boat forward to cross the river. Minto found this odd. She did not understand the pilot's intentions, and the more she tried, the more frustrating it became. As a layperson, it was impossible for her to make heads or tails of the navigational situation, especially since the boat was drifting downstream instead of sailing directly across the river.

And just as Minto was about to give up, the pilot began sculling the boat from the right-hand tip at the stern. The new manoeuvres were, at the very least, predictable. According to Minto's observation, the pilot was attempting to steer the boat towards a predetermined location, potentially an imaginary wharf on the opposite side of the river. Minto observed in amazement as the pilot expertly navigated through rapids, torrents, and whirlpools, maintaining perfect balance with each stroke. It was truly a remarkable display of skill and precision.

At first, the pilot's unorthodox attempt to allow the boat to drift with the river's currents seemed accidental. However, in hindsight, it became apparent that the pilot was in full control of the entire process. The passengers would later come to understand that the pilot was making use of the natural kinetic energy of the river channel to conserve his own energy. This was crucial for the later stages of the journey, when the pilot would be called upon to propel the boat westwards across choppy waters under unfavourable conditions.

With the river unfolding before them, the pilot suddenly noticed a whirlpool forming about ten metres ahead. Despite his attempts to navigate clear, the boat was ensnared by the swirling waters. His initial instinct was to execute a quick gybe, yanking the fore-and-aft sail rig to swivel the vessel, but this proved to be too little too late. The boat slammed into the vortex, catapulting it off the water into the air and ejecting the pilot skyward from the driving seat. Minto, observing the pilot's unexpected ejection from the controls, shut her eyes, and started to recite a prayer for the dying.

In a moment of sheer brilliance, the six-foot-five pilot performed an acrobatic turn in mid-air and pulled the sail boom just in time to shift the boat's direction of sail from left to right, regaining control of the boat. With the boat back under control, the pilot lowered the sails to reduce the sail area and minimize stress on the boat. He also adjusted the rudder to steer the boat back in the desired direction. The pilot's quick thinking and expert sailing skills saved the day, averting what could have been a disastrous situation. He was indeed a maritime wizard.

During a tumultuous moment on the boat, Minto found herself panicking and swearing repeatedly as the vessel rocked violently. Surprisingly, she felt a sense of relief after swearing. She recalled learning about a trauma response called the "amygdala hijack" in school. The amygdala hijack is characterized by a surge in adrenaline that provides a temporary natural form of relief from pain or fear. These memories gave her a solid reason to continue swearing, despite the disapproving looks from other passengers. At this juncture, their opinions did not matter, as long as she found solace in the temporary respite from her panic attacks. Minto was convinced that the whirlpool incident was the beginning of the end. Miraculously, the boat recovered from the turbulence and stabilized. Oddly, Minto attributed the boat's miraculous recovery not to the pilot's skills but to divine intervention.

Minto's opinion was biased. If anything, the pilot had so far demonstrated beyond reasonable doubts that he was a skilled navigator, highly capable of reading the river conditions and making split-second decisions to avoid obstacles and navigate aggressive currents.

Crossing the river was an intense experience, leaving everyone silent for the remainder of the journey. Benjo, however, noticed that he had wet his pants in the process but chose not to draw attention to it. He struggled to recall the exact moment when the embarrassing accident had occurred, with his only recollection being tightly gripping the mast of the boat, bracing himself for the worst. Amidst the confusion, Benjo could not determine whether the wetting of his pants was the result of splashing from the river rapids or otherwise, leaving him in a state of perplexed embarrassment.

After the mid-river drama, the boat sailed smoothly and finally reached a safe distance from the shore, much to the passengers' relief. However, in another peculiar yet unsurprising turn of events, the pilot unexpectedly picked up speed towards the shore. Minto found this decision irrational, as it seemed counterintuitive to increase the boat's speed barely fifty metres from the shore. Typically, one would expect a boat to slow down in preparation for docking. Nonetheless, the pilot had been unpredictable throughout the journey anyway, and, therefore, one more surprise move did not make a difference. Besides, the pilot had the final say in the matter.

The passengers were filled with horror as they watched the pilot activate the improvised bow motor, providing an additional surge of power to the boat. His action was subtle, yet it sent a clear message to Minto and his team to stay out of the pilot's decisions. Despite building up confidence in the pilot from all the milestones he had achieved throughout the journey so far, the passengers were back on tenterhooks. It was impossible to predict how this journey was going to end, but they prayed for a safe and successful outcome.

The pilot killed the bow motor and deftly adjusted the trim to an angle of approximately eighty degrees to the wind, propelling the boat forwards with impressive force. With rapid sculling, he approached the foreshore at a remarkable speed, expertly hitting the beach berm with such precision that the boat came to a firm stop exactly where the pilot intended. Evidently, the pilot's manoeuvres were not mere trial and error, but rather the quintessential skills that he had practised and perfected over many years of experience. It was truly an impressive display of nautical mastery.

The passengers were jolted by the boat's sudden acceleration followed by an abrupt deceleration to dock. The resulting collision left Minto feeling rattled and muttering a few more obscenities under her breath. Despite hard landing, the pilot's skilful manoeuvre was nothing short of genius.

Although the boat was in a state of disrepair, it was truly impressive on the water. However, much of the successful river crossing should be attributed to the flawless co-ordination and precision with which these two brothers conducted their business. Their passion and complementary skills, coupled with their infectious youthful energy, had earned them a reputation as industry leaders, attracting passengers from all corners of the country.

Nevertheless, despite the team's successful journey across the Thika River, Minto's recovery from her psychological trauma required more than merely crossing the river safely. Her trauma was deep-seated and long-lasting. Her maternal uncle, Mr. Nzau, had died in a capsized boat accident at the same river-crossing point, and the cause of the accident remains unresolved to this day. This tragedy made it difficult for Minto to overcome her mental disturbance every time she visited the Thika River, as she was always apprehensive about crossing the same waters that had claimed Uncle Nzau's life.

The Kamba people have a proverb that cautions against marrying a widow without first investigating what caused her husband's death. This adage was pertinent to Minto's situation, considering that her uncle tragically drowned at the same Syukoni crossing. The loss of Mr Bullock Nzau shook the very foundation of humanity, to say the least. Prior to his untimely passing, Mr Nzau was the undisputed heavyweight boxing champion of the Yatta district and Minto's closest uncle. He was a pre-eminent pugilist whose fame was known far and wide. However, fate had other plans, and Mr Nzau, along with four others, drowned in a massive whirlpool in the middle of the Thika River. His sudden and tragic death remains a topic of discussion in the local community to this day.

Minto found it difficult to erase the memory of Uncle Bullock's passing. However, she found consolation in yet another Kamba proverb encouraging victims of drowning to continue drinking water even after a child drowns in a river. Nonetheless, every visit to the Syukoni crossing reignited memories of her beloved uncle. This was one of the harsh realities of life that Minto had to accept and live with forever.

In contrast, Benjo was exhilarated by the thrill and fright of crossing the Thika River. Each surge of the river beneath the boat infused him with an intoxicating rush, akin to ecstasy, and he relished every pulse-pounding moment of this monumental odyssey. Given the chance, he would do it all over again. Unlike Minto, the experience taught Benjo that even within the very jaws of danger, there lie hidden opportunities for joy and profound personal transformation.

The ship gracefully docked at the shore, and the passengers disembarked safely onto the sand berm. Minto, the family treasurer, paid for the ferry services and joined Wasa and Gaati to climb up the riverbank towards the floodplain, the intended assembly point to begin the second leg of their journey. Meanwhile, Benjo remained standing momentarily on the sand at the banks of the river, admiring a flotilla of anglers downstream who were struggling to pull out a giant African mudfish from underneath the roots of a mangrove tree.

The mudfish was putting up a fierce fight, and it seemed unlikely to give up anytime soon. The river monster was using its powerful tail muscles to clasp onto the roots of nearby mangroves, making it difficult for the fishermen to reel it in. Benjo couldn't help but joke to himself that the fish must have declared to itself, "Let death come before surrender." Or perhaps the fish was aware that any slight mistake could lead to its defeat, and its body would end up on display for sale at the nearby Kwa Kulu Market in just two days' time. In any case, its adversaries were no ordinary men but serious fishermen who supplied fish stocks to the local market mongers.

Regardless of the outcome of the battle between the men and the fish, the future of the African mudfish remained bleak, if not dystopian. It was a sad reality that these magnificent creatures were being hunted unsustainably and sold for profit, with little consideration for their significance role in maintaining the local river ecosystem.

Meanwhile, Minto cast a quick glance over her shoulder and noticed that Benjo was still lingering at the riverbank. She called out to him and scolded him for being distracted and not sticking to the journey's protocols. Minto scolded Benjo as if to follow rules, whereas in reality, she was trying to release the tension and fear that had built up during the river crossing. In any case, Benjo was an easy target. A short while ago Minto could not reprimand or issue orders to Benjo. She had been as quiet as a mouse, partly due to her fear of water and partly because of an unwritten Kamba maritime law that prohibited anyone from issuing orders while crossing a river.

The second leg of their journey promised a completely different experience. The team eagerly anticipated traversing the breathtaking African savannah, crossing the Yatta Plateau, and reaching the mystical Nzambani Rock. The Yatta Plateau, lying between the Thika river valley to the west and the Yatta village to the east, presented a stark contrast to the treacherous terrain and tempestuous waters of the river valley. After crossing the river and climbing out of the valley, Minto's team encountered the flat Yatta Plateau, which offered them the freedom to choose their movements and space. Spanning over three hundred kilometres, the Yatta Plateau is the world's longest phonolite lava flow, stretching from Ol Donyo Sabuk in Machakos County to the Tsavo National Park in Taita-Taveta County in Kenya. It is a geological wonder with a rich and fascinating history. However, despite appearing to be a mere eighty kilometres as the crow flies, attempting to cross the plateau in a straight line between the Thika River and the Banda Salama Ranges across the savannah would be ill-advised for Minto's team. The imposing Nzambani rock outcrop, positioned directly in the center of the plateau, presents a treacherous obstacle to navigate.

The Nzambani Rock is an imposing batholith and a remarkable landmark revered by the local Kamba people. Legend has it that this rock possesses mystical powers capable of altering one's gender. It is believed that if a man walks around the outcrop seven times, he will transform into a woman, and a woman doing the same will become a man. However, should such a transformation occur accidentally, it can reportedly be reversed by walking around the rock seven times in the opposite, anticlockwise direction. Despite the legend, the Nzambani outcrop remains a fascinating and intriguing geological formation, captivating the imagination of the Kamba people for generations.

The rock held a certain allure for Benjo, drawing him to its mystical powers. Since the announcement of the trip to Banda Salama, he was consumed by wild imaginations of what to expect during his visit. He even fantasized about breaking away from his team to challenge the legend by walking around the rock seven times. His willingness to consider such a risk was bolstered by assurances that the gender transformation could be reversed. Nonetheless, his aspiration wasn't to change his gender permanently but rather, to put the gods to the test.

The team climbed out of the river valley and gathered under a magnificent African fig tree, right at the beginning of the tableland. This fig tree held great cultural significance to the local people, given that it was once a sacred shrine for the Atangwa clan. Although it was no longer in use, it remained taboo for women and children to approach the shrine.

The clan shrine was considered powerful and dangerous, and therefore, restricting access was intended to protect vulnerable individuals such as women and children from the potential risk of harm during confrontations between evil and good spirits. As a result, the designated assembly point was moved to a weeping wattle tree, at a safe distance from the shrine.

Beneath the rustling branches of the wattle tree, Sosh's family gathered to receive a briefing from Gaati on their itinerary for the odyssey through the savannah. Unfazed by the formidable challenge of circumnavigating Nzambani Rock, Gaati, the chaperone, casually gave the outline of the route without delving into finer details. In any case, it was of no use giving more details, which meant nothing to the rest of the team who were not familiar with the terrain. However, he bolstered their spirits with a few words of encouragement, emphasizing the importance of their quest. In a display of dry-wit humour, Gaati jested with them, saying that the journey is not about the destination, but about how one travels it. He concluded by telling them that he could not control the wind, but he could at least adjust the sail for them. Following that short moment of connection, Gaati adjusted the quiver on his shoulders and led the way into the savannah grassland.

Minto found herself captivated by the breathtaking beauty of the African savannah. The endless expanse of grassland stretched to infinity, punctuated by the occasional acacia, teak, or African padauk, and teeming with a diverse array of wildlife. As the wind whipped through her hair, she felt a surge of freedom and excitement, a stark contrast to her scary encounter with the Thika River and reveled in the comfort of being back on dry land.

Gaati made a cursory assessment of the team's energy level, average speed, and estimated time of arrival, and decided to take the optimal route via the windward side of Nzambani rock. Before this decision, he had carefully evaluated and rejected the alternative route on the leeward side due to its numerous obstacles, such as overhanging cliffs, tors, boulder heaps, and insular rock domes, which were nearly impossible to navigate. In contrast, the windward side offered permanent and navigable elephant tracks, making it the practical choice.

Despite Gaati's best intentions to make the team's journey as comfortable as possible, not everyone was pleased. Barely three kilometres into the chosen route, Minto began to whine about the longer distance to be covered on the windward side and the less user-friendly elephant tracks. She was frustrated by the overhanging tree branches that scratched her face and the hooked burrs and other hitch-hiking weeds that clung to her, pricking her skin through her clothes.

Gaati was infuriated by Minto's criticism, especially after investing a significant amount of time and mental energy into planning the journey. Despite his attempts to remain composed, Minto's continuous grumbling pushed him to his limit. Overwhelmed with frustration, Gaati finally snapped, shouting, "Turning around does not bring the buttocks to the front!" The intensity of Gaati's scowl silenced Minto, effectively putting her in her place. After the outburst, an uncomfortable silence lingered over the group for a considerable duration, which was precisely the outcome Gaati had intended.

The journey continued through the vast savannah grassland, dotted with whistling thorn trees that provided occasional shade from the blazing sun every hundred meters or so. For Benjo, this was the ideal moment to test his slingshot skills. Seizing the opportunity, he began hunting birds and small rodents, using pebbles as his ammunition. Benjo had been preparing for this moment well before the team entered the Kwa Mulinga tributary. He had discreetly gathered a significant collection of expanded shale pebbles for his slingshot and filled his pockets, ready to spring into action whenever the opportunity presented itself.

The team snaked their way past a deserted homestead, overshadowed by a large umbrella thorn tree standing tall in the courtyard. This giant thorn tree was a remarkable sight, offering shelter and sustenance to thousands of birds that lived in colonies around it. Its lush foliage, gnarled trunk, and branches that reached up into the sky provided a sanctuary where the feathered guests could rest, sing, and build their nests. The birds ventured out from their nests to find food, returning with forage to feed the hatchlings, before repeating the same cycle over again.

Benjo looked up and spotted hundreds of birds perched on the branches, feeding on spiked flowers. The birds chirped and cheeped, completely oblivious to Benjo, who was lurking under-neath them, unnoticed due to his pint-sized body. His intention was to test his slingshot on any one of the unsuspecting birds.

He waited patiently; his sights locked onto a grasshopper buz-zard perched alone on a dead branch. He had meticulously identi-fied this poor bird as his first target. With unwavering hands and a sharp eye, he held his breath and homed in on the target before releasing the shot. To his dismay, nothing happened. Confused, he quickly looked up to understand why the shot had failed and found Gaati towering above him, holding the slingshot by the leather patch that housed the stone missile.

Benjo's attempt to shoot the grasshopper buzzard was thwarted by Gaati, who reminded him of the customary law of the Kamba people: according to their beliefs, it is considered taboo to shoot birds that are nesting or perched on a tree within a residential com-pound. The presence of migratory or native bird colonies on a tree inside a residential compound is believed to bring blessings of wealth and good health to the home dwellers. According to legend, the Kamba people believe that birds, soaring high over vast dis-tances, occasionally touch the spirit world. It is for this reason that birds are revered as messengers from ancestors or deities, deliver-ing blessings and good fortune Therefore, it is strictly forbidden to harm or chase the birds away.

The team leader dismissed the incident as a minor learning expe-rience and resumed the journey southward, maintaining a watchful eye on the horizon to keep the team on course. Gaati was an experi-enced travel guide and a navigational expert who, having traversed the jungle many times, relied on traditional methods like observing the sun, mountains, and other landmarks to navigate safely to their destination. His expertise earned him the respect and admiration of those he led through the jungle.

Gaati's navigational ingenuity was a combination of his deep understanding of topography and his remarkable ability to utilize the natural features of the terrain to his advantage. He triangulated the team's position by observing multiple landmarks, including the mountain peak's position relative to the sun and the shadows cast by the mountain. It is for this reason that he kept an eye on the geological gap between Mount Banda and the Banda Salama Ranges to remain on course.

The team trekked along elephant trails, making significant progress deeper into the savannah. The open sky, scattered trees, flat grasslands, and lowlying shrubs provided ample light, helping Minto move with ease without fear of lurking snakes or spiders. However, the physical demands of walking for long hours, compounded by the heavy load on her back, began to take a toll on Minto.

To Minto's pleasant surprise, Gaati noticed her exhaustion and called for a much-needed break under a nearby baobab tree, known locally as the monkey-bread tree. The team was relieved to find themselves in a well-known rest area frequented by long-distance travelers and visitors en route to Banda Salama. They settled into makeshift seats, making themselves comfortable and taking in the beauty of their surroundings. However, Benjo remained standing, in awe of the baobab's colossal trunk, so massive that he likened it to a giant water-storage tank.

Minto took full advantage of the break to catch her breath, relishing the peacefulness of her surroundings. A wave of relief washed over her as she finally set down the heavy basket from her back. Gasping for air and wiping the sweat from her forehead, she marveled at the breathtaking beauty of nature that enveloped them. For a moment, she forgot all about her exhaustion and simply basked in the tranquility of nature.

During the break, Minto reached into the basket, retrieved a small gourd, and offered Benjo some cold sour porridge. This pause provided a much-needed opportunity to nourish Benjo, who, unlike the adults, could not endure long hours without sustenance. Meanwhile, Wasa and Gaati took the chance to leisurely stroll and relieve themselves behind the bushes. Observing their interaction, or the lack thereof, Minto mused about the silent tension between Wasa and Gaati, who never spoke outside official matters. She speculated it might be due to Gaati's inner demons clashing with Wasa's puritan spirit.

Suddenly, a fork-tailed drongo emerged from the blue sky and perched atop the boab tree, directly above Benjo. The bird began to sing a virtuoso aria, accompanied by a befitting jig that involved swinging its upper body from right to left and back again in a continuous loop. The uninvited melodist was a striking little black bird with red eyes, a hooked beak, and a forked tail, presenting a unique presence. Its persistent and indefatigable efforts to sing suggested that the drongo was on a mission.

With all due respect to the drongo's musical talents, Minto and Benjo found its song both bothersome and intrusive, especially after a well-deserved rest from their long and tiring trek. The last thing they wanted was this offensive noise from an unannounced orchestra. Benjo, in his irritation, even swore to teach the bird an unforgettable lesson with his slingshot, once he had finished quenching his thirst.

Meanwhile, in a secluded corner of the rest area, Gaati was alerted by a coded message he intercepted from the premonitory drongo. The fork-tailed African drongos are renowned for their remarkable ability to act as sentinels. They have the sensory ability to spot predators before they strike and warn other animals, and even humans, by emitting auditory alarm calls. The bird's message was urgent, prompting Gaati to act fast. Just as he was preparing to respond to the emergency, his worst fears were unequivocally confirmed by a nearby group of gazelles. The mother gazelle snorted, prompting the entire herd to stand at attention, hackles raised. This state of hypervigilance was a dual warning: it alerted other animals to the presence of a lurking predator and preemptively notified the predator that it had been detected, thereby reducing its chance of a successful surprise attack. The writing was on the wall; from Gaati's bush experience, he knew that a lead mother gazelle does not snort and raise her ears without reason. The urgency of the situation was undeniably palpable. Gaati knew he had to act quickly to protect his companions, who until now were unaware of the looming danger. But first things first, he needed to identify the source of the threat.

In response, Gaati escalated the alert to a full-blown emergency, hastening toward Benjo and Minto to ensure their safety.

Undoubtedly, Sosh chose Gaati as the chief pathfinder for her family's journey for good reason.In the Yatta village, Gaati was admired for his unparalleled bravery and fearlessness, facing down both beast and human adversaries with equal valour.

He was predisposed to react to challenging situations by fighting, so he needed little prompting or forethought to take such action even if it meant going to the ends of the earth. In fact, he once triumphed over a hyena in single man-to-beast combat, armed with nothing more than his bare hands. Gaati's toughness was legendary, and none of his peers in the twelve villages of the Yatta sub-county and beyond could match his grit.

According to accounts from Gaati's older neighbours, who watched him grow up, he consistently found it challenging to adopt a peaceful stance during arguments, disputes, or conflicts. This predisposition towards confrontation significantly influenced his early life, leading him to become a child delinquent. This lifestyle compelled him to leave home at the tender age of thirteen and ultimately choose never to marry.

Unfortunately, Gaati's unpleasant demeanour made it difficult for him to initiate and maintain relationships, especially when it came to courting for marriage. However, when people asked him about his conspicuous bachelorhood, he would often quip that a naked man does not put his hands in his pockets. Nevertheless, despite his attempts at humour, most people chose to avoid him due to his off-putting behaviour.

Gaati, much like many bullies and dictators, did not possess striking good looks. However, his towering height and commanding presence exuded an air of confidence and strength. He was never one to shy away from confrontation or to be polite when defending his beliefs. In fact, he was known to be quite rude at times. His unwavering determination and fearlessness were the defining traits that set him apart from the rest.

There was a tale of a violent altercation that occurred once upon a time between Gaati and a mason named Fundi at a popular local drinking joint. Fundi had just arrived, exhausted from a long day's work, and had barely taken a sip of his drink when Gaati started hurling insults at him for no apparent reason. Understandably agitated, Fundi delivered a swift left-hook punch to Gaati's left ear, knocking him unconscious. The attack happened so quickly that Gaati only felt a sharp blow and grogginess in his head before losing consciousness, partly due to the haze induced by alcohol.

Gaati remained motionless on the ground for several hours, his body bearing the marks of his ordeal, languishing in a stupor induced by both the alcohol and the trauma of the blow. When he finally woke up, his first clear thought was about hurting Fundi. Fortunately, Fundi had already left for home. This left Gaati simmering with unresolved anger, plotting his next move in the shadow of the night's events.

In a fit of rage and frustration, Gaati burst into a nearby store, his eyes ablaze with unbridled anger. He emerged shortly clenching a curved cutlass in one hand and a wooden mallet in the other, his grip tight and unyielding. Driven by an intense focus, he scoured the area for Fundi, his heart heart pounding the rib cage with an urgent need for vengeance, to exact retribution for the pain inflicted upon him.

With meticulous attention, Gaati scoured every corner of the compound, frenziedly rummaging through belongings and examining every nook and cranny of the hang-out. Despite his best efforts, Fundi was nowhere to be found. Frustrated and boiling with anger from not finding his attacker, Gaati directed his fury towards his fellow patrons, vowing to crush anyone who dared stand in his way, like a pesky fly.

As Gaati's escapades escalated, a sizable crowd of inebriated spectators formed around him, their anticipation for chaos palpable in the air. Tragically, instead of dissuading him, many among the throng spurred him on, their judgment clouded by alcohol, egging him to exact his revenge. Amid the cacophony of taunts and jeers, a solitary figure, Muuo—Minto's brother—stood firm, trying to inject a dose of sanity into the frenzy. He warned that seeking solace in alcohol and vengeance would only spiral into further despair. Yet, his pleas for peace were lost, swallowed by the drunken mob's raucous calls for retribution, their shouts of "Get him!" and "Fix him!" echoing louder than reason.

The next day, unbeknown to him, Gaati arrived at Fundi's compound at dawn. He sat on a stool in the middle of the courtyard, eagerly waiting for Fundi to wake up and face him in a decisive new round of combat to determine the true embodiment of manhood. Known for his relentless nature and refusal to concede defeat, Gaati was adamant about fighting Fundi until one of them emerged victorious or died in combat. Reflecting on their previous encounter, he scornfully compared Fundi to a reckless child provoking a sleeping buffalo.

Despite Gaati's arrogance, Fundi was no pushover. Among the masons, he was renowned for his impressive physical stature. The moment Fundi knocked Gaati out with a single, decisive punch, a bystander humorously remarked that the true measure of a man's strength might well lie in the size of his wrist. Indeed, Fundi's fist, when clenched, measured a whopping thirty-eight centimetres, complemented by forearms as robust as steel rods. Fundi's clenched fist surpassed even those of the reigning heavyweight boxing champion of the Yatta district in size. Such physical attributes made him a truly formidable opponent.

Before the altercation last night, Munyua, a long-term drinking buddy of Gaati, had advised him against confronting Fundi. Despite Munyua's firsthand account of Fundi's extraordinary strength—demonstrated when he single-handedly restrained a giant bull that had refused to enter the footbath at a local cattle dip—Gaati ignored the warning, dismissing it as mere cowardice.

In contrast, Fundi was a wise and strategic. He fully understood that choices have consequences. It was not lost on him that engaging a formidable adversary on his own property could lead to damage and loss on him. He wisely heeded his clan's proverb that cautions a one-eyed person against fighting on the sandy ground for obvious reasons.

After carefully assessing the situation, Fundi decided to negotiate peace, signalling his willingness by raising the white flag. This decision, however, came with its own set of demands from Gaati. As a condition of the truce, Gaati demanded that Fundi publicly recognize him as the superior fighter at the very drinking spot where he had suffered defeat. Moreover, Gaati couldn't resist taunting Fundi, declaring, 'Every man has a plan until he gets punched in the mouth. Next time, pick your fights more wisely little boy.' This public humiliation, inflicted in front of Fundi's closest friends and family, was Gaati's way of inflating his ego while diminishing Fundi. With a triumphant swagger, Gaati then left the courtyard, exiting Fundi's compound.

Within minutes of arriving, Gaati identified the lurking danger alerted by the drongo. With his expert woodcraft, he surveyed the area for signs of animal activity — tracks, spoor, or burrows — and listened for any movement, like the rustling of branches. Then, the wind shifted, bringing a light westerly breeze that carried a strong musky scent towards him. Drawing on his jungle experience, Gaati instantly recognized the predator he was dealing with from the scent.

Turning into the wind, Gaati spotted a massive nine-foot-long African rock python concealed amidst the leaves under a nearby bush-willow tree. The python, stealthily prowling through the underbrush, was clearly on the hunt for a quick meal. Drawing once again from his knowledge of animal behavior in the wild, Gaati understood the danger. A hungry python, especially one that had already set its sights on its prey, could be incredibly obstinate and dangerous. Despite Gaati's hunting experience giving him a potential upper hand in this situation, Minto and Benjo, completely unaware of the lurking threat, remained vulnerable.

Despite feeling vulnerable and exposed, their confidence in Gaati's situational awareness and control remained unshaken, perhaps naively so, considering pythons rarely attack humans. In this instance, the reptile's menacing presence seemed focused on the chickens nestled in the crib Wasa had placed beside them, momentarily absent while answering nature's call.

Gaati carefully observed the python's movements, analysing its behavior and anticipating its next move. He understood the importance of remaining calm and collected, as any sudden movements could provoke the python and put him in harm's way. A nine-foot-long python could easily weigh up to a quarter of a tone. Given that the python's body was composed of incredibly powerful and elastic muscles, used to wrap around its prey and squeeze until it died from suffocation or cardiac arrest, Gaati stood no chance of freeing himself from its grip should the python decide to strike.

Amid the tense situation, Gaati wisely decided against killing the python. Instead, he opted to dismantle the intrusive human camp and relocate his team away from the reptile's habitat, acknowledging the critical role of pythons in controlling rodent populations and the necessity of conserving them. Otherwise, Gaati could have eas-

ily sliced the python's head in two with a single arrow from his collection of cyanide-tipped arrows, thereby killing the python within
minutes. However, he refrained from such a decision by drawing
on his grandfather's conservation training, which emphasised the
important role that every species plays in maintaining a balanced
ecosystem.

With utmost caution, Gaati swiftly disassembled the resting
camp and instructed his team to form a single file on a wildlife trail
to resume their journey. He held a large, forked branch ready to defend his team against the python should it attack. In the jungle, there
is an unspoken understanding between humans and animals dictat-
ing their interactions. According to this natural order, the python
would likely not attack Gaati and his team if they retreated peacefully. On the other hand, should the python become aggressive,
Gaati reserved the right to defend his team by harming the reptile. It
was a delicate balance of respecting the jungle's natural order while
ensuring the team's safety.

Following their chilling encounter with the serpent, the team
pressed on through the vast savannah grasslands, making steady
progress towards a small town situated southeast of the Nzambani
Rock. At one point, Benjo entertained the idea of breaking free from
the group to walk around the legendary Nzambani Rock seven times
to test the gods. However, after careful consideration, he decided
against it, realizing the potential risks far outweighed any potential
benefits.

After trekking for about five kilometres, Gaati made the impulsive decision to take a short cut through what appeared to be unfamiliar private property to save time. It's crucial to understand,
though, that the concept of private property in this context is
markedly different from conventional interpretations. In the Kamba
community, all land was communal, belonging not to individuals
but to the community, stewarded by a trust for the benefit of all its
members.

Nevertheless, despite the potential risks, it was common for long-distance travellers to take short cuts through vast areas of land, such as tribal trust lands or open jungles, to shorten the distance between two points in this region. However, it appears that Gaati may not have taken heed of the adage that the road to hell is paved with good intentions.

The team navigated through the revised route and came across an imposing batholith that forced them to slow down and circumnavigate it. Suddenly, all hell broke loose. A sharp arrow whizzed past Gaati's temple and lodged itself deep into a nearby tree trunk. The team was under attack, and they had to act fast. Without hesitation, Gaati commanded everyone to take cover as a second arrow hurtled towards him like a heat-seeking missile. Gaati ducked in the nick of time to avoid a fatal blow to his forehead. The second arrow ricocheted off a rock outcrop behind him and fell to the ground.

As soon as Gaati's team hit the ground to take cover, a commanding voice echoed off the rock outcrop, instructing the invisible marksmen to disable the lead slasher. The attack was meticulously coordinated and choreographed, complete with a command centre directing the field soldiers to immobilize Gaati. As a seasoned warrior, Gaati understood "immobilization" in a war context as a tactical measure to pin him down to his current position so he couldn't flee or gain a tactical advantage by moving elsewhere. It was evident that the invisible merchants of death had been scouting Gaati's team for some time and had identified him as their most significant threat. Unfortunately for Gaati, the enemy held the upper hand, having already taken full control of both the situational awareness and the war arena.

Gaati kept his cool in the face of peril. He understood that his team's safety was his responsibility, so he cautiously slithered on his stomach and retrieved the discarded arrow from the ground to inspect it. He made a quick scrutiny of the patterns and intricate carvings on the arrow shaft and right away recognized that type of arrow missile as belonging to the belligerent Akimi clan.

The Akimi clan had a unique preference for crafting their arrow missiles, utilizing red milkwood for the shaft and glossy ibis feathers for the flight end. On the other hand, Gaati's own Aombe clan preferred highland bamboo for their arrow shafts and white-backed vulture feathers for the flight end. This clear contrast between the two clans made it effortless for Gaati to distinguish the enemy's missile.

However, what truly set the Akimi clan's arrows apart was their clan totem – the African scops owl – embossed on the flat part of their barbed arrowheads. This unique symbol confirmed beyond a doubt that the missile belonged to the Akimi warriors.

Gaati's worst nightmare began to sink in: the last thing he wanted was to be taken captive by the Akimi warrior. The mere thought sent shivers down his spine. The Akimi warriors were notorious for their use of barbed arrowheads with pointed spurs, a cruel tactic designed to inflict excruciating damage to their victims' body tissues. The result was a slow and agonizing death from bleeding and poisoning. But that was not all. According to the village historian's account, the Akimi people were cannibals who roasted their victims alive. Gaati found himself in the most perilous situation of his life, tasked with protecting innocent civilians who had no combat training.

Given the high stakes, Gaati's exceptional skills in hostage negotiation were required now more than ever to save his life and that of Sosh's family from the clutches of the Akimi warriors. Gaati's extensive experience in dealing with dangerous armed conflicts, gained as a former member of Yatta District Inter-Clan Conflict Negotiations and Reconciliation Council.

The Akimi warriors were infamous for their ruthless and barbaric tactics, leaving no survivors in their wake. Gaati understood the urgency of the situation and knew that he had to act quickly and with caution to ensure the safety of his team. With a stealthy roll onto his back, Gaati pulled out his handcrafted ocarina and played a unique sound as loudly as he could muster. He waited anxiously for a response, but all he heard was a deafening silence. It was a morbid silence that could only mean one thing – death.

Two minutes passed, but it felt like an eternity. Gaati's fate and that of Sosh's family hung in the balance. It was the longest wait of his life, surpassing even the nerve-racking experience of requesting a truce during the bloody Mau Mau battle of Ol Donyo Sabuk Forest against the mechanized division of the British army.

As each minute passed, Gaati's heart raced with anticipation. The deafening silence was a clear indication that the Akimi warriors were not going to back down. Gaati knew that these could be his last moments on earth. Nonetheless, he was determined to protect Sosh's family from being taken hostage by the savages, even if it meant sacrificing his own life.

In a dire situation, Gaati found himself caught between a rock and a hard place. He was outnumbered and outgunned by the Akimi cannibals, but he remained calm and resolute in his determination to achieve a favourable outcome. As the minutes ticked by, the silence from the cannibals became more and more unsettling, but Gaati refused to let fear take hold. The rest of the team was in the dark about what was happening, but they had faith in Gaati's ability to lead them out of this dangerous situation alive.

Suddenly, the piercing sound of a bugle echoed through the air like a sonic boom, signalling a response to Gaati's request for a truce. Never in his life had Gaati been so relieved to hear a bugle. The reveille originated from an Akimi scout perched high up on a flat-crown tree to the north of the team's position. Gaati had not noticed the scout until now, but that was not important at this point. What surprised and pleased him at the same time was the fact that the Akimi savages had accepted his request for a ceasefire. It was a moment of relief and disbelief.

Having served in the Signal Corps Division of the Kenya Land and Freedom Army, Gaati was uniquely equipped to decode the military signal granting them amnesty. Yet, before sharing the good news with his comrades, he needed to verify the signal's authenticity. This required completing one final procedure to confirm that the signal was neither a ruse nor a trap.

Gaati unfurled a white handkerchief and waved it seven times in the air, signalling his intentions for peace. In a reciprocal gesture, the Akimi scout dropped down an arrow into the neutral ground between them, laying his shield next to the arrow. It was at this moment that Gaati was assured beyond all doubt of the amnesty's authenticity. Such an event was exceedingly rare, given the Akimi's reputation for ruthlessness. Overwhelmed yet relieved by the turn of events following the ambush, Gaati believed that the morning's blessing from Sosh had contributed to their extraordinary survival. However, he chose to keep these thoughts to himself, unwilling to show any vulnerability before his team.

Despite the Akimis' reputation for violence, Gaati couldn't help but feel a sense of admiration for their bravery and tenacity. Witnessing their pinpoint accuracy in setting a death trap not only challenged his perceptions but also fostered a grudging respect for his adversaries. The team had survived a death trap and that was all that mattered to Gaati now. It was a small victory, but it was a victory, nonetheless.

With a profound sense of respect, Gaati stood up slowly and bowed three times to the three Akimi warriors who stood just ten metres away from the site of the planned homicide. The three rough-looking warriors waved their rhino-leathered shields, signalling Gaati and his team to continue their journey. However, Minto remained sceptical about the cannibals and walked with a sideways glance, ever watchful for any sign of danger. It was not over until it was over. Meanwhile, Wasa and Benjo strode ahead confidently, determined not to let the savages intimidate them. They were fuelled by the inherent yet overconfident belief among the Aombe clan that let death come before surrender.

Gaati and his team swiftly formed a single file and departed from the scene, cautiously walking past the warriors and avoiding any eye contact that might provoke an attack. However, Benjo couldn't resist the temptation to steal a quick peek at the warriors. As the Kamba saying goes, the devil often comes as everything you've ever wished for. In this moment, Benjo accidentally locked eyes with one of the warriors, whose eyes glowed red like fire—a shocking sight that underscored the warrior's notorious reputation for consuming marijuana and tobacco. This encounter sent a wave of fear crashing over Benjo, causing his knees to weaken and his stomach to coil into knots.

As Gaati and his team trudged forwards, a heavy silence hung over them. Each member was lost in their own thoughts, the tension in the air almost tangible. The fear of the Akimi warriors lingered – not just in their minds, but permeating every aspect of the atmosphere around them. It was an experience each one of them wished to forget sooner rather than later.

However, amidst the unease, there was a silver lining. The encounter with the Akimi warriors had etched the Jogoo family name into the annals of history. From that day onwards, they became the only known humans, dead or alive, to have faced the alleged Akimi cannibals and lived to tell the tale. It was a stroke of luck, if not a happy accident, but one that would be recounted for generations to come.

After their harrowing escape, Gaati made the decision to abandon the revised shortcut through the Akimi trust land and revert to the original route through the bushland. Their destination remained the same: a small town nestled amidst rolling hills, where they hoped to find some much-needed rest and respite after their long and arduous journey punctuated with an ambush.

Before they could see the town itself, an unexpected yet welcoming scent of freshly baked bread wafted through the air, heralding their approach and igniting a sense of homeliness they hadn't felt for hours. As the group approached Kwa Kulu Town, the sight of smoke rising from the chimneys of the houses and the distant sounds of people going about their daily lives brought a profound sense of relief. Finally, there was a sign of civilization after the ten kilometres they had covered in silence, ruminating about their near-death experience. Despite the harrowing journey, they were all grateful to finally arrive at Kwa Kulu Town, a place that promised rest and a momentary escape from their recent ordeals.

Kwa Kulu Town was a small trading centre with only one main street, yet it boasted about two dozen shops and a large open market area. Despite its size, the town had a disproportionately large population, estimated by Minto to exceed two thousand people. At first, it was unclear why the town was so overpopulated. However, as Minto's team explored the town, it became apparent that its capacity was simply insufficient to accommodate the vast number of people who came from far and wide to attend the designated market day on Fridays.

The town derived its name from Mr Kulu, a nomadic Maasai herder who roamed the Yatta Plateau in the eighteenth century. During the dry seasons, with a shortage of pasture in Maasailand, Kulu would bring his livestock to graze in the lush savannah grassland of the Yatta Plateau. As a result, Kulu consistently pitched his manyatta (temporary dwelling) at the same spot, which organically grew into what is now known as the Kwa Kulu trading centre in postcolonial Kenya, as permanent farming migrants settled in the area.

When nomadic grazing activities were restricted by the colonial administration after recommendations from the Agricultural Commission and Carter Land Commission in 1929, Kulu's dwelling became a permanent fixture in the area. The Kamba people, who migrated into the region, referred to Kulu's dwelling as 'Kwa Kulu,' with the prefix 'kwa' meaning 'the place of.' Hence, the name 'Kwa Kulu' was born.

As the team ventured deeper into the town, they were met with less-than-ideal living conditions, appalling yet expected given the population pressure on the town's infrastructure. The narrow and congested lanes, cluttered with makeshift merchandise stalls, created a chaotic and overwhelming atmosphere. The air was permeated with the stench of cow dung and general animal waste from a nearby large open market selling livestock. The lack of proper sanitation facilities was evident, as offensive odours of ammonia and sewage wafted from behind the shops. People seemed to have little regard for waste recycling, carelessly tossing banana skins and sugarcane leaf sheaths onto the streets, resulting in a landscape littered with garbage and debris. It was clear that the town's overpopulation had severely impacted its infrastructure and resources, significantly detracting from the quality of living conditions.

A typical day at Kwa Kulu is characterised by a vibrant and bustling crowd of people from all walks of life converging at the trading centre to showcase and trade their wares. The diversity of products on sale is truly remarkable, ranging from fresh farm produce to smoked fish, live animals, delectable food, and all sorts of retail merchandise. Everywhere you look, vendors tout their merchandise, with buyers haggling over prices and peddlers filling the air with raucous cries of "Come buy this! Come buy that!"

Minto stumbled upon a large abandoned landfill located at the southern end of the town whilst exploring. The dumpsite was overflowing with a mishmash of waste, strewn across the ground and spilling into the surrounding bushland. The site had become a haven for scavengers, from marabou storks to domestic cats, all foraging for food amidst the rubbish. This landfill served as a stark reminder that the town had once operated an efficient waste management system before the town council either became overwhelmed and abandoned the effort or ran out of resources.

Nonetheless, despite its small size, Kwa Kulu Town played a crucial role in the economy of the region. Its strategic location on the boundary between three populous districts, inhabited by the Kamba, Kikuyu, and Maasai tribes, attracted a significant influx of people into the town, all drawn by the opportunity to participate in commerce.

Without a doubt, Kwa Kulu Town was a vibrant hub of activity, brimming with a symphony of sounds, lively chatter from vendors, a colourful array of fresh produce, and the aroma of delicious food wafting through the air, tempting visitors to sample the local cuisine. From dawn to dusk, there was never a dull moment in this bustling town. It also served as a melting pot of cultures, with people from various backgrounds coming together to trade and socialize. Consequently, most inhabitants across the three districts served by the municipality were multilingual, fluently speaking Kamba, Kikuyu, Maasai, and Swahili.

Benjo was charmed by the vibrant energy of the town. Unlike in his village, where he held a position of power among his peers as a prince, he found himself struggling to understand the urban patois. As the team made their way to the town centre, Benjo couldn't help but stop more than a dozen times to take in the lively chaos of itinerant merchants haggling over prices with their clients, and local hawkers touting their wares to potential buyers. However, the diversity of the town was not limited to commerce, as Benjo soon discovered. He observed idlers sauntering about in all types of outfits, from casual wear to formal clothing. Of particular interest to him was the large number of young people in tawdry jeans and T-shirts, either smoking cigarettes or chewing khat. He couldn't help but wonder if these teenagers attended schools or colleges at all.

After criss-crossing the town for a while, Benjo grew weary of the raucous behaviour of the townspeople and decided to take a leisurely stroll towards the outskirts. He meandered along and noticed a political rally taking place about two hundred yards ahead on the eastern side of the town. His curiosity was immediately piqued, and he decided to investigate further.

He moved closer to the crowd and listened to the lively chatter of the local attendees. It quickly became apparent that the rally had been organised by a local politician who was vying for a seat in the upcoming county assembly elections. The supporters of the aspirant were effusive in their praise, describing him with ridiculous adjectives such as "the holy one", "honourable", "prince of peace", and even "our saviour!" To an outsider, it would have seemed as though the politician was being worshipped like a deity.

It was no secret that, in Africa, politicians held an enormous amount of power and influence. Superficially, a politician was regarded as the most important human being the society. Thus, an aspiring son of the Akimi clan was determined not only to make a mark for himself and his tribe in the country's political arena but also to ensure that he secured a share of the national cake on behalf of his tribe.

Unlike many of his peers, the aspirant, Mr. Tambi, had been educated in Catholic boarding schools by European missionaries before Kenya gained independence. This education set him apart from other members of his community and provided him with a unique advantage in politics. However, Tambi's current bid for the Kwa Kulu seat was not his first attempt. In the previous election, he was defeated by a competitor with more financial resources, illustrating the challenges faced by candidates from humble backgrounds. Unfortunately, in this region, voters often base their decisions more on financial influence and partisan loyalty than on merit. Winning an election in Africa is challenging without significant financial backing.

Benjo was not interested in politics. He couldn't understand why three hundred people in their right senses would abandon their daily chores to listen to a package of platitudes from someone who sounded like a con artist. Specifically, Benjo pondered how a mere county assembly member could fulfill the multitude of promises he was making to his constituents, from constructing hospitals, local roads and schools to providing piped water to every household. It seemed implausible to Benjo that one person could accomplish so much.

Despite the politician's grandiose proclamations, draped in the cloak of pretension and hollow promises, the atmosphere among the crowd was electric with genuine hope. Here stood a man whose words were woven with the threads of ambition and ostentation, yet his audience, driven by a sincere desire for transformation and improvement in their lives, hung onto his every utterance. The contrast between the politician's insincerity and the crowd's authentic yearning for change was stark. As he delivered his speech, adorned with pledges he scarcely intended to keep, the crowd, blinded by their fervent wish for a better future, erupted in cheers and applause. They were captivated, not by the truth of his intentions, but by the mirage of progress he skilfully painted before their hopeful eyes.

Enraged by the politician's blatant deception, Benjo left the political rally and wandered north until he reached the end of town. Surprisingly but not unexpectedly, he stumbled upon a Christian crusade. The transition from a political campaign rally to a praise and worship crusade was akin to moving out of the frying pan into the fire! As Benjo approached the gathering, he was struck by the fervour and passion of the worshippers. The quintessential claque of revivalists belted out one of their most popular canticles with such intensity that a stranger would have been convinced that it was the worshippers' last day on earth before an eschatological rapture. Benjo drew closer to investigate the crusade anyway.

No sooner had the song died down than a holier-than-thou-looking man of God climbed onto a makeshift rostrum and began pontificating loudly to proselytize the Akimi people. He thundered unapologetically, urging the people to abjure their maimu (demons) allegiance. His sermon was amplified across the town and its environs by a sophisticated sound system, projecting his message from a large loudspeaker mounted on a tree in the middle of town to ensure that no one missed a bit.

In the Kamba language, the term maimu was frequently used to describe malevolent demonic spirits and, regrettably, the local pastor was insinuating that the Akimi people were devil-worshippers. It was apparent that the preacher's attitude was influenced by preconceived attitude about the Akimi people's connection with God, as well as an ardent desire for confirmation bias. This deceitful propaganda resulted in the preacher's belief that the Akimi people were uncivilized and idolatrous, which was not only incorrect but also insulting.

The preacher's sermon stirred up quite a bit of controversy among his listeners. One irate listener who was visiting the town from Kiambu district went as far as threatening physical violence against the pastor if he persisted in his religious discrimination. The pastor's words also caused a commotion among the native congregants, who until now only heard rumours of Christian missionaries denigrating their local deity as demonic. They got even more irked after hearing it straight from the horse's mouth.

The tension in the outdoor arena was palpable, and it seemed as though things were about to boil over. In response, the pastor wisely decided to increase security around the pulpit. He knew all too well that a missionary had been killed in this very town, not long ago, for using derogatory language about the local deities, and he wasn't about to take any chances.

Benjo was unfazed by the preacher's discriminatory remarks. Instead, he was enthralled by the clamour of the crusade, if not the madness of the strange ways of the urban people. Even though the preacher's sermon was tinged with religious discrimination against the Akimi people, Benjo found the opinion and reaction of the protestor from Kiambu district to be expressively impious. But it was not within his powers to give counsel to counsel to strangers.

Undeterred by the disapproval of his audience, the preacher continued to read from the book of Matthew, focusing on the Baptism of Jesus Christ. He paused to offer an explanation as to how and why Jesus was baptized, but Benjo took special exception with a logical conflict in the syntax of the preacher's explanation. In Benjo's understanding, the Biblical content did not align with the lexical analysis by the man of God.

Traditionally, baptism has been administered by a priest who invokes the name of the Father, the Son, and the Holy Spirit. Benjo, a regular attendee at the local parish, had witnessed this ritual many times before. However, on this occasion, Benjo found himself lost in thought. He couldn't help but wonder: Since Jesus was the Son of God and also the person being baptized, did John the Baptist ever find this choice of words confusing? For instance, did John the Baptist say, 'I baptize you in the name of the Father, *in your own name*, and in that of the Holy Spirit?' This question left Benjo racking his brain.

Benjo often thought deeply about things he read in the Bible. Once, he even got kicked out of his catechism class because he argued that Adam and Eve's lives must have been boring since they were devoid of childhood experiences. His troubles started when he asked the catechist if Adam and Eve, being created as fully grown adults, missed out on the typical childhood phase of growth and development like everyone else.

In response, the catechist initially requested that Benjo return home and come back accompanied by either or both of his parents for counselling. However, after careful consideration, the catechist decided to instead suspend Benjo from classes for two weeks, instructing him to recite the Act of Contrition twice daily during this period as a form of punishment. This change of mind was influenced by the realisation that Benjo was more likely to return accompanied by his grandmother, a choleric woman known for her confrontational and sometimes even violent demeanour. The catechist had been informed by Benjo's discipline master at school of an incident where Benjo's grandmother had slapped the discipline master for administering corporal punishment to Benjo for being late to school. Wishing to avoid any potential conflicts, the catechist opted for a course of action that minimised the risk of confrontation.

Like everyone else, Benjo's dad, Wasa, seized the opportunity of the interval at Kwa Kulu to immerse himself in the local culture and explore the open market. He interacted with the amiable locals and even purchased some snuff and toiletries. Echoing the wisdom of the Kamba proverb, "when a tortoise dances in the market square, it is about to gain something," Wasa's evident enthusiasm was rooted in the anticipation of enjoying the freedom to be alone, a prospect he deeply cherished given his love for solitude.

Wasa's demeanour shifted from reserved to lively, reflecting his unique personality blend. Preferring solitude, he usually appeared timid and unassertive among strangers, yet among close friends, he was known for his irreverent stance on customary laws, frequently dismissing them with his sharp, larrikin humour.

To put it simply, Wasa's mysterious character can best be explained by the wisdom of Kamba sages who believe that people with extraordinary minds often find themselves isolated. Could Wasa have possessed a form of genius that was unrecognised by those around him? Despite his mysterious aura, Wasa preferred to spend time in common meeting spaces with like-minded peers, who were often mistakenly considered to be idle gossipers by other villagers. Sometimes, they were even disparagingly regarded as crooks. Fundamentally, when a person is secretive and taciturn with information about themselves, people tend to fill in the gaps with their own negative opinions. Intriguingly, Wasa seemed indifferent to the negative public perception of himself. He once told a close friend that he didn't care about being perceived as a crook, musing that while all the crooked trees remain standing in the forest, the straight ones have been felled.

Despite his infamous reputation for being a loafer, Wasa was surprisingly a master of observational humour. According to his best friend and confidant, Mr Tamasha, Wasa honed his wit by closely observing the daily foibles of the villagers, always keeping his quips fresh and up to date. Indeed, Wasa was bohemian. It's no surprise then that Minto was shocked to find her usually thrifty husband actually spending money at the busy Kwa Kulu Market.

I n every law, there is always an exemption, and that was certainly the case with Wasa, an enigma to many. However, little did most people know that there was one individual who knew Wasa better than anyone else – his mentor and circumcision godfather, Mzee Pembe. Mzee Pembe's rare insight into Wasa's personality came to light during the courtship period, when the suitors' party visited Minto's parents. The groom's reception party assigned Mzee Pembe the task of providing an account of Wasa, as required by Kamba customary law.

According to Mzee Pembe, Wasa possesses an unquenchable desire to stand out and be remembered, even if it meant being viewed negatively. While his actions may have been misunderstood by many in the village, it was crucial to consider the possibility that he possessed a unique perspective that wasn't readily apparent to others. Despite Wasa's character remaining a mystery, his story served as a reminder of the importance of making an effort to understand and appreciate those who may be different from us.

Mzee Pembe's insightful commentary on Wasa's character proved to be a pivotal moment in his life, as it earned Wasa a wife. Hitherto, Wasa's in-laws could not make head or tail of his complex demeanour but even to categorize him within the five fundamental human traits.

Mzee Pembe's insightful commentary on Wasa's character proved pivotal in his life, as it earned Wasa a wife. Until then, Wasa's in-laws had been unable to understand his complex demeanour or categorize him within the five fundamental human traits. Mzee Pembe's courageous account before Wasa's in-laws provided the much-needed breakthrough in their understanding of their prospective son-in-law, leading to a newfound appreciation for his unique qualities. From that day on, Wasa was able to forge a deeper connection with his in-laws and establish a more harmonious relationship with them.

Despite Wasa's peculiar habits, when Minto discovered that he had been spending money without her approval, she immediately confronted him. She demanded to know why he was shopping alone and for whom. Sensing Minto's foul mood, Wasa hesitated to answer. Until that moment, he had been enjoying a peaceful moment of solitude during his short break and had no interest in engaging in unsolicited conversations. However, as the Kamba proverb goes, a coward often becomes hungry for a fight when they see someone they think they can beat. In this scenario, Minto saw her husband as an easy target and swiftly moved in for the confrontation.

Thankfully, Wasa was wise enough to recognize that discretion was often the better part of valour. He also understood that a bird doesn't sing because it has an answer, but rather because it has a song. So, he painstakingly mumbled a laconic answer in response to Minto's initial question, claiming that he was shopping for a Mr Spit-It-on-the-Floor without providing any further details. Wasa's answer was a non-responsive nonsense answer designed to shut Minto, but it was sufficient to divert Minto's attention and preserve Wasa's tranquillity.

Since Wasa's answer to Minto's question was a white lie, and given that falsehoods can lead to multiple outcomes, Wasa hoped that he would not be challenged to repeat the same answer in the future. He was afraid that, if it happened, remembering the exact same answer would be unlikely. Nevertheless, he had successfully deflected Minto's verbal attack for the time being, and that was all that mattered at the moment. However, Wasa seemed oblivious to the fact that, when assisting a blind person with peeling groundnuts, it's crucial to keep whistling so that the blind man knows you're not eating from his bowl.

Minto decided to stop nagging Wasa, but it was a tactical retreat. Her silence marked the beginning of a well-planned grand scheme to harass Wasa through incremental steps until she completely cornered him. No wonder Wasa occasionally found himself questioning societal norms that officially designated men as the heads of households, yet, in practice, married women wielded substantial power within a marriage.

Minto's temporary incertitude gave Wasa a glimmer of hope to break free from his wife's manipulative ways and focus on his own business. He wondered why someone who claimed to love him would constantly nag him about insignificant matters. Wasa believed that true love meant highlighting each other's strengths, not weaknesses. In Wasa's opinion, this was a clear violation of one of the age-old tenets of the nuptial union. Unfortunately, Minto deliberately chose to ignore this fundamental aspect of their marriage. She enjoyed seeing her husband in distress.

The Kamba people have proverb that bad things often come in pairs. Just as Minto and Wasa were about to end their uncomfortable exchange of words, Gaati, who had been silently observing from a nearby stall, saw an opportunity to intensify the conflict. Without targeting anyone specifically, Gaati approached the couple and loudly proclaimed that while a fish and a bird may fall in love, they cannot build a home together. He paused, letting the insult sink in, before further inflaming the situation by adding that most married couples are like buttocks: always in friction, yet inseparable. Gaati aimed to deepen the couple's already tense mood. And he succeeded. His comments propelled Minto into a furious rage, while Wasa chose to ignore him and walked away. Gaati's remarks were a dig at their contrasting personalities.

Minto was a woman of strong will and determination. She refused to let anyone take advantage of her and was not one to take an insult lying down. However, she was wise enough to choose her battles carefully and not act impulsively.

Driven by rage, Minto contemplated taking a blunt object to split Gaati's skull open with a single blow to teach him a lesson. However, after careful consideration, she realized that delayed action was the best remedy for anger. She took a step back to reflect on the situation, understanding that those who are hardest to love are the ones who need love the most. For this reason, she decided to take the high road and put the matter to rest.

Following the brief argument with her husband and the hurtful remarks from Gaati, Minto realized the significance of establishing boundaries to safeguard herself from further frustration, disappointment and hurt. She recognized that protecting her emotional and physical well-being was crucial, and she was determined to do so with grace and tact.

In contrast, Wasa deliberately chose to steer clear of the self-centred contests between Gaati – whom he saw as the devil incarnate – and Minto. He foresaw the possible emotional damage that these contests could inflict and made a conscious decision to avoid them. He was fully aware of Minto's ambitious nature and her unwillingness to settle for anything less than the best. As Briffault's law dictates, it iwas the female who sets the conditions for the animal family, and Wasa was not about to challenge a universal law of nature. He knew that Minto was not one to play in the repechage league. When she withdrew from their verbal exchange, he saw an opportunity to discreetly tuck away the items he had procured into a small leather bag strapped across his body.

Wasa's reclusive nature had taught him a valuable lesson: in this case, the best way to heal from an encounter with toxic people is by distancing oneself from the source of pain. Consequently, he moved away from Minto and retreated into a world of his own, completely oblivious to the activities around him.

Admittedly, Wasa's misanthropic demeanor can be traced back to an authoritarian upbringing by his condescending mother, Sosh. This situation was further exacerbated by the absence of a father figure, resulting in a tragic episode that reads like a cautionary tale out of a book on how not to raise a child. Adding insult to injury, Wasa's father, Mr. Jogoo, passed away during the Mau Mau war when Wasa was just ten years old, leaving him under the guardianship of his namesake grandfather, who was already a hundred years old and frail.

Regrettably, Mzee Wasa was well past his use-by date, with little to offer his grandson in terms of active guidance. As a result, young Wasa was left to navigate the murky world of growing up on his own, often relying on his own quirks and quiddities punctuated by Sosh's terror and tyranny. Despite the challenges he faced, Wasa remained determined to forge his own path and make a name for himself.

But to be fair to all, Wasa's problems have their origins in events before his birth. Even when his parents were at the height of their lives, Wasa's mother, Sosh, held significant influence over her husband in both familial and social spheres. Interestingly, prior to their marriage, one of Jogoo's maternal uncles, Mr. Peter Manyi, had foreseen Sosh's potential domineering nature over Jogoo. Uncle Manyi even went as far as to caution Jogoo with a proverb, warning against a man who does not heed the signs of a domineering woman, implying he may end up in an undesirable marriage.

In addition, Manyi cautioned Jogoo in a musing manner that, although having an ex-spouse was not uncommon in society, demoting his own kin to the position of ostracized family members by choosing the wrong partner was unacceptable. Uncle Manyi was insinuating that the spouse Jogoo had chosen could potentially alienate him from his extended family.

Tragically, Jogoo was blinded by Sosh's irresistible charm and failed to heed his uncle's wise words of caution. In the end, his ill-fated love affair and infatuation with Sosh led him down a path of misery and despair, culminating in what turned out to be a marriage from hell.

In the end, Uncle Manyi's prophecy was fulfilled. The upbringing Wasa received from an alpha female and a subservient male as parents proved disastrous for his personality. To make matters worse, society's attitude towards Wasa's damaged personality only worked to worsen the situation. For example, most villagers perceived Wasa as a lazy individual who enjoyed lounging in village hangouts and engaging in self-righteous debates with other daydreamers who shared his views. Yet in private, Wasa saw himself as a decent person, a good listener in a world full of chatty busybodies. He also believed in the importance of developing oneself into a positive father figure if one was not fortunate enough to have a good father.

Despite Wasa's strong beliefs in his leadership abilities, a psychoanalytic examination conducted after his unsuccessful application to join the Kenya Defence Forces revealed a different truth. His case officer and the lead consulting psychiatrist at the Nairobi Forces Memorial Hospital concluded that Wasa suffered from a chronic condition of schizoid personality disorder. This condition had compromised his ability to form meaningful relationships and engage in social interactions. In fact, Wasa himself admitted to Minto that he did not hate people, but rather he felt better when he was alone.

Eventually, after a one-hour break, Gaati ordered his team to fall in line and prepare to depart from the bustling Kwa Kulu trading centre. The team promptly obeyed the command and assembled at the forecourt of one of the shops, ready to depart. With the discipline of migratory wild beasts, they set off in a single file towards Dipu, a small village nestled between Kwa Kulu Town and the edge of the Yatta Plateau. After walking for a short distance, Wasa noticed that Benjo was conspicuously absent from the group.

He scanned around for him and, after a brief search, spotted him in the distance, mingling with a group of local hunters. Benjo was completely engrossed, captivated by the sight of roasted squirrel and dik-dik meat skewered on sticks over an open flame, utterly oblivious to the journey ahead and the scheduled departure. Seizing the moment, one hawker approached Benjo, enticing him with a free sample of the roast, hoping to make a sale. After tasting the delicacy, Benjo simply walked away without uttering a word, an action that did not perturb the hawker in the slightest. Accustomed to the unpredictable nature of passers-by, some of whom became customers while others remained just fleeting visitors, the hawker shrugged it off with ease.

Meanwhile, Benjo's mother shouted angrily at him to hurry up and catch up with the rest of the team. Startled by his mother's sudden outburst, Benjo exclaimed, "Eek!" He had been caught napping. Since arriving at the Town of Kwa Kulu, Benjo often found himself lost in thought, distracted by the exotic activities of urban life that were strange to him. However, after awakening from his mother's call, he regained his focus and scurried south to catch up with the rest of the team.

They set off and travelled for another two hours, making significant progress towards their next waypoint, the village of Dipu. As they drew nearer, Minto began to hear a commotion in the distance - the sound of people shouting angrily. The clamour and chaos were reminiscent of a public shaming, although a cluster of euphorbia trees obstructed their view, preventing them from seeing any details. Minto couldn't help but ponder the peculiarities of the people in this seemingly peaceful town. They quickened their pace, fuelled by curiosity and eagerness to reach the source of the commotion.

As Minto's team neared the entrance of Dipu, they witnessed a heated discussion between the locals. Observing the discussion, it was clear that a young man had been accused of a serious act of theft, stealing food from an elderly woman's home. The villagers were divided on the appropriate punishment, with some advocating for severe consequences while others sought mercy for the thief.

However, the arrival of Minto's team had a calming effect on the situation. As outsiders, they were able to offer a fresh perspective and suggest a peaceful resolution. One old lady suggested that the young man should be publicly reprimanded to ensure that others wouldn't dare to commit such an act again. Another middle-aged woman supported this suggestion, adding that the young man should be made to walk around the village with a sign that read "I stole."

Despite the suggestions, the debate continued without resolution, lacking a moderator to oversee the discussion and ensure a fair outcome. However, the villagers rejected Minto's team's offer to mediate, dismissing them as uninvited strangers.

As the team finally arrived at the crime scene, they were met with a flurry of activity that immediately caught their attention. Minto, with her prying eyes, quickly scanned the crowd and noticed a small group of villagers huddled around a man whose hands and legs were bound with sisal ropes. The victim had fresh wounds on his torso, hands and lower body, suggesting that he had been brutally assaulted. In addition, the victim was bleeding from the temple and nostrils, and his skin was lacerated.

Minto was eager to know what was happening first-hand. She approached a bystander to inquire about the situation. With her heart racing from curiosity, she moved closer to the commotion. Hesitantly, she approached a woman observing from the fringes, her weathered face etched with concern. "Excuse me," Minto began, "may I enquire what's happening?"

The woman, her gaze fixed on the unfolding drama, replied in a low voice, "The young man there, he was caught taking food from Mama Amani's house. Now, they're holding a baraza, a public court, to decide how to handle his misdeed."

Minto's eyebrows shot up. "A public court?" she echoed, surprised. "Is that common here?"

The woman nodded slowly. "In these parts, the community gathers to settle minor disputes like this. It's a way to ensure everyone has a say and that justice is served, fairly and promptly."

Minto's team was shocked by the severity of the punishment for such a minor offence. Minto agreed that stealing was wrong, but also believed that the punishment should fit the crime. Surely, stealing food to abate hunger did not justify the aggravated injuries on the victim's body. As they looked around, they saw the fear in the eyes of the villagers and realized that this was a community living in constant fear of punishment.

A deep sense of pity and sadness washed over Minto as she looked upon the young man lying before the crowd. Posing a question to the air, directed at no one in particular, she sought to engage the onlookers: Would it not have been wiser to report the suspect to the local police station instead of taking the law into their own hands? She hoped to spark a discussion about the need for a fair and just legal system that protected the rights of all citizens. Before anyone could weigh in, however, Gaati cut in with a cold stare. "Steer away from this matter, woman!" he commanded, his voice cutting through the crowd's murmurs. "You do not invite locusts to a feast and then blame them for enjoying it."

Minto's heart was heavy with frustration, recognizing that Gaati had no interest in justice or fairness. His complacency in maintaining the status quo, even at the expense of the innocent, was clear. While she acknowledged that it is not easy to change the minds of those who were set in their ways, she pledged internally not to be deterred by those who preferred oppression. This commitment meant pursuing justice and fairness tirelessly, even if it required standing in solitude.

Minto navigated through the crowd towards the young man, intent on understanding the full context of his actions. Meanwhile, she cautioned Gaati against taking sides until all facts were known, but her words fell on deaf ears. Instead, he too continued to push his way through the crowd, muttering something about a lion not caring about the opinion of an antelope.

Privately, Minto firmly believed that when an individual was in dire need of basic human necessities, such as food and water, but was unable to access them due to societal barriers, they may feel compelled to subvert existing social norms and challenge these barriers as a means to avoid the indignity of hunger. Unfortunately, Minto's attempts to convey this perspective to Gaati were unsuccessful, as he seemed either unaware of the situation's severity or incapable of understanding the message.

Gaati, however, outright dismissed Minto's explanation, labelling the suspect a social deviant who merited punishment for his actions, a response that ignited a surge of anger within Minto. Yet, despite the instinctive urge to retaliate, she managed to maintain her composure, choosing not to stoop to exchanging insults. This moment of restraint led Minto to a deeper realisation: justice should not be solely left in the hands of the victims. Often, out of indignation, they might lack the broader perspective necessary to understand the complex social and economic factors driving certain behaviours.

All eyes were fixed on the poor young man as he struggled to explain away his crime and convince those around him that he deserved mercy. According to Kamba customary law, the probative burden of proof lay with the accused. In this case, the accused man knew that he had to make a compelling case if he wanted to avoid punishment. He was running out of time.

With a heavy heart, he began his prayers before the village headman, who was under express instruction from the local area chief. 'Do not forsake me!' he cried out. 'My Lords, I only took enough food to satisfy my hunger, and I had no criminal intent. I humbly ask for leniency.

Despite his heartfelt plea, the request for mercy fell on deaf ears. To everyone's horror, the village headman drew a chicote whip and mercilessly lashed the vulnerable defendant four times in quick succession. The unfortunate young man writhed in excruciating pain. The chief's henchman added ten more lashes on the victim's bare upper body and the air filled with a deafening shriek of fear and death. As the lashes cracked into the victim's skin, they tore through soft tissues, drawing blood and raw flesh, until Minto couldn't bear to watch anymore. She turned away and vomited, unable to stomach the brutality. In stark contrast, the sound of the defendant's shrieks and cries for mercy sent Gaati into a frenzy of wild celebration, revelling in the suffering of a fellow human being.

The young man cried like a banshee, but his tormentor showed no mercy. It was a brutal and heartless display of power that left the defendant reeling with shock and despair. The scene was harrowing evidence of the cruel and unforgiving nature of justice in this village.

After five minutes, the headman was completely drained, his body trembling with exhaustion from the merciless beatings he had just inflicted upon the helpless suspect. He paused, gasping for breath, with sweat pouring down his face in rivulets. He resembled a hunter exhausted from the chase, panting and wheezing, fighting to regain his composure.

With trembling hands, he scooped up a handful of soil from the ground, rubbing it onto the chicote whip to improve his grip. The headman was not finished with the suspect yet, a fact the suspect was painfully aware of, bracing himself for what was yet to come. Crafted from the tough hide of a hippopotamus, the chicote whip was a vicious weapon, designed to inflict maximum pain. Regrettably, the village headman, who was meant to serve as a neutral arbiter in village disputes, overstepped his bounds by assuming the roles of judge, jury, and executioner.

As Minto witnessed the brutal beatings, she couldn't ignore Gaati's disturbing reaction. With each lash of the whip, Gaati seemed to convulse with pleasure, as though the pain inflicted on the helpless suspect provided him with ecstasy. Minto was appalled – Gaati appeared to derive a perverse satisfaction from the violence.

It wasn't only his convulsions that alarmed Minto. On closer observation, she saw Gaati sweating profusely and drooling from the corners of his mouth, his twisted sense of pleasure unmistakably evident. Minto was left to conclude that Gaati was either suffering from a profound psychological disturbance or she was witnessing an extreme case of masochism.

Minto's razor-sharp insights into Gaati's psyche left her questioning the very foundations of problem-solving. In her lay opinion, Gaati's obsession with corporal punishment was akin to that of a person whose only available tool is a hammer and who therefore sees every problem as a nail, or a bird born in a cage that believes flying is a disability. He was bigoted. Minto surmised that Gaati was highly likely to be a victim of narcissistic personality disorder, given his mechanical approach to problem-solving. But what really irked Minto was not so much the corporal punishment meted out to the victim, but the community's widespread acceptance of mob justice without a fair trial. This, coupled with Gaati's presumption of the suspect's guilt, was too much malevolence for Minto to bear. It was a blatant disregard for the rule of law and a violation of basic human rights.

On the one hand, Gaati was aware of Minto's disapproval of his demeanour, but it was the least of his concerns. He was convinced that even if he were to perform a graceful dance in the water, Minto would still find a way to accuse him of stirring up dust. In reality, Gaati was not unfairly accused. He openly expressed his chauvinistic views towards women with his signature saying, 'Every woman is beautiful until she opens her mouth to speak.' This attitude earned him the disdain of many women in Yatta village.

Despite their differences, the conflict between Minto and Gaati was fiercely contested, and it was unlikely to end in their lifetime. It was a battle of wills, a clash of personalities, and a struggle for dominance in which Minto sought to put Gaati in his place, while Gaati saw an opportunity to assert his dominance.

Nevertheless, if discipline was making a choice between immediate desires and long-term goals, Minto opted for peace over war and decided to disengage from the verbal sparring with Gaati, at least for the time being. After all, she was wise enough to realize that it was impossible to reason with a tiger when your head was already inside its jaws. Eventually, after a gruelling battle of wits, the team finally departed southwards towards the Banda Salama Ranges. However, Minto was left feeling utterly exasperated and fed up with the flagrant injustice that had been inflicted upon the village petty thief. It was enough to make her want to throw both hands up in despair!

Three

Chapter 3 – To Hell and Back

The final leg of the journey to visit the medicine man was arduous, winding between the mystical Nzambani Rock and the rugged Banda Salama Ranges, through Dipu Canyon. The previously flat Yatta Plateau gradually gave way to a dense, primeval rainforest, teeming with wild landscapes and dense chaparral vegetation. Venturing into such uncharted territory was a bold move if not daring for the group, fraught with hardships and perilous obstacles that tested their courage and strength to the fullest.

The mere thought of navigating through a primitive jungle, fraught with dangers, ranging from treacherous ravines to venomous snakes, elicited mixed feelings of an adrenaline rush and nervousness. The group was filled with a sense of daring excitement, one that not even the breathtaking views of lush flora and exotic fauna could temper. To add fuel to the fire, the only way to access the emergent layer of the tropical rainforest was by going through a three-kilometre transitional belt that was densely populated with stinging nettle.

Despite facing seemingly insurmountable odds, the team remained resolute in their determination to cross the transitional belt. This ecotone, a stunning overlap of the receding savannah bushland and the equatorial rainforest, was a true natural wonder. However, unbeknownst to the team, deciding to travel through the belt would lead to untold consequences. As fate would have it, they soon discovered that the zone was home to both the dreaded stinging nettle and spotted jewelweed. The stinging nettle, a harmful plant, has needle-like hairs on its leaves that release formic acid upon contact, causing a tingling burning sensation followed by severe itching and unpleasant rashes on the skin of unsuspecting humans and animals.

Given the daunting circumstances facing them, the team's success hinged on their ability to execute their plan meticulously and flawlessly. One wrong move and the journey would turn into a disaster, if not a medical emergency. The team somehow had to start with the basics and work their way up to achieve the impossible. However, there was one obstacle that stood between them and success: the stinging nettle.

The sages advise that when the going gets tough, the tough get going. This ethos and wisdom are precisely what the team embraced to overcome the daunting challenge of navigating through the poisonous leaves. Among them, Benjo, the reigning triple-jump champion at Yatta Primary School, developed a hop-step-and-jump technique. This strategy involved taking a deep breath, initiating a quick sprint, and executing a significant leap over the shrubs. Engaging in such a gamble was filled with risks, yet Benjo's belief in his ability never wavered. Whatever he did, he had to be careful not to land on the noxious plants.

Minto, on the other hand, had to rely solely on her wits and strength to navigate through the treacherous thicket, carefully avoiding the poisonous leaves that lurked within. Despite her heavy-set frame and the weighty burden she carried on her back, Minto fearlessly forged ahead, determined to find a safe path. Unlike Benjo, who had the luxury of agility, Minto's success depended on her unwavering determination and her ability to circumvent the dangers while keeping a safe distance from the clusters of weeds.

Despite the team's impressive creativity in surviving the harsh conditions of the jungle, Minto and Benjo's techniques proved to be necessary but not sufficient. For instance, when faced with a dense cluster of weeds covering a large area, Benjo's jumping abilities were inadequate. It was a tall order for Benjo to leap seven metres in the air between two glades. Similarly, an encounter with a copse of stinging nettle forced Minto to wander far away from the designated route to circumnavigate the cluster of weeds before navigating back onto their course at the earliest available weed-free space. These challenges and other unforeseen obstacles significantly affected their rate of progress to reach the tropical rainforest.

Quarter way through the epic journey, Minto recalled a wise Kamba proverb: 'One does not insult the crocodile's mouth while still crossing the river.' This saying reminded her not to share her past harrowing experience with the stinging nettle, as it might discourage her team. Yet, deep inside, she was itching to tell the story. As the story goes, Minto once made the grave mistake of using leaves from a stinging nettle to cushion her back while carrying a load of dry firewood. It was her first encounter with a stinging nettle shrub, and therefore she had no idea that its leaves were poisonous. The experience was so excruciating that by the time she arrived home from the forest and unloaded the firewood, Minto was horrified to discover severe hives covering her back. She was immediately rushed to the local clinic for emergency treatment. From that day on, the mere mention of the devil's weed left a repugnant taste in Minto's mouth.

The family's journey through the transitional belt was a harrowing experience and, to say the least, a rollercoaster of emotions. What started out as an exciting adventure quickly turned into a nightmare. Despite their best efforts to avoid the nettles, every step forward was met with pain and discomfort. Sometimes, they contemplated turning back, but deep in their minds, they knew they had to push through and endure the hardship. It was a journey they would never forget; one they would live to tell for the rest of their lives.

After a gruelling battle with the invasive weed, the team finally arrived at the entrance of the rainforest biome. From their vantage point, they paused to take in the breathtaking view of the emergent layer of the tropical rainforest. The beauty was truly awe inspiring, so much so that even Minto, who until now had been preoccupied with navigating through the prickly underbrush, forgot all about the twists and turns of the epic journey to enjoy the captivating beauty of the tropical rainforest. She imagined the ineffable biome as an inexhaustible treasure trove, with every step leading to a new and exciting discovery!

Meanwhile, Benjo couldn't help but feel a twinge of nostalgia as he gazed at the stunning cusp between the receding savannah grassland behind them and the lush greenery of the tropical rainforest ahead. He knew he would miss the hunting opportunities that came with the savannah grassland, but he was also eager to explore the uncharted depths of the rainforest.

The vast expanse of savannah grassland stretching out to the horizon evoked a flood of halcyon moments, conjuring up the full spectrum of memories from their epic journey through the Yatta Plateau—ranging from Benjo's experiences hunting wild birds with a slingshot to the terrifying encounter with a giant rock python. Yet, the hearts and flowers of their tragic adventure now seemed like distant memories, overshadowed by the fresh concerns about the daunting task ahead. The untouched wilderness before them, with its ancient trees, marshy lands, deep gorges, and steep hills, presented a formidable challenge. The sight of jagged peaks merging into a complex maze of riverbeds and connected ridges drained Benjo's energy, making him acutely aware of the monumental task of climbing the mountain range ahead.

Delving further into the tropical forest, Gaati recognized the need to brief the team on the potential dangers ahead. He presented the information in a straightforward manner, explaining that the charming, beautiful foliage they were seeing was actually a facade, hiding some of the world's deadliest predators. Knowing from experience that the best way to make information memorable was to add drama to the presentation, Gaati cleverly concealed his intentions. He then stopped next to a group of bromeliad plants, ready to dramatize his message with an element of suspense.

With a long piece of dry branch, Gaati rustled aside the damp leaves beneath the bromeliads, revealing the damp substrate layer. The team didn't notice anything out of the ordinary, only the earthy scent of the forest floor and the glistening silver trails left by snails. Gaati moved closer and pushed away a dry, rotted log in crumbly condition, exposing colonies of sow bugs and pill bugs. Ignoring the startled crustaceans, he pointed towards the base of a vibrant leaf rosette, and there it was—a golden dart frog no bigger than his thumb, with metallic yellow-gold colours that shimmered and shone in the light. Its sleek body and bold hues were unlike anything Benjo had ever seen. It was a creature of pure, dazzling beauty.

As Benjo moved closer to get a better view, Gaati stopped him in his tracks by blocking his way with the tree branch he was holding. He explained that, beautiful as it was, the golden dart frog was perhaps the most poisonous animal on earth. The skin of an average golden dart frog produces enough poison to kill ten standard human beings. Benjo felt goosebumps forming all over his body. He couldn't imagine that such a beautiful creature could kill him in seconds Gaati took this opportunity to emphasize to the team that the forest was home to other deadly creatures just like the deceptively beautiful golden dart frog, including marauding forest elephants, venomous snakes, and ferocious slender-snouted African crocodiles, just to mention but a few.

However, Gaati didn't want to dampen the team's spirits completely. He also informed them that the same perilous forest was home to some of the world's most magnificent wildlife, such as diurnal primates, pygmy chimpanzees, peafowls, mandrills, and pygmy hippopotamuses. The fecundity of the forest was truly remarkable.

After completing the precautionary briefing, the team ventured through a desolate area to reach the lush gateway to the forest. The boundary between the two microclimates was clearly marked by a magnificent artesian spring at the base of an escarpment. As the team approached, Benjo was overwhelmed with excitement at the sight of the limpid water of the spring, a stark contrast to the murky Thika River they had seen earlier that day. Meanwhile, Minto couldn't resist the urge to quench her thirst. She carefully navigated potential hazards, such as unstable ground and a nearby sinkhole, before filling her water gourd and seeking shade under a nearby tree. The exhilarating relief from her thirst and heat exhaustion was the most invigorating feeling Minto had experienced in a long time. After enjoying a moment of respite, she refilled her bottle to the brim and the team continued their journey.

Unlike his mother, Benjo didn't bother to check the safety of the foreground. Instead, he boldly slid through the mud, cutting across a caravan of bull ants, and landed toes first in the cool, refreshing water of the spring. With a quick glance over his shoulder, he cupped his hands together to create a makeshift bowl and dipped them into the stream to quench his thirst. The water was a boon on his parched lips, relieving him of the heat exhaustion that had been building up inside him all day long.

Benjo seized this rare opportunity, immersing himself in the fountain's refreshing waters, relishing the cooling sensation on his feet. He also splashed some water over his head and body to escape the scorching heat. The spring water was remarkably transparent, unlike anything Benjo had ever witnessed. The acme of potable water. Pausing in awe, he couldn't help but admire the vibrant marine life visibly thriving at the chasm's depths. A school of red-silver killifish captivated his attention, their synchronized swimming forming a breathtaking echelon, their vivid red, silver, and black colours accentuating the spectacle. It was a sight that left him breathless.

Suddenly, Minto's sharp voice shattered Benjo's reverie. "Focus, Benjo!" she shouted, startling Benjo, who had been trailing about a hundred meters behind the team, lost in thought. Minto was livid, with good reason—the peril of the jungle made sticking together vital. Her reprimand prompted Gaati to step in and remind the team of their mission's gravity. He cautioned them, saying, "A hunter in pursuit of an elephant does not stop to throw stones at a small bird." Their mission was bigger than any distractions or sideshows.

Gaati's words restored order, at least for the time being. Benjo quickly caught up with the rest of the pack, determined to toe the line and stay focused on the task at hand.

In the interest of time, Gaati selected a route running parallel to the Banda Salama escarpment, which was more navigable and avoided challenging subalpine terrain. He believed that choosing this less demanding path would conserve energy, sparing the team additional calories for their ascent of Mount Banda. Strategically, this route would reduce the distance and steepness of their climb by approaching the mountain from the west, nearer to the medicine man's residence. Despite its benefits, Gaati's choice was not without challenges. Navigating through a couloir deeper into the forest, the team encountered dense, energy-sapping vegetation, prompting Gaati to adjust their approach, including using walking staffs to clear obstructive branches. Nonetheless, given that the benefits of walking parallel to the escarpment outweighed the risks of alternative routes, Gaati stuck to his guns and committed to his plan.

To minimize the struggle of navigating through obstacles, Gaati took a right turn and tagged along a spoor to bypass overhanging branches and the dense undergrowth that was beginning to impair visibility. At the earliest opportunity, he made another right turn, weaving through a stand of raffia palms to merge onto an unusually wide animal trail leading to a clearing. This tranquil glade, bathed in dappled sunlight filtered through the canopy of towering palms, brought relief to the team. All but Minto rejoiced at the sight of open space for the first time since their forest entry. However, Minto harboured reservations about the safety of following such an expansive trail, drawing a parallel to an old Sunday school lesson that equated wider paths with perilous outcomes. Upon reflection, though, she rebuked herself for succumbing to such pessimism and chose to keep her fears to herself, aiming to prevent unnecessary alarm among her companions. With a swift shake of her head, she cast aside her apprehensions, determined not to invoke misfortune.

As the team navigated the terrain, they came across a large pile of decaying organic matter beside a cluster of elephant bush and cautiously skirted around it. Unfortunately, Wasa's foot accidentally plunged into the mass, sinking up to his lower calf muscle and causing him to trip. Reacting quickly, Gaati sprang into action, squatting beside his fallen teammate to assist him. Gaati's priority was identifying the animal that had left the dung, for safety reasons.

After a brief examination, Gaati identified the deposit as freshly dropped elephant dung but chose to downplay the possibility of elephants nearby to prevent panic. Nevertheless, as the saying goes, "if there are spiders in the house, one does not ask who wove the web." The presence of abundant elephant-bush shrubs in the area was sufficient evidence that it was a natural habitat for elephants. These shrubs, rich in high water content, make them a highly appealing source of food for elephants, helping them hydrate their massive bodies.

With the potential security risk looming, it was the perfect opportunity to test Gaati's expertise in wild-game tracking. Although trained by Yatta village's finest animal trackers, his team had yet to witness him in action. Gaati had begun his foray into hunting by joining his uncle, Kilunda, on big-game hunting expeditions in his early twenties where he learned his ropes. Notably, Kilunda is among the top five certified archers and elephant hunters among the Kamba people in the south-eastern division of the Yatta district, with his name meaning "arrowhead" in Kamba.

Given Gaati's impressive training, it came as no surprise to the team when he confirmed their worst fears with a single peek: they were staring at fresh elephant droppings that had been left behind barely thirty to fifty minutes ago. Despite the gravity of the situation, Gaati did not want to convey any sense of doom and gloom to the team. Instead, he quietly upgraded the potential risk of an elephant attack to an emergency level of alertness and kept the information confidential.

Drawing on his jungle experience, Gaati knew that elephants live in close-knit family herds of between eight and one hundred animals, depending on the terrain and family size. As soon as he upgraded the security alert to an emergency, his first instinct was to scan the surroundings to gain a better understanding of the local herd.

As a safety measure, Gaati directed his team to maintain composure and to stand still under the shelter of a towering tree. Meanwhile, he employed a range of investigative techniques to determine the distance and direction of the elephants from the team's current position. He sidled between the trees, attuning his ears to the sound of trumpeting elephants to pinpoint their location. Additionally, he scrutinized the broken branches and trampled grass to identify their active trail. Furthermore, he examined the stripped barks of trees to confirm the direction in which the elephants were traveling, among employing other hunting techniques.

Drawing on his extensive hunting experience, Gaati understood that situational awareness was the first step towards gaining control over a threat. According to Gaati's uncle Kilunda, situational awareness is the ability to observe and anticipate on-the-ground activities in a hunting area of interest. In simple terms, it is the hunter's knowledge of what is happening on the hunting ground. Armed with this wisdom, Gaati was aware that an analysis of situational awareness was necessary for two reasons: firstly, to identify if there was an immediate danger to human life and decide whether to activate a survival management plan; and secondly, to gather sufficient information to decide on a course of action commensurate with the magnitude of the danger.

Based on the intelligence gathered, Gaati decided against evacuating the team, instead instructing them to take cover behind the nearest tree trunk on the windward side and remain motionless. This might appear to be an unusual request, yet it was a strategic move to minimize the risk of the gentle giants detecting the team's human scent. Elephants, with their exceptional sense of smell, can detect water sources up to twenty kilometers away. To reduce the likelihood of detection, Gaati advised against team members taking shelter under the same tree, as doing so would increase the concentration of human scent in the air per unit area.

Unlike his wide-eyed teammates, Gaati knew all too well that elephants could outrun humans. While the average human running speed is between nine and sixteen kilometres per hour, elephants can reach speeds of up to sixty-five kilometres per hour. Aware of this critical difference, Gaati made it a priority to maintain a safe distance between his team and the animals.

After ensuring that a safety management plan was in place, Gaati began to track the beasts by spooring every footmark. He carefully examined the markings under a nearby iroko tree and noticed a dozen fresh footprints measuring approximately forty centimetres long and fifty centimetres wide, with a depth of thirty centimetres. The toenails on the pentadactyl limb marks were facing east, indicating that the animals were travelling in that direction. Yet, Gaati's experience in the jungle taught him that relying solely on one indicator was not enough.

To put the jigsaw together, Gaati needed to gather more information. He climbed up a mammoth lombi tree and conducted additional reconnaissance. From his vantage point, he was relieved to see that the elephants were about one and a half kilometres away from the team's current location and heading away in the opposite direction. He made a mental note of the herd's location before climbing down.

With the newly acquired precise intelligence, Gaati was in a comfortable position to manage the threat. As a result, he revised the security alert from an emergency to low risk under observation. Moreover, he revised the route and followed a nearby canyon that ran parallel to the escarpment. His intention was to stay as close to the edge of the escarpment as possible and avoid the elephants' grazing corridor.

As they journeyed along the new route, they stumbled upon an ancient granitic rock formation with a deep grotto, formed over many years by the combined forces of water and wind erosion. The cave did not significantly interest the leading three members of the team, who ignored it and continued down the path. However, Benjo's curiosity got the best of him, and he decided to take a peek inside the portal, a decision that would haunt him for the remainder of their journey.

Immediately after Benjo glanced into the grotto, two spotted eagle owls burst from the cave's roof, soaring over him before vanishing into the valley below. The abruptness of their departure and the booming noise they made triggered a reflex in Benjo that paralyzed him with fear. The unexpected encounter with the disturbed Strigiformes left him profoundly shaken. As if the shock wasn't enough, Gaati erupted in fury, berating Benjo, who was now standing prominently in front of him.

"Lord the distributor!" Gaati exploded, his hands clasping his head in dismay. "Benjo has disturbed a sacred dwelling! Sacrilege! Sacrilege!" he ranted, seemingly to the air around him. His behaviour was akin to someone witnessing a grave taboo. It was the first instance where he appeared truly terrified. Owls, especially during the day, were considered harbingers of misfortune or even messengers from the spirit world in their tradition. This unexpected encounter had shaken Gaati to his core, a stark contrast to his usual composure.

"Can I have everyone's attention, please?" Gaati finally screamed, this time facing the team directly. When everyone stopped to listen, Gaati spoke in a subdued whisper. Examining Gaati's unusual behaviour, it was apparent that the only thing that scared him was the wrath of the gods.

Gaati informed the team that Benjo had committed a serious offense by desecrating a sacred shrine. He explained that, according to Kamba customary law, it was mandatory to perform the *ng'ondu* appeasement ritual to pacify the Numen of Banda. This ritual would not only protect Benjo from potential divine retribution but also cleanse the team from any subsequent misfortunes that might arise.

The team was taken aback by the severity of Benjo's actions and the potential consequences. Gaati explained that the *ng'ondu* appeasement ritual was a sacred ceremony passed down through generations. It involved immolating an unblemished male animal to propitiate angry gods from taking revenge on both the offender and his community. However, if the offender was a child, the ritual would also include offerings of traditional herbs, prayers, and sacrifices to appease the spirits and seek their forgiveness.

Regrettably, Benjo, in his foolishness, not only encountered the owls in broad daylight but also deliberately provoked them inside a sacred cave, incurring a grievous offence against the ancestral spirits. As a result, a *ng'ondu* rite was necessary to appease the gods and restore balance to the community. While others were mourning the tragedy, Benjo attempted to play the victim by curling up in a foetal position to appeal for mercy. However, Minto saw through his ruse and scolded him for his reckless behaviour. Indeed, Benjo learned that a cockroach cannot feign ignorance among fowls, and such ignorance would not shield him from the consequences of his actions.

Blind to the unseen forces at play, Benjo's youthful curiosity led him to explore an ancient cave. Unaware of the significance owls held in Kamba tradition, his innocent act was misconstrued as a grave offense. Bound by the community's customary law, he faced the consequences anyway, a stark reminder that even the purest intentions can have unforeseen repercussions.

The urgency surrounding the *ng'ondu* ritual demanded swift action. Traditionally, only ordained priests hold the position of lead celebrant. Bypassing customary protocol, Gaati appointed himself as the lead celebrant and began delegating tasks. He did this to save time, even though he knew that Wasa was older and therefore technically more eligible. However, in Gaati's opinion, Wasa lacked the necessary speed to manage the intricate tasks involved in the *ng'ondu* rite. To conceal his illegitimate appointment, Gaati swiftly assumed the role of the celebrant, officiating the rite as if he held the formal designation.

As per the *ng'ondu* rite, the celebrant must personally prepare the designated site for the shrine. For this purpose, Gaati unsheathed his Somali sword and cleared the undergrowth of honeysuckle vines and mangrove ferns beneath a nearby fig tree he had earmarked for the shrine. Assuming full authority, he then delegated duties to the rest of the team members before disappearing into the deep forest without explanation. The remaining team, accustomed to following the celebrant's orders, dispersed in different directions to perform their assigned tasks.

After what felt like an eternity, Minto and Benjo finally returned to the makeshift shrine, their arms laden with wild-banana leaves harvested from the perilous slopes of a hidden box canyon deep in the heart of the jungle. They had followed the celebrant's instructions to the letter, ensuring that every detail was perfect so as not to upset the strictures of the *ng'ondu* rite.

Minto and Benjo found Wasa emerging from the brushwood, his broad shoulders hunching under the weight of a hefty bundle of firewood. With a grunt of exertion, he launched the logs toward the southern end of the shrine, the bundle rolling to a stop with a satisfying thud. Sweat clung to his shirt, a testament to his arduous climb up the steep slope. Minto, ever the devoted wife, offered him a cool gourd of spring water from her basket. A small gesture, yet one that spoke volumes of her unwavering support.

Wasa set to work preparing the fireplace next to the shrine, the celebrant's instructions echoing in his mind. A single misstep could disrupt the delicate balance of the ritual, potentially invoking the gods' wrath. He meticulously arranged seven layers of basalt screes, forming a solid base for the fire. Following the *ng'ondu* canon, he selected seven dry logs of the African mangosteen tree and meticulously laid them over the fireplace in a perfect rectangle.

After completing this solemn part of the ritual, Wasa exhaled a sigh of relief, having successfully navigated the prescribed procedures without a single misstep. He likened the strictures of the *ng'ondu* rite to diffusing a bomb in a war zone, given the celebrant's stark warning of divine retribution for any misstep, whether by omission or commission. Now, with the fireplace complete, Wasa set about the next task, the fear of offending the gods temporarily abated.

Wasa carefully selected seven additional sekelbos logs from the pile and placed them on top of the basalt screes. He then filled the gaps with sand and gravel to create a sturdy foundation for the fireplace. To complete the cooking grid, he ingeniously used a makeshift sledgehammer to drive five giant bamboo stakes into the ground. Each corner of the rectangular fireplace was secured with a stake, and a fifth, central stake was placed to suspend the cooking grates.

To wind up, Wasa moved on to tidying up the shrine. He was grateful to work through this task quickly because he had, at least, been given carte blanche to complete the remaining tasks as he saw fit without the fear of retribution from the gods.

With military precision and newfound enthusiasm, Wasa completed the first assignment in record time. Minto, however, was taken aback by her husband's sudden burst of productivity. This led her to wonder why Wasa wasn't as productive at home. Attributing his current success solely to fear of the ancestral spirits rather than his own abilities, Minto dismissed his efforts. However, it was evident that her current attitude stemmed not just from this specific instance, but from a long-held assessment of her husband's overall character.

Despite Minto's lack of recognition, Wasa, accustomed to disappointment in this regard, felt a surge of pride and accomplishment for completing the assignment. He also took a moment to instruct Minto and Benjo on how to create a beautiful carpet using the wild banana leaves around the fire pit, adding a touch of lush greenery to the sacred space.

Motivated by their shared goal of appeasing the gods, Minto and Benjo dove into the task. With great care and attention to detail, the duo started to weave what turned out to be one of the most beautiful makeshift bush carpets, surprising even Wasa and Gaati. The task, to their delight, proved less challenging than anticipated, leading them to engage in lively conversations about their past experiences and future aspirations. In contrast, Wasa remained quiet and focused on removing the green waste left behind by Gaati during the land-clearing exercise, a stark reminder of the hurried preparation for the shrine's construction.

Suddenly the trio heard a strange heavy trampling in the adjoining bushland. They stood frozen in fear as the sound of cracking branches and rustling leaves filled the air. Minto whispered in terror, pulling Benjo towards her, convinced that they were under attack from marauding elephants given their past encounter with the giants. But, just as they were about to take flight, the commotion died down and Gaati emerged from the forest, carrying the carcass of a large-sized zebra duiker on his right shoulder and a bunch of devil's horsewhip shrubs in his left hand.

Gaati looked like a beast of burden. Covered from head to toe in leaves, vines, nectar, and the bristly pods of goose-grass, a quick glance at his appearance was enough to demystify the earlier rampaging noise mistaken by the duo to be that of a marauding wild animal pushing through the thicket. Standing at six feet five inches, Gaati's body frame was big enough to shake and rustle tree branches like a wild animal.

Gaati's presence provided relief and a sense of security. For this reason, Minto's historical loathing of Gaati seemed to abate, at least for the moment. For the first time in her life, she was happy and relieved to see him. She nearly hugged him in appreciation of his presence. The mistaken animal-scare incident had left Minto petrified – so much so that her heartbeat could be heard drumming inside her ribcage, while her palms were completely drenched with sweat.

Gaati's dramatic return to the shrine was met with excitement from Wasa's family. However, his focus was on the position of the sun, as he was determined to keep track of time. The shadows cast by nearby trees served as a warning that time was running out, causing him to become increasingly worried.

In a flurry of activity, Gaati quickly ordered Benjo to assist Minto in spreading wild-banana leaves around the shrine. This task was both a delegated duty for Benjo and a punishment for his previous misdeeds. To the amazement of everyone, the duo replicated their earlier feat and created a spectacular carpet-like corridor around the shrine, drawing on their previous experience of laying banana leaves at the fireplace.

Gaati took Wasa through a woodcraft drill, teaching him how to light a fire in the jungle without a lighter. After imparting the necessary knowledge, he handed Wasa the tools and essential materials needed to ignite a blaze. Wasa skilfully carved a spindle and fireboard from dry red-cedar wood and began to spin the hand drill to create friction. After a few attempts, he saw wisps of smoke rising from the fireboard, followed by amber sparks, before the tinder nest burst into flames. "Bingo!" he exclaimed. Benjo stood in awe, his mouth agape, his lower jaw dropping in utter astonishment. He had never seen anyone start a fire without a lighter before. It was a thrilling experience.

In the meantime, Gaati expertly split open the duiker carcass with his Somali sword and stretched it out across four bamboo stakes, preparing it for barbequing. He secured the meat on the cooking grate by tying the rear and front shanks of the duiker with raw agave-plant cords. The carcass sprawled perfectly over the five stakes above the fireplace, ready to roast.

The *ng'ondu* rite commenced in earnest with a brief prayer invoking the blessings of the ancestral spirits upon them, followed by a sprinkling of lustral water to bless the shrine. Gaati, the self-appointed celebrant then moved to the side of the shrine and melded a purificatory elixir by mixing spring water with a grey powder made from pounded African sage weed, roots and stem, along with a pinch of salt harvested from a natural mineral deposit. Minto observed the ritual with great interest, as it was her first time witnessing the rare *ng'ondu* ceremony.

The participants were called forth to form a single line, ready to be cleansed and purified. With a bunch of devil's horsewhip weed in hand, the celebrant sprinkled the lustral water on each participant to purify them. After a short prayer of atonement, Gaati sprinkled the remaining water over the shrine and the surrounding area before concluding the session with another brief prayer, imbued with a smooth, supplicatory tone. Finally, he carefully placed the ritual items under the makeshift ciborium and genuflected to venerate the shrine.

Once the most solemn section of the ceremony was over, Gaati announced to the participants that they were free to break from the line and join him at the firepit to inspect the meat. Gaati instructed them to stand on one side of the flames while he took his position opposite them, alone. With a practised hand, he used a skewer to carefully retrieve the roast liver from the fire, placing it on the mantelpiece to cool. The transformation was striking – the once reddish-brown meat now shimmered with an iridescent sheen.

Without hesitation, Gaati drew his Somali sword from its sheath. With a swift movement, he sliced through the liver, carving off a sample. He closed his eyes, savouring the robust, earthy flavour and the hint of pungency. Despite a touch of singeing on the exterior, the liver was perfectly cooked, its core devoid of any rawness. It was ready to be served.

Gaati proceeded to chop the liver into small, chewable pieces and served them on a wild banana leaf. The aroma of the freshly cooked liver wafted through the air, tantalising their senses.

After offering a blessing for the food, Gaati extended an invitation to Wasa and Benjo to join him in enjoying the roast. However, the father and son politely declined his offer. To outsiders, this might have seemed strange, but the Kamba people had a long-standing tradition that prohibited members of the Asii clan from consuming liver meat, whether from any animal or bird, including domesticated livestock. Wasa and Benjo, as members of the Asii clan, were bound by this tradition and therefore could not accept the celebrant's generous offer. Violating this tradition would be costly for Wasa and Benjo, necessitating the payment of seven bulls each and enduring seven years of banishment to the land of their mother's kin—an inordinate price they were not willing to pay.

According to the clan taboo passed down through generations, the Asii believe that eating liver will make their eyes develop a watery discharge and eventually impair their sight. To avoid this misfortune, any member of the Asii clan who consumes liver must undergo a costly and time-consuming cleansing ritual. It is for this reason that the clan council of elders imposed hefty fines on anyone breaking the taboo, effectively discouraging members of the clan from indulging in liver consumption.

The situation was further complicated by Gaati's omission of Minto from the invitation to share the liver meat. As Benjo would later learn, the Kamba people traditionally reserved the liver from freshly killed animals exclusively for hunters and other male participants chosen by invitation. Female members of the community were excluded from this tradition, as hunting was a male-only activity at the time.

Unfazed by the lack of company, Gaati accepted his fate and savoured the delectable liver all by himself. As per the strict ng'ondu rite, the roasted liver had to be consumed before any other meat. Thankfully, Gaati was a man of considerable stature and appetite, having been down this same path before, officiating at similar ceremonies in the past. Without wasting any further time, the celebrant found a large boulder to sit on and relished the roast.

In the meantime, the rest of the meat continued to cook undisturbed above the smouldering fire, fuelled by seven hefty logs. Gaati had used an indirect roasting method, suspending the meat over bamboo stakes about seventy-five centimetres from the direct flames. This technique allowed Gaati to see to other duties without fretting about the meat charring or needing to constantly turn it over the fire.

After savouring the last morsel of liver, Gaati, the celebrant, returned to the fireside, his lips still slick with the succulent flavour. With a deft flip, he checked the red meat and was pleased to find it cooked to perfection – tender and well-done with a mouth-watering caramelisation on the outer crust. In fulfilment of one of the final dictates of the *ng'ondu* rite, Gaati meticulously selected the most tender portions of the loin, shank, and rump steaks, chopping them into fine pieces to be served on a separate banana leaf as an offering to the gods.

As per the sacred decree of the ritual, the gods were served first, before any human could partake. It was a sign of respect and reverence for the divine. For this reason, the gods received the finest meat – precisely the cuts with the least amount of connective tissue and collagen, which were often found in the muscles that did little work in the animal's body, hence the choice of loin, shank, and rump steaks.

After the gods were fed to their satisfaction, the celebrant proceeded to offer them libation and prostrate himself before the shrine in a humble plea for divine favour. As per the sacred *ng'ondu* ritual, the gods must be appeased by the offerings before the celebrant and members of the public could partake of the feast. Once the spirits had given their approval, the celebrant rose to his feet, clapped his hands, and declared, "My dear friends, it is time to enjoy the banquet!"

Minto was taken aback by Gaati's sudden display of impeccable manners. It was as if a malevolent spirit had performed a miraculous transformation, turning him into a virtuous saint. She wished that the gods who had witnessed this transformation would accompany them on the rest of their journey to continue taming Gaati's wild ways.

After six excruciating hours without food, Benjo finally found himself face-to-face with a tantalizing plate of duiker ribs. His mouth watered at the sight of the golden-brown roast, and he couldn't wait to tuck in. However, his initial excitement curdled into disappointment with the first bite. The meat was bland and flavourless, leaving him unsatisfied and hungry.

Little did Benjo know, the *ng'ondu* rite forbade the use of salt to season meat for the ritual. Any participant caught breaking this rule would face punishment multiplied tenfold by the gods. Despite the risk, Benjo toyed with the idea of stealing some salt from the cellar to spice up the tasteless meat. An internal battle raged within him. One side, fuelled by desperation, screamed for a sprinkle of salt.

The other, a voice suspiciously like his mum's, reminded him of the vengeful gods. Thankfully, sanity emerged with a white flag.

Instead, Benjo focused on filling his empty stomach and chose to ignore his tastebuds. He gratefully and ravenously devoured the meat without minding the taste, like a sick person downed prescription medication to get healed even though the medicine was bitter. Though he didn't enjoy the flavour, he knew it was necessary to eat it in order to survive.

After the lavish feast, the celebrant concluded the ceremony by sprinkling blood on the shrine. This blood had been collected earlier, when Gaati hunted and slaughtered the sacrificial antelope in the forest. The blood had been concealed in a small gourd and fastened to Gaati's loincloth in accordance with the ritual.

To conclude the festivities and ensure the safety of the camp, Gaati mobilized the entire team to extinguish the fireplace completely by covering it with damp soil. This effectively eliminated the risk of embers sparking a bushfire from spontaneous combution. Additionally, the team dug a pit to bury all the bones, leftover food, and other discarded materials, including the banana leaves used to cover the walking areas. Leaving such materials to dry in the open air would make them potential fuel for wildfires.

Minto was impressed by the effectiveness of the team's teamwork, which reminded her of her grandmother's famous saying: "Many hands make light work." Finally, it seemed the gods were pleased with Benjo – at least for now. If he could manage to tame his curiosity, perhaps the gods would continue to look favourably upon him in the future.

The journey resumed, and the team pressed on with renewed determination, bolstered by the belief that the gods were now on their side after the offering to appease them. Gaati had set an ambitious goal: to reach the medicine man's place before sunset. Failing to do so would be disastrous; navigating the treacherous landscape of Mount Banda in the inky blackness of night would be a fool's errand. In the meantime, Benjo tried his best to forget about the bizarre grotto incident and focus on the task at hand.

After trekking for about three kilometres, the team encountered a treacherous section of terrain. The once-comfortable path gave way to a steep descent marked by jagged obsidian rocks, making it feel like walking on metal spikes. This, however, was merely a warm-up for the true challenge that awaited them below.

Reaching the canyon floor at the base of Mount Banda, the team came face-to-face with the dreaded basaltic volcanic rocks known locally as "*A-aa!* rocks." This name originated from the agonizing cry "aa—argh" uttered by victims who stepped on the sharp clinkers of the rock, piercing their skin.

Fortunately, each member of Gaati's team was wearing tough African akala sandals, a crucial advantage on this challenging terrain. These sandals were made from discarded car tyres – a resourceful way to create durable footwear. The anti-puncture rubber soles of the akala sandals provided not only enough friction to descend the steep slope safely but also the strength to resist the pressure of the sharp, rugged surface. In short, the *A-aa!* rocks posed no match for the heavy-duty akala sandals.

The team navigated the steep slope with relative ease, their sturdy rubber sandals providing good grip on the treacherous *A-aa!* rocks. They skilfully made their way down the basaltic terrain until they reached the canyon floor. Gaati paused atop a pile of scree to consider the ascent of Mount Banda. Despite his reputation as a skilled decision-maker, he seemed to be struggling with decision-making fatigue on this occasion. Unfortunately, Gaati wasn't one to seek the opinions of others, especially his subordinates, and was desperate to hide his uncertainty.

To avoid revealing his indecisiveness, Gaati scanned the environment until a solution presented itself. He spotted the long-stemmed woody vines of the liana plant, firmly rooted in the soil and twined around giant tree trunks like overhead power cables. In the cords of the vines, Gaati saw the perfect winch to hoist his team out of the canyon and onto the mountain. He relished this defining moment of finding a solution from an unexpected source, keeping the details of his plan to himself.

The lucky discovery reminded Gaati of an old saying: even if you don't have enough water for a bath, at least wash your face with it. In other words, make the most of what you have, no matter how limited it seems.

Gaati was a man on a mission, and he quickly set out to test the strength of the liana twines of the Banda Salama Ranges. With his towering six-foot-five frame and giant feet firmly planted on the ground, he reached out and grabbed one of the twines, and with all his might he pulled the twine down the slope, but the twine did not snap! To ensure that the results of his experiment were not a fluke, Gaati repeated the test with Wasa, and the twine withstood the combined weight of the two men, which was about 200 kilograms.

Gaati's two experiments gave him a reasonable degree of confidence to believe the centuries-old claim that the liana twines of the Banda Salama Forest were indestructible. Buoyed by this confidence, Gaati secured himself with one of the twines. He held out Wasa's arm to form a two-man human chain and winched Benjo and Minto up the slope to a safe landing using the human chain as a pulley. Gaati's plan was a success!

Once everyone was winched to safety, Gaati suddenly shouted, "Batten down the hatches!" It was his way of breaking the ice and grabbing their attention before delivering a serious briefing before they set off. As a responsible leader, he knew the stakes were high. Their safety hinged on the liana twines as they faced the monumental slope of Mount Banda. However, Gaati was determined to succeed. The twines were a make-or-break factor for their safety, so he gave the pre-departure briefing the weight it deserved.

With the gravity of a drill sergeant, Gaati outlined the dual purpose of the liana twines: they would act as both climbing ropes, propelling them up the slope, and as safety harnesses to prevent nasty tumbles down. He stressed the importance of keeping a constant grip on the twines – there was no room for mistakes. To ensure this message sank in, Gaati repeated it, this time the austere look on his face speaking more than his words.

With a final nod, Gaati organised the team into a line. He took the lead position, Wasa brought up the rear, and the others slotted in between. It was time to put his theories into practice.

The team began their ascent, making steady progress. They'd left behind the lush savannah for a stark contrast – a forest floor carpeted with moss and lichen, thriving in the low light filtering through the canopy. While this lack of vegetation made the climb less frustrating, the craggy terrain presented a daunting and unpredictable challenge.

Inching their way upwards with meticulous care, the team adhered strictly to the safety guidelines. Wasa, ever the watchful guardian, kept a close eye on Benjo, ensuring his grip on the twines remained firm and his footing on the rocks secure. Yet, disaster struck when Benjo impulsively decided to experiment with using only one hand on the twines. As he reached for a handhold, his left foot slipped on a slug's slimy trail, sending him tumbling down the slope.

Benjo's desperate scrabbling for any handhold proved futile as he spun and tumbled down the mountainside. It wasn't until his body collided with his father's legs, a near-tragedy averted much like a goalkeeper stopping a hockey puck, that he finally came to a jarring halt.

Despite this harrowing ordeal, Benjo emerged remarkably unscathed. The team, shaken but more determined than ever, pressed on towards the summit.

The team ascended the slope without further problems, finally reaching a ledge at its shoulder. Huddled together, they rested on a flat, narrow shelf, gasping for fresh air. The journey had been incredibly demanding, especially for Minto. Carrying an impressive one hundred and twenty-seven kilograms in addition to a heavy backpack, it's no surprise the team needed a break.

As they paused for a well-earned break, Minto wrinkled her nose at a sudden, offensive whiff wafting around them. The combined body odour, likely worsened by the occasional toot, was proving unbearable for someone with her type of hyperosmia. Gasping, she excused herself from the malodorous huddle and retreated to the ledge's edge, seeking refuge in the welcome north-easterly breeze. Fresh air finally filled her lungs, a sweet relief after the ordeal.

During the break, Gaati seized the opportunity to scrutinize his navigational charts. With a cartographer's practiced eye, he meticulously compared the map to his mental map, putting his ground-truthing skills to work by verifying key landmarks. This verification process wasn't straightforward. It necessitated scaling one of the towering, sun-drenched afrormosia trees to gain a bird's-eye view of the surrounding terrain. Though simple and time-consuming, the technique remained highly effective for assessing the physical characteristics of the landscape features below.

To Gaati's delight, the actual map closely matched his mental map, suggesting he was right on course. There was no better time than now for the clansmen's wisdom to ring true: "There is no friend as loyal as a well-known road." However, not everyone was pleased with the progress. Benjo, wearied by the endless steep climbs, began to question Minto about the wisdom of following their unpredictable guide. He also pondered aloud whether they would ever reach their destination and what their expected time of arrival might be.

In a final jibe, Benjo challenged his mother to wake up and smell the coffee. "Only a foolish fly follows a corpse to its grave," he warned ominously. Despite Benjo's negativity, Gaati remained focused on the task at hand: leading the group towards their destination.

Buzzing with excitement, Gaati hurried down from the towering tree. He couldn't wait to share the good news and lighten the load his team carried. Finding the descent too slow, he took a leap of faith, jumping the last three metres with a wince. "We're only nine hundred metres from Mue's gate!" he announced triumphantly. "Mue," he explained, "is the Numen of Banda", and the name also means 'sage' in the Kamba language.

In a bid to boost morale, Gaati quipped, "A rolling stone gathers no moss!" His lighthearted remark, along with his own unwavering determination, spurred them onward. With renewed vigour, they followed him through a saddle and up a steep ridge, reaching the second ledge. The journey was far from over, but Gaati's zest and resolve were contagious. They felt re-energized, prepared to tackle whatever obstacles lay ahead.

Four

Chapter 4 – The Numen of Banda

Miles of relentless sun-baked travel had left Minto's feet sore and weary. Sweat drenched their skin, adding to the discomfort as they trudged along the dusty path. Minto gazed in wonder at their elongated shadows stretching out behind them, a testament to the distance they had covered. As the day wore on and the sun began to dip below the horizon, Minto's shadow slowly shrank behind her.

As the team trudged along the narrow mountain ledge, they suddenly found themselves in a cul-de-sac, facing a daunting timber gate. The gate stood bizarrely before them, crafted from two uneven tree trunks that rose from a colossal stone plinth. A third trunk lay across the top, braced by a sturdy stanchion, giving the structure an eerie and formidable air. The team noticed a large bough of blackthorn acacia wedged tightly between the gate frames, sealing the entrance with an almost impenetrable barrier. The bough was so tightly jammed between the tree trunks that not even a tiny mouse could possibly squeeze through.

The colossal gate dwarfed even the six-foot-tall Gaati, but it was the presence of a non-native *Acacia mellifera* tree deep in the heart of the rainforest that truly left the team baffled. This species was known to thrive only in dry savannah climates, yet here it stood, deep inside a tropical rainforest: half a ton of wood defying all logic and reason. The team could not figure out how on earth the massive acacia tree bough somehow made its way up the mountain to this mysterious location.

The superimposed acacia was stranger than fiction, a dead branch that added an air of mystery to the scene. Nonetheless, standing before the gate, the team couldn't help but feel a sense of intrigue and excitement. Minto took another look at the gate from another angle and thought to herself that Hell's gate looked more inviting. Without doubt, Numen's gate, with its formidable presence, must have held secrets even more closely guarded and mysterious than she could imagine.

Meanwhile, as the others were engrossed in theorising how the acacia tree had travelled from the savannah grasslands of the Yatta Plateau to the peak of Mount Banda, Minto's attention was captured by the peculiar gatepost. Upon closer inspection, she noticed a brass plate with a skull-and-crossbones emblem hanging on the top right-hand corner of the post. Despite the ominous presence of the emblem, Minto ignored it and continued to explore the infrastructure, heading towards the left-hand side. She paused briefly at the middle of the gate to marvel at the massive mortise and tenon joint connecting the left tree-trunk frame to the top log. It boggled her mind how on earth the two giant frames, weighing over a tonne each, were lifted and joined together without a giant crane.

Minto was unable to unravel the mysteries of the dovetail joint, prompting a shift in her focus. Her new interest led her towards the left side of the gate, near a gothic portico, where her attention was captured by a dry human skull hanging from copper wire parallel to the gate's frame. The sight of the human remains sent shivers down her spine, and she began to frantically wave her arms in the air, hoping to alert her team members to the eerie discovery. Frustratingly, no one noticed her distress. Instead, the blokes seemed engrossed in a heated discussion about the mysterious acacia tree, deliberately avoiding Minto's unsettling find of unidentified human remains.

Unfazed by the snub, Minto chose to leave the blokes alone and ventured fearlessly into the mysterious land of the dead, eager to uncover its secrets. She walked past the massive gate and navigated a natal plum bush to get a better view of the human skull from a different angle, when she stumbled upon a peculiar metal disc hanging from a cable. Intrigued, she moved closer to inspect it, but her view was obstructed. Undeterred, Minto climbed to higher ground, achieving a perfect view.

After examining the disc from a better vantage point, Minto realized it was an improvised bourdon bell, ingeniously crafted from a discarded tractor plough. Yet, the enigma deepened: how had 350 kilograms of pure steel been transported up a steep mountain slope and hoisted seven metres up a redwood tree trunk without the aid of a forklift or pulleys? Adding to the mystery, Minto found it challenging to read the griffonage inscriptions on the lower tip of the disc, possibly some faded manufacturer's markings. The disc, evidently, had weathered many years.

In the meantime, while the rest of the team was excited to reach Mue's mysterious gate for the first time, Gaati attempted to draw the attention of the gatekeeper by throwing stones at the bell. Gaati was acquainted with the entry procedures from his previous visit. He finally managed to haul a sizeable stone after several attempts, and the sound of the ding reverberated down the mountain ridge, echoing through the valley below and causing a flock of red-billed weaver birds to swarm over them. The flock was so massive that it blocked the sun's rays, creating a momentary shadow.

The team waited with bated breath for what felt like an eternity. Finally, a gargantuan figure emerged from behind the delicate silk mimosa trees. Standing at an impressive height of nearly six foot eleven, the man was a sight to behold. His large ears, long arms and deep brow-ridge bone gave him a gorilla-like appearance. His muscular physique was so impressive that his chiselled chest was the size of a small table, and his biceps looked like the articulated arm of an industrial robot.

With little effort, the man pushed aside the gigantic bough blocking the gateway and approached the team. His bare knuckles were scarred and callused, resembling someone who had punched a rhinoceros head several times. He was enigmatic, to say the least. Minto, the self-appointed team detective, noticed that the man's pinkie finger was missing, replaced by a growth of black mass. The giant was clad in a groin cloth. He was sporting a bizarre tattoo on his glabella, and a copper ring piercing through his aquiline nose.

"We have company," Minto quipped, breaking the silence. As the gatekeeper approached, he immediately recognized Gaati from their previous meeting two weeks prior and extended his anaconda-sized arm to shake hands. "Welcome back!" he greeted warmly, and the two men exchanged pleasantries and brief commentaries about the weather. Meanwhile, Benjo observed something unusual in the brief exchange between the two men. Despite the gatekeeper's enormous size, his voice was as gentle as a dove and as warm as morning sunbeams, starkly contrasting with the preconceived biases Benjo had formed about the stranger. He had expected the earth to vibrate when the giant spoke.

Despite Benjo's prejudices, the stranger went around shaking hands with the rest of team. Minto felt the calloused immensity of the giant's hand engulf hers, extending down her wrist like a massive mitt. It felt more like shaking the blade of a large bulldog shovel than a human hand. Even more curious, the gatekeeper's palms were incredibly dry and rough, like sandpaper. They could easily graze the skin off Minto's arm.

The giant bypassed the men, greeting Minto, the only woman present, first. Perhaps it was a gesture of respect, or a subtle way of offering protection, duties that the team would much later discover extended far beyond mere greetings – he was, in truth, a Praetorian

Guard, tasked with safeguarding Mue's Fort. In contrast, the giant introduced himself as Mue's concierge, describing his role as welcoming and seeing off guests at the medical facility. This encounter left Benjo with a newfound respect for the gatekeeper and his role, serving as a stark reminder that first impressions can be deceiving and that it is always important to keep an open mind when meeting new people.

As the last rays of the setting sun cast long shadows, the concierge closed the gate and guided his final group of outpatients for the day. They were headed towards Mue's Fort, a sprawling compound marked by a curious mix of contrasting architectural styles, visible in the distance. It was 6:30 pm. After walking for about three hundred metres, they reached a built-up area marked by insalubrious structures of mudbrick walls and thatched roofs. The concierge stopped and asked the team to wait on a flat wooden bench outside the first hut while he disappeared into another windowless one, presumably to consult with the resident diviner.

The diviner's role functioned similarly to a triage nurse in a hospital, quickly assessing the severity of a patient's condition to determine the appropriate level of care. They also used divination practices to assess patients beforehand and recommend whether they should see the Numen of Banda for specialized treatment.

The diviners of Banda Salama wielded immense authority, granted carte blanche by the Numen of Banda to make independent decisions. They possessed the power to deny prospective patients access to the medicine man if suspected of witchcraft. In some cases, any queue-jumpers who dared bypass the diviner and head straight to the doctor would face swift retribution. Such arrogance would not be tolerated. The offender would be forced to go back to the end of the queue and start all over again, a harsh reminder of the diviner's absolute authority. The diviners, however, weren't entirely inflexible. In rare cases they allowed a patient they deemed or appraised to have a clean soul to bypass the examination and proceed directly to the medicine man.

The diviners' facility operated as a fully fledged spiritual diagnostic laboratory, independent of the Numen of Banda. Despite this autonomy, the diviners were intricately linked to the medicine man, who retained the ultimate authority to hire and fire them. The professional relationship between the diviners and the Numen of Banda was complex. This paradox is best captured by the anecdotal belief that two experts can never agree, or by a local Kamba saying, which asserts that living next to a cemetery means one cannot mourn every deceased person. Nevertheless, due to the high demand for diviner services across multiple medicine men in Banda Salama, the diviners wielded significant bargaining power, making their work peripatetic in nature. In other words, although the diviners were professionally subordinate to the medicine men, no medicine man could afford to employ them on a permanent basis.

As the team waited for the concierge, Minto felt exhausted and reached for a low bench to rest. She sat down heavily, and the rudimentary timber bench, clearly not built for a woman of Minto's robust stature, snapped under her weight. Minto, a buxom woman from the Aimu clan, landed with a surprised yelp in a muddy puddle, sparking a blush that rivaled the setting sun. Though she attempted to shrug it off with a laugh, Benjo's snickers, persistent as a gadfly, continued to annoy Minto.

As the saying goes, 'a mouse that mocks a cat should ensure there's a hole nearby to take cover in case of a retaliatory response.' Amidst the titter, Benjo realized he was close enough to be within reach of Minto's retaliatory slap, and he cautiously moved back five meters. In any case, he was confident Minto couldn't outrun him. Eventually, Minto regained her composure.

However, the commotion, marked by Benjo's playful snickering, alerted the Diviner to the patients waiting outside. As Wasa's family entered the consultation room, Gaati, adhering to the facility's strict protocols, found himself waiting outside with the Concierge. This protocol forbids accompanying guides from engaging in any activity within the facility until the patients' full treatment is complete. It's partly a security measure, but more importantly, because some guides might be unwitting agents, posing as innocent companions while secretly carrying out retaliatory curses on behalf of those who inflicted evil magic on the patients. This very protocol explains Gaati's absence during the consultation with the Diviner and his inactivity throughout most of the family's stay at the medical fort.

For centuries, tales of diviners' arcane practices and supposed spell-casting shrouded them in mystery and fear. Benjo was no exception to this disquiet. Yet, his preconceived prejudices were shattered upon meeting their diviner – a surprisingly affable and easy-going woman, though well past her prime. By Benjo's reckoning, she must have been in her mid-seventies.

At the earliest opportunity, the diviner offered Minto and Benjo some black tea, perhaps to show her human side or to gain their trust. Reaching out, she poured sweetened black tea from a burnt-out teapot into a rusty metal cup and handed it to Benjo. To her delight, Benjo promptly accepted the tea and took a sip. However, before the diviner could repeat the gesture with Benjo's mother, Minto quickly declined the offer. Nonetheless, the diviner was happy to have won over Benjo and, by extension, his mother – or so she thought. She was not bothered about Wasa who sat stoically observing the exchange.

In truth, Benjo accepted the tea simply to please the diviner and appease the local deity, the Numen of Banda, in case his visit stirred memories of his mistake at the mountain grotto. Meanwhile, the diviner began preparing her tools for telling fortunes. Always, before touching any of her talismans, she retrieved a tiny gourd from a leather pouch and offered some tobacco to the gods on the floor. Taking a pinch, she stuffed it into both nostrils and inhaled deeply. The snuff hit the right spot, forcing a powerful sneeze out of her.

Diviners rarely take the time to explain their craft to their clients, and Benjo's diviner was no exception. Reaching for a large sisal basket in the corner of the room, she pulled out an assortment of animal horns among them ram's horns and antelope horns, a small gourd filled with cowrie shells, and a stunning necklace adorned with variegated beads and polished stones. Without any explanation, she placed these items on the left side of a monkey skin that was spread out on the floor. In an unexpected move, she took another sniff of tobacco and then froze in one position for about a minute, her eyes fixated on a single spot on the ground between her seat and Benjo's legs. The room fell silent with anticipation, but the diviner remained transfixed on the same spot, not uttering a word.

Despite the oddity of the situation, the patients remained composed, perhaps believing this to be a necessary part of the divination process or a sign of the spirit's manifestation. However, the septuagenarian struck Benjo as more likely to be either unhinged or under the influence. Benjo couldn't shake the memory of his grandfather's favourite proverb: "A silent dog bites first." Unease gnawed at him. He knew he'd wronged the clan spirits, and guilt, as they say, is a fearful companion. Nonetheless, he feigned composure to on his face.

The diviner consultation was barely a minute in, but the proceedings were becoming increasingly arcane and baffling for mere mortals like Wasa, Benjo, and Minto. Despite their pressing questions which they kept to themselves; the strange happening was far beyond their grasp. Suddenly, and without warning, the diviner erupted in a violent sneeze, unleashing a spray of bodily fluids straight onto Benjo's chest and face. It was a revolting experience, to say the least. To make matters worse, the diviner didn't even bother to apologize to Benjo; instead, it was Benjo who stammered an apology for the involuntary sneeze. In reality, Benjo was utterly mortified and disgusted by the appalling crudity of the situation, and he fought back nausea. Fortunately, Minto quickly came to his aid, yanking out her kitenge scarf from her basket to clean the filth off him.

After displaying strange behaviour, the diviner decided to take a break and indulge in her tobacco habit, much to Benjo's passive resistance. He wasn't thrilled about the prospect of another round of the pungent experience. As the diviner reached for a rusty iron cylinder for an improvised spittoon, Benjo braced himself for the inevitable stench. With three powerful chomps, the diviner spewed a generous glob of tobacco into the spittoon and slammed the lid shut with a clang. But it was too late. The air around them was rapidly filled with an offensive odour – a noxious blend reminiscent of curdled human waste. The stench was overpowering, like a fertilizer truck colliding with a skunk outside a garbage dump. In a desperate bid to escape further punishment, Benjo scrunched his nose in disgust and swivelled his face towards the doorway. Minto, on the other hand, resorted to her scarf, covering both her mouth and nose in a desperate measure to mitigate the putrid odour.

In stark contrast, the diviner was unfazed by the putrid odour that permeated the air. Her body language suggested that the foul smell was the least of her worries, and her brusqueness left Minto wondering if she was immune to the stench or had developed a superhuman tolerance after years of exposure. The chasm between the diviner and the rest of the team was obvious.

Suddenly, without provocation, the diviner snapped: 'Shut up or go jump in a lake, for all I care!' Her vehement reaction to Benjo's discomfort left everyone taken aback. For all intents and purposes, Benjo had been protesting silently, unaware that his body language would give him away. Little did he know that the rule of nonverbal communication states that body language accounts for fifty-five percent of meaning. However, the inscrutable diviner did not specify who she was scolding, but the impact of her words was unmistakable. Benjo nearly jumped out of his skin in fear and never uttered a word again unless he was addressed directly from that moment on.

After firmly putting Benjo in his place, the diviner resumed her work, her face adorned with a mean-spirited smile as she whistled a cheerful tune. Her behaviour was perplexing yet not surprising. Nonetheless, she effectively demonstrated that she was a force to be reckoned with.

Following the minor spat, the preparations for divination resumed earnestly. The diviner deftly picked up a hunting bow and wedged a calabash between the wooden limb and the leather string, creating a crude yet intriguing musical instrument. She strummed the string to test the instrument and carefully positioned the tool on the right-hand side of the mandrill monkey skin spread out on the floor. Minto, with her sharp eye, noticed a pattern in the way the diviner arranged the items on either side of the monkey's skin. It was clear that the exercise was not mere extemporaneous guesswork but rather a predetermined and methodical process.

The Kamba proverb that warns one person's fate is another's lesson resonated with Minto after witnessing Benjo's admonishment. Despite her curiosity, she wisely kept her thoughts to herself, understanding it was none of her concern how the diviner worked, as long as she could unveil Benjo's future. After all, there is a clan proverb, which advises that a woman who sells oil beans in a marketplace has a better understanding of the intricacies of her trade, including minor peculiarities such as the fly that has one eye. This was the diviner's domain, and Minto respected her expertise.

However, the series of events in the diviner's consultation room sparked a new question in Minto's mind: what truly defines a consultant? She considered a consultant to be someone who could precisely tell you how to solve your problems but might not necessarily be able to solve their own. This reflection was influenced by the diviner, who was quick to prescribe solutions for Minto's problems. Ironically, despite her apparent wisdom, the diviner herself was struggling with poverty.

After what felt like an eternity to Benjo, the diviner finally took three hearty gulps of the mysterious brew that had been steeping in a calabash on the floor since the team's arrival. This was just the first step in a series of rituals preceding the séance. Benjo, fearing retribution from the clan spirits for his past mistakes, wished for the diviner's consultation to end as swiftly as possible. The fortune-telling moment was always a solemn and eerie affair, involving a paranormal manifestation of the spirit of divination, which unnervingly took control of the diviner's soul, body, and mind. In other words, the divination moment represented a complete takeover of the diviner's personality by a supernatural being, during which the diviner's will and natural thought process were disabled or rendered powerless. Nevertheless, the disenfranchised patients had no choice but to sit and observe the arcane proceedings of the diviner with a sense of awe and trepidation.

The diviner uttered a brief incantation and then fell silent, her body language conveying a sense of deep concentration, as if she were straining to hear faint whispers. Suddenly, she began to hiccup and speak in an incomprehensible tongue that erupted into full-blown glossolalia. The scene that followed was unlike anything Benjo or the others had ever witnessed. The diviner's trance deepened, her body trembling uncontrollably. It was as if a powerful presence had taken hold of her.

In that moment, they were witnessing a rare and extraordinary event – a visitation by the clan spirit. Ancestral spirits, protectors of the bloodline, are seldom seen, but on this occasion, it seemed the spirit had descended to honour Benjo, the heir apparent to Sosh, the family matriarch. The spirit's purpose, however, remained shrouded in mystery.

After a few harrowing moments, the trance subsided as abruptly as it began. The diviner, drained but composed, regained control. Her first words, though, sent a jolt through the room: "Benjo," she declared, "Kiseko has chosen you. You go first."

The pronouncement settled like a shroud over the room. No explanation followed, leaving the words to hang heavy in the air, thick with unspoken questions. Who was Kiseko? What did 'going first' entail? How had this mysterious Kiseko arrived at their decision for Benjo to go first? The diviner offered no answers, her lips sealed shut. Her silence, coupled with the secrecy surrounding Kiseko's identity, forced the patients into a tense acquiescence. Perhaps it was the fear of the unknown that kept them silent, a hesitancy to challenge the enigmatic figure before them. Whispers even began to circulate among them, speculating that Kiseko might be a mere alias, a shield protecting the true name of Banda's all-powerful deity – the Numen of Banda.

Despite the secrecy surrounding Kiseko's choice, it gradually dawned on everyone that Benjo's being chosen to 'go first' meant he would be the first to undergo the individual consultations. In fortune-telling, each person is assessed separately, even when they come as part of a family group. Therefore, considering both tradition and the special favour granted by the clan spirit's visitation, it was Benjo's turn for the much-anticipated clinical assessment. A mixture of fear and excitement churned within him as he prepared to face the diviner's test.

The preparation for the consultation was a meticulous affair. With purposeful, practised movements, the diviner unfurled a large, cured mandrill monkey skin in the centre of the dimly lit room. The pungent odour of the hide filled the air, mingling with the faint aroma of black cat oil. She then spread a rough burlap sack atop the skin, creating a seating area that was both clean and symbolically grounded. Benjo, feeling a cold sweat prickling his skin, was directed to sit on this makeshift throne. With his back to the door and legs close together, he faced the diviner, whose presence cast a complex aura in the flickering light.

Benjo sat on the burlap-covered monkey skin, following the diviner's exact instructions. The room's dim, flickering lights made long shadows on the walls, making the smell of herbs and black cat oil stronger. The diviner's presence was both soothing and scary, which made Benjo feel even more troubled inside. He realised how important this moment was; it would break or shape his future. Being close to the clan spirit now, Benjo felt nervous, remembering the sacrilege he committed at the sacred grotto.

The diviner reached for a small, mortar-like container. Inside, a pungent mix of ground herbs lay melded with black cat oil. With practiced movements, she dipped her fingers into the paste and painted narrow, irregular white marks across her face, hands, and legs. The stark white against her dark skin sent a shiver down Benjo's spine. After adorning herself, she donned a beaded necklace that clicked softly against her chest. Then, with a nod towards the earthen floor, the diviner took a pinch of tobacco and offered it to the unseen gods. Finally, she brought a pinch to her nostrils, inhaling deeply as if to calm her own nerves.

The diviner dipped her fingers back into the pungent herbal mix, a glint in her eye that sent a tremor through Benjo. This time, instead of adorning herself, she pinched the paste and thrust it under his nose. "Inhale deeply," she commanded, her voice a low rumble.

Benjo hesitated, the sharp, herbal scent stinging his nostrils. But under the unwavering intensity of her gaze, he obeyed. A potent mixture of herbs and black cat oil exploded in his senses. He lunged forward, a violent sneeze erupting from his chest, shaking him to his core. It morphed into a spasmodic cough that wracked his body for what felt like an eternity. The room spun, and Benjo clung to the arms of the makeshift throne, gasping for air. The diviner remained a statue, her gaze locked on him until the coughing subsided.

Her gaze still fixed on Benjo, the diviner reached out a hand, her fingers trembling slightly. From the array of mystical objects scattered beside the monkey skin, she snatched a slender gourd bottle filled with cowrie shells. Despite its worn appearance, the diviner held the gourd with reverence, blocking its mouth with her right thumb. The burgundy hue and shiny surface of the gourd were enough testaments to its frequent handling and polishing with ghee, which had given it a timeless, classic look. With a swift shake, the diviner invoked the ancient powers of the Numen of Banda, before releasing the choke to reveal a single cowrie shell on the ground. The diviner froze with excitement, knowing that this was the climactic moment that everyone had been eagerly awaiting. To ensure the accuracy of the results, she meticulously repeated the experiment, achieving the same outcome. ''"This is incredible!"'' she exclaimed animatedly.

The parents of Benjo, having observed the diviner's rituals, were left bewildered by the arcane proceedings. Wisely, they kept their questions unvoiced, haunted by the knowledge that the last person to challenge the diviner's work and by extension the clan spirit was buried upside down at the base of Mount Banda. This macabre detail sent a shiver down Minto's spine as she recalled the unidentified human skull dangling ominously at the medicine man's gate. She quashed the rising curiosity within her, aware that such inquiries might lead her to a grim end. Yet, the nagging thought lingered: could that skull be a grim testament to another defiant soul who had dared to question the diviner?

After repeating the test on Benjo a third time with a different tool, just to be on the safe side, the diviner's face broke into a wide grin. In a sudden burst of excitement, she shot up from her seat and vigorously shook Benjo's hand. The gourd placed on her lap tumbled to the floor with a clatter, yet she barely noticed. Turning to Minto with a beaming smile, she declared, 'Your son is the most protected child I have ever seen in my fifty-five years of divining! Absolutely the most protected!' Her joy was infectious. Although Minto did not fully grasp the significance of the message, the diviner's smile was undeniably genuine, crinkling the corners of her eyes, even as it inadvertently revealed a few tobacco stains on her teeth. Caught up in the excitement of the discovery, she seemed blissfully unaware of the slight mishap.

The brief celebratory commotion subsided, and the diviner gracefully resumed her seat. Her demeanor, once focused and intense, softened as she turned to Minto with a warm smile. Now, it was time to explain the results of the divination. Her explanation was clear: the single cowrie shell spilling from the gourd signified a good omen from the ancestral world, *Zamani*. It was a unanimous decision – Benjo was to become Sosh's heir apparent, and in essence, a living saint. As a result, the dominion of *Zamani*, the council of ancestors in the spiritual realm, had granted Benjo an extraordinary protection. No evil eye, witchcraft, or any other malevolent force could penetrate this shield. Benjo was, quite literally, untouchable.

The second translation of the divination held equal significance. Benjo had been given a clean bill of health, allowing him to proceed to the next stage of the treatment procedure, presided over by the Numen of Banda himself. This news was a moment of great hope and optimism, a stark contrast to the despair that had shrouded Minto ever since the miscarriages. While their primary purpose in visiting the medicine man was to diagnose and potentially treat Minto's fertility issues, the visitation by the clan spirit presented a rare and special opportunity. It allowed Benjo to receive a diagnosis as well, a blessing not readily bestowed to mere mortals.

Benjo was overwhelmed with relief when the gods declared him sound of body. He had been certain his transgression at the mountain grotto would invite punishment. Instead, this unexpected outcome fuelled his faith, reinforcing his belief that the gods worked in mysterious ways.

To conclude the session, the diviner retrieved two hartebeest horns from a cache on the floor. She instructed Benjo to grasp them by the opposite ends and support himself as she lifted him off the ground. Once Benjo was back on his feet, the diviner simply said, "Wait outside." Relief and gratitude washed over Benjo; a feeling more profound than anything he had ever experienced.

The diviner remained motionless in her seated position for a long time after tending to Benjo. Minto, already plagued by a growing ache in her own back, couldn't help but wonder about the woman's tolerance for discomfort. With no answer forthcoming, Minto suspected the diviner either possessed superhuman resilience or had more pressing battles to fight. Suddenly, it was Minto's turn. The consultation seat, habitually dreaded by all, awaited Minto. Just moments ago, she'd silently mocked Benjo for his fear. The old adage echoed in her mind: "Those who have not yet crossed the river should not mock those who are drowning." It was time for Minto to face her own test at the hands of the enigmatic diviner.

Minto took Benjo's place on the burlap sack and underwent a series of tests similar to those used for him. However, there were three key differences. First, the diviner performed a preliminary touch examination on Minto's stomach before continuing with the main ritual examination. Second, and most unexpectedly, the diviner instructed Wasa to sit back-to-back with Minto in a curious arrangement. Minto would later learn that including her husband in the diagnosis was mandatory, as conception was considered a couple's affair in the eyes of the spirits. The third, and most striking, difference was the cowrie shells calabash test. Unlike Benjo's experience, the diviner's gourd spewed forth a multitude of coloured cowrie shells, scattering them across the floor.

Minto sat in awe and trepidation as she watched the diviner's gourd spew out about two dozen cowrie shells. She couldn't help but feel uncertain about what the analysis of the test results would reveal about her. She was wary of the outcome because she knew that the results would have a significant impact on her future. Would the gods smile upon her, or would they reveal a darker fate? Despite her anxiety, she was determined to face the diviner's test with courage and hope.

Leaning closer, the diviner interpreted the eerie sequences and patterns displayed by the cowrie shells, seeking to foretell Minto's story. To the untrained eye, the mere skeletons of the dead molluscs scattered on the ground may have seemed insignificant. However, to the diviner, the patterns and sequence of the shells contained a decipherable message from the gods that was key to unlocking Minto's prosperity.

The diviner delivering both good news and bad. A believer in the power of positivity, she started with the brighter side: the couple had aced the divination test, granting them access to the next crucial stage of treatment – a personal audience with the revered Numen of Banda.

However, the bad news was that Minto's womb had been blocked using potent juju imported from a foreign land, hence the miscarriages. Despite this evil spell, the diviner reassured the couple that it was reversible. This was one of the unique advantages of consulting diviners before the main treatment – their ability to accurately predict whether a curse or spell could be reversed, and by what type of practitioner.

The diviner's announcement was a mixed bag of emotions. Yet, the invaluable insight she provided gave Minto a much-needed glimmer of hope. With the knowledge that the spell could be reversed, the couple was able to move forward with their treatment plan with renewed hope, thanks to the diviner's invaluable guidance.

To facilitate the couple's progression, the diviner utilized the same hoisting ritual she had previously employed on Benjo. Using two massive horns from a giant eland antelope, she lifted each member of the couple from their seated positions onto their feet. This ancient ritual served as a symbolic stepping stone to a new phase in their lives. The diviner's mastery of this tradition was evident as she effortlessly lifted Minto, who dwarfed the diviner's own frame, from a seated position.

The pronouncement complete, the diviner's eyes flicked towards Wasa. A silent command understood instantly. Wasa dipped his head and crossed the room, the clink of coins echoing as he deposited the diviner's fee into a worn wicker basket perched precariously on a rickety stool in the shadows. A satisfied grunt escaped the diviner's lips. Then, with a surprising burst of energy for someone who'd spent hours seemingly frozen in meditation, the diviner rose and ushered them out, a strange, almost manic cheer in her voice. Back to the waiting game, back to the unknown.

The concierge resumed his role as a guide, leading the patients deeper into the expansive Mue compound. As they made their way through the courtyard, Minto couldn't help but notice the stark contrast between the dilapidated structures they had seen earlier at the diviner's quarters and the idyllic beauty of the rest of the compound.

The courtyard was immaculately kept, with neatly trimmed hedges, rustling palm trees, and magnificent flowers. However, idyllic beauty was marred by a jarring sight: a dozen squat, grass-thatched huts huddled incongruously along the path. Their ramshackle appearance clashed with the manicured hedges and vibrant flowers.

The meticulous care bestowed upon the compound far surpassed Minto's expectations. Sculpted hedges formed emerald walls, and immaculate flower beds burst with colour, their sweet fragrance scenting the air. Yet, this idyllic scene was shattered by a cacophony of disturbing sounds emanating from the grass-thatched huts lining the path.

Benjo, drawn by morbid curiosity, approached the huts to investigate the source of the unsettling noises. From the first hut, a guttural shriek pierced the air. The next hut unleashed a mournful wail, followed by a whimper so pathetic it sent shivers down Benjo's spine. Together, these sounds coalesced into a haunting a cappella that seemed to echo from the depths of hell. The atmosphere was so oppressive that a cold sweat slicked Benjo's skin. He couldn't help but wonder if the strain of the day was causing him to hallucinate.

Concerned, Benjo paused to speak with a frail old man leaning heavily on a walking stick nearby. The man revealed that the huts were inpatient wards for critically ill individuals. Multiple fractures, rheumatoid arthritis, and acute pancreatitis were a few of the severe conditions the patients endured. A wave of empathy washed over Benjo as the overwhelming sense of human suffering permeated the compound.

The tranquility of the compound was shattered by a piercing scream from somewhere in the middle. Pandemonium ensued, followed by a loud explosion echoing from the direction of the diviner's quarters. Abandoning Benjo's team, the concierge sprinted rapidly towards the source of the commotion, disappearing into the diviner's hut. Determined to protect the lives and property of the Fort, the concierge had no idea what awaited him. Every second counted in what seemed like a matter of life or death, and he was prepared to do whatever it took to ensure everyone's safety.

Feeling disoriented and abandoned after the Concierge's sudden departure, Minto's team huddled together in the cloister, unsure of their next move. A voice, roughened by time and hardship, then echoed across the courtyard, offering a much-needed explanation.

The voice came from a long-term resident of the medical facility, a stranger to them, yet evidently familiar with the inner workings of the Fort. He took pity on their disorientation and decided to inform them.

'The giant you encountered,' the stranger boomed, his guttural voice taking Minto's team by surprise, 'is not a mere gatekeeper or concierge as you presumed.' His long, gnarled finger extended, pointing directly at Benjo. 'Yes, you there, with the worried frown drawn on your face. That imposing figure—mind you, is not just any gatekeeper or concierge!' He chuckled, emitting a low, humourless rumble that sent shivers down their spines. 'That, my friends, is the Chief Security Officer of Mue's Fort, a man ominously nicknamed "The Tragedian." His sudden appearances often herald unfortunate events, hence the name bestowed upon him by the patients here.'

The stranger's revelation illuminated their previous encounter with the giant at the gate. But before Minto could express her newfound curiosity, the resident disappeared as swiftly and mysteriously as he had arrived, leaving them with more questions than answers. Perhaps he was wary of being implicated in revealing the Chief Security Officer's true identity.

There was a compelling reason the imposing figure they'd encountered wasn't addressed by his real name. Before joining Mue's camp as the Chief Security Officer, he resided on death row at Kamiti Maximum Prison for murder during an armed robbery. Among his fellow inmates, he was known solely by the Swahili nickname "Pasua," meaning "to split." His release came through a highly political presidential pardon for hundreds of inmates just before a general election. Mue, having heard whispers of Pasua's reputation as a ruthless and fearless fighter, strategically recruited him as his personal security chief.

Shortly afterwards, the Concierge emerged from the diviner's hut, firmly holding a young man upside down. The man's feet were clamped in the Concierge's right hand, his own hands flailing in a futile attempt to escape. The Concierge led the way towards the courtyard, with the young man's family pleading for his life.

A large crowd hurried past Benjo's team and stopped outside the second-to-last hut before the palace. The Concierge blew his emergency whistle three times, and two assistants emerged from the medicine man's quarters holding powerful torches, illuminating the entire courtyard.

The scene was tense, the air thick with anticipation. The young man's family stood beside him, worry etched on their faces. The Concierge, however, remained stoic and unwavering. It was clear he was in complete control, and nothing would deter him from carrying out his duty.

What unfolded next resembled a well-rehearsed disaster recovery plan in motion. A fifth figure emerged from a different structure behind the medicine man's house. He carried a small, ornate pot resembling a psykter and handed it to one of the Concierge's assistants. Without hesitation, the assistant, likely a posologist, scooped a handful of the unknown powder and, with brute force, shoved it deep into the restrained young man's nostrils. He then clamped a hand over the victim's nose for several seconds, seemingly waiting for the incapacitating agent to take effect.

The young man's response was horrifying. He wheezed uncontrollably and convulsed violently, his body jerking like someone in the throes of a severe allergic reaction. This bizarre punishment continued until his eyelids slammed shut in a spasm and his vision faded. The young man then slumped unconscious, his body wracked with tremors and foam bubbling from his mouth.

The tense atmosphere was unexpectedly disrupted by the arrival of a new figure: Mue's resident peacekeeper, a senior diviner named Amara. Emerging from the palace with a serenity that contrasted sharply with the chaos unfolding in the courtyard, she glided towards the commotion. Her calm voice, seasoned with authority, cut through the tension as she cautioned the security team against using excessive force on a patient.

This admonition sparked a heated exchange of words between Amara and the Chief Security Officer (formerly mistaken for a Concierge by Minto's team). "Sir," Amara retorted, her voice firm yet laced with a hint of empathy, "I think you have gone mad with power!"

The Chief Security Officer, however, remained unfazed. "Of course, I have!" he shot back with a sardonic grin. "Have you ever tried going mad without power? It's boring!" His menacing glare, however, instantly diffused Amara's aggression, bringing an abrupt end to their verbal sparring.

The soporific barbiturate acid in the mysterious powder effectively subdued the unruly young man. By blocking dopamine, a key neurotransmitter in the brain, it rendered him unconscious – a brutal coup de grâce.

The Chief Security Officer approached and checked the victim's pulse. He then made a discreet hand signal, and two of his assistants emerged to remove the comatose body. The young man was a sorry sight, his body wracked with tremors, mucus discharging from all orifices, and his clothes soiled. The assistants swiftly transported him to one of the unoccupied post-treatment recovery care units, where they instructed the carers to keep him under close observation.

Minto pondered the bizarre operation. While she partly agreed that challenging Mue's authority within his domain was a foolish decision for the young man, she vehemently disagreed with the security team's response. In her opinion, resorting to coma-inducing chemicals was not only brutal but entirely disproportionate to the transgression. It was akin to swatting a fly with a sledgehammer. This swift and inhumane elimination of a perceived threat solidified Minto's belief that it was such security concerns that prompted Dr. Mue to hire a physical enforcer as his Chief Security Officer.

The Concierge as they knew him approached Minto's team, profusely apologizing for abandoning them abruptly. He attempted damage control by explaining that the powerful sedative administered to the young man was necessary to prevent the chaos a delusional and potentially violent episode could have caused. However, Minto wasn't convinced. Despite his attempts to downplay his role and obscure his past, Minto had already pieced together the truth: the Chief Security Officer was essentially Mue's personal guardian of brute force.

While the Chief Security Officer dealt with the commotion, Minto managed to gather some crucial information about the young man. She spoke with his mother, who shared a concerning story. According to the mother, a powerful river spirit had taken control of her son, using him to attack the Diviner. Apparently, the benevolent powers of the Numen of Banda were irritating the malevolent river spirit. The mother also revealed that the medication used to restrain him would keep him unconscious for nine hours. She knew this because it was the exact same medicine, they used on him during their previous visit for a similar incident.

Minto was furious. The mother's scary story and her growing suspicion about the security chief's reasons for doing what he did made her imagine him on trial for crimes against humanity. She believed she had enough evident to edict the security man. But then she remembered this wasn't a real court, and her dream of a judge hitting the gavel to stop him disappeared.

Despite her belief in the unseen realm, Minto couldn't shake the feeling that the young man's case was more earthly than demonic. The erratic behaviour pointed more towards a complex medical issue – perhaps a cocktail of undiagnosed conditions (comorbidity) or even a misdiagnosed case of highland malaria, a nasty bug plaguing the mountain people, including those from Banda Salama. However, logic seemed to be lost on the distraught mother, who clung fiercely to her belief in demonic possession.

Indeed, Minto was an invaluable asset to the team, a walking encyclopedia of practical knowledge, life skills, and situational awareness. Nonetheless, Gaati loathed her for her deep understanding of modern education and her ability to navigate these situations. However, as soon as they entered the treatment place, the rules changed. Gaati could no longer boss Minto around due to protocol restrictions. As a result, Minto seized the opportunity and took charge of the conversation, which further fuelled Gaati's resentment. With Wasa barely speaking at all, given his reclusive demeanour, Minto had the stage all to herself and relished the opportunity.

The reputation of a great man often precedes him like his shadow, sometimes stretching larger than life. Such was Mue, a man whose fame bestrode Yatta administration district like a colossus. Mue's public acclaim rested on a rare combination: his mastery of herbal treatments and unmatched prowess in magical healing, drawing people from far and wide to consult him.

To the tens of thousands who benefited from his benevolence, Mue stood at the intersection of power and the powerless, a towering authority in both medicine and magic. Patients from all walks of life flocked to seek treatment from the renowned medical expert. His popularity was so widespread that, during peak times, patients endured waits of up to a week for a consultation. These extended delays could be a source of immense frustration, especially for those with serious medical conditions.

Interestingly, the harvesting season of pigeon peas proved to be the most chaotic of all the cyclical peak periods. This season coincides with an inexplicable surge in mental health cases, leading the local Kamba community to nickname it the "Harvest Season of Madness" due to the dramatic increase in the number of people experiencing mental illness.

In stark contrast to the delays experienced by the general public, Sosh's family received a red-carpet reception, treated like esteemed VIP visitors. Unbeknownst to them, Mue was well-informed about Sosh's distinguished reputation. Sosh was a commander in the Kenya Land and Freedom Army and a highly respected member of the Yatta district community.

The team later discovered that Mue's source of information was Sosh's elder brother, Corporal Mbibo. Both Sosh and Corporal Mbibo served together in the Kenya Land and Freedom Army during the Aberdare Forest Mau Mau uprising. Interestingly, Sosh was Mbibo's regimental commander in the Aberdare battalion. Their shared experience forged a strong bond of friendship and loyalty that would last a lifetime.

According to confidential information Corporal Mbibo shared with his brother, Dr. Mue, the Aberdare Forest Regiment was a specialized unit tasked with conducting surprise attacks to disarm and confiscate firearms from British farmers who also served as army reservists. Additionally, the regiment neutralized armed African members of the Home Guard. These Home Guards were comprised of trusted African natives recruited, trained, and armed by the British colonial government to protect their local communities from Mau Mau infiltration, particularly in regions perceived to be sympathetic to British rule.

As a result, the Aberdare regiment specialized in ambush operations designed to destabilize the Home Guards. Their operations were brutally violent, intended to send a chilling message to other Africans contemplating joining the Home Guard reserves.

During the Mau Mau Revolt, the Aberdare Forest Regiment emerged as a formidable force, striking fear into the hearts of both British settlers and African Home Guards alike. Their cunning and effective tactics, carried out with precision and skill, made them a force to be reckoned with. Their legacy lives on as a symbol of resistance against colonial oppression.

Their tactics were cunning and effective, and they were able to carry out their operations with precision and skill. They were a force to be reckoned with, and their legacy lives on as a symbol of resistance against colonial oppression.

Besides sharing military experiences, Mue fondly remembered his elder brother, the late Corporal Mbibo, as a gifted storyteller. Mbibo would captivate audiences for hours with tales of his wartime exploits. One of his most unforgettable stories recounted the daring raid on the Makutano Home Guard command post. Led by regimental commander Sosh, a group of Mau Mau fighters infiltrated the post undetected under the cloak of night and brutally killed the five Home Guards on duty.

Mbibo described in vivid detail how Commander Sosh, with nerves of steel, infiltrated the outpost from behind enemy lines, armed with a machete. She eliminated the Home Guard commander in seconds before disappearing into the darkness.

It's important to understand that the Mau Mau, an insurgent group fighting against British colonial rule in Kenya, had a unique rank structure. Unlike formal militaries, Mau Mau ranks were often awarded based on experience, leadership skills, and battlefield performance, drawing inspiration from the Second World War experience of many fighters. While some ranks ensured clear reporting lines, others were bestowed in recognition of exceptional bravery or battlefield prowess. Sosh's title of regimental commander reflected her exceptional leadership, and her subsequent recognition as a field marshal was even more extraordinary.

Among the Mau Mau, the title of Field Marshal was a rare and coveted honour, bestowed upon only the most legendary warriors. Sosh wasn't just a whirlwind of steel in close combat; she possessed an unmatched talent for mobilizing operations and coordinating fighting units from the front. Unlike formal militaries with their rigid hierarchies, the Mau Mau recognized greatness in the crucible of battle.

Sosh's body count was a testament to her skills, but it was her unwavering courage and tactical brilliance that truly set her apart.

In response to the brutal attack, the Chief Native Commissioner of Kenya Colony placed a hefty bounty of fifty thousand pounds sterling on Sosh's head. This was an enormous sum of money at the time, reflecting the desperation of the colonial authorities.

Despite the hefty bounty and the governor's urgent directive, Sosh remained a ghost, evading capture throughout the war. This cat-and-mouse game continued for years until 1960, when the fighting finally subsided. She remains the highest-ranking Mau Mau woman to have never surrendered, been captured, or been killed by the colonial government.

Kenya's long-awaited independence arrived in 1963, heralding a new political landscape. The newly formed government negotiated an amnesty for the Mau Mau, giving them an opportunity to lay down arms and return home safely. This shift in perspective recognized the Mau Mau as "freedom fighters" in the struggle for independence, contrasting sharply with the outgoing colonial government's stance, which had branded them as outlawed rebels and terrorists on the police wanted list. Under these transformed conditions, Sosh finally emerged from the shadows and surrendered, ready to rebuild her life in a free Kenya.

Unfortunately, Mbibo wasn't as fortunate. He lost his right leg to a sniper's bullet during the Battle of Kahigaini Valley in Nyeri. The war wounds eventually led to complications that claimed his life.

The time to be ushered to see Mue finally came. He graciously invited Sosh's team into his opulent home and led them directly to a secluded VIP lounge. This space was typically reserved for society's elite – politicians, community leaders, and Mue's old acquaintances who'd built impressive careers. Thanks to Sosh's connection, the family received full VIP treatment, a delightful surprise. Even though Sosh and Mue never met in person, Mue knew a great deal about her and held her in high esteem.

Bound by the strict protocols for guides escorting patients within the facility, Gaati remained on the periphery, observing the lavish treatment bestowed upon the group. While impressed by the VIP treatment, it wasn't entirely unexpected for him. He, too, received a taste of the courtesy extended to Sosh's family, a subtle acknowledgment of his role as their guide. Nevertheless, a deeper sense of satisfaction stirred within him, far more rewarding than any outward display of privilege. This satisfaction stemmed from his immense contribution to the success of linking Sosh and Mue.

The medicine man's home was a sight to behold – a grand, modern structure adorned with stunning blue and black awnings that graced the leeward veranda. Its grandeur, befitting a king, stood in stark contrast to the surrounding compound's traditional grass-thatched mud houses, which housed staff and inpatients. If houses could hold court, this one would surely command a king's presence. Its superimposed presence was akin to stumbling upon the eighth wonder of the world, set unexpectedly in an isolated expanse.

This wasn't just a house; it was a mountain fortress, a monument to human ingenuity rising from the untamed wilderness. Sprawling across 1,200 square meters of land, the house boasted nine bedrooms constructed with rustic, brown-coloured brick walls. Large French windows offered breathtaking views of the surrounding landscape, while the corrugated iron sheet roofing and modern water gutters combined functionality with undeniable style.

The construction of this magnificent abode spoke volumes. Intricate awning details and sturdy brick walls exuded luxury and refinement. It was a testament to the medicine man's wealth and power, a man of undeniable means.

Minto stood awestruck before the architectural marvel. The creators' genius was evident in every detail, from the meticulously manicured courtyard garden to the intricate espalier and grand, pea-gravel-filled allée. The topiary standards were truly outlandish.

Despite her admiration, a logistical question niggled at her: How did these massive quantities of building materials traverse the treacherous slopes to reach this remote location? The answer remained elusive. Perhaps, as the saying goes, it is the crooked wood that shows the best sculptor; the monumental challenge may have brought out the best in the builders. Did they employ giants in a Herculean effort, or did the medicine man himself utilise his magic to haul the stones up the escarpment? Minto pondered these possibilities as she continued to marvel at the beauty surrounding her.

Minto and Benjo pushed open the heavy oak doors of the reception room, followed by Wasa and Gaati. The silence that greeted them was thick and unsettling, broken only by the creak of the hinges. The room was devoid of any occupants, an unsettling emptiness that hung heavily in the air. Undeterred, they settled into the plush armchairs, hoping for a receptionist or perhaps Mue himself to appear.

Twenty minutes crawled by, each tick of the grandfather clock echoing in the oppressive stillness. A shared sense of unease settled over the group. Minto, ever the pragmatist, tapped her foot impatiently. Benjo's brow furrowed in concern. Gaati, ever vigilant, scanned the room, his gaze lingering on the shadows in the corners, poised to always protect Sosh's family. Even Gaati, usually stoic, seemed to tense slightly. Despite the growing disquiet, they trusted the process.

Waiting rooms were Minto's personal nightmare. Stuck with nothing to do, they amplified her every worry. She remembered all too well her past experience at a postnatal clinic, filled with wailing infants and cold nurses. The memory flashed back into her mind, making her even more jittery now. Waiting was never easy, but prolonged uncertainty demanded a particular brand of patience, one that Minto wasn't sure she possessed. From the moment they entered the silent reception room, she felt claustrophobic, accompanied by a tightness in her chest. Even as she tried to calm herself by telling her inner self that everything would be alright, she couldn't shake the feeling of unseen eyes watching them. It felt creepy.

As if to amplify the sense of unease, the room boasted a collection of strange furniture and unnerving decorations. However, nothing chilled her to the bone quite like the table nestled against the wall. Carved from a massive chunk of African ironwood, it was unmistakably crafted to resemble a human figure contorted into a disturbing crouch. The tabletop curved like a human back, the front legs mimicking grasping hands, and the back legs replicating human feet. The surreal design sent shivers down Minto's spine. Her heart hammered in her chest, an erratic drumbeat against the oppressive silence. Her breath quickened, shallow and ragged. A long night stretched before them, filled with a growing sense of foreboding.

The eerie atmosphere of the room, illuminated by a dozen cressets arranged in a radial pattern casting dappled light on the floor, spurred the concierge onward. Unfazed by the unsettling ambience, he took a left turn and followed a long corridor to the far end. There, he knocked on the last door with a resolute rap. A brief pause followed, then a response came through in a language that flowed like water, yet remained incomprehensible to the rest of the team. The concierge's response was swift and unequivocal. He dropped to his knees; his head bowed in reverence. It was a kowtow, a gesture of complete submission that spoke volumes about the power he acknowledged behind the door.

Minto drew a startling conclusion from the concierge's peculiar behavior. The incomprehensible language, his complete deference in the form of a kowtow – a gesture usually reserved for deities – suggested a secret communication between humans and beings of immense power. Until now, the concierge had exuded an aura of authority. People made way for him without question. To see him so humbled, reduced to his knees in reverence, spoke volumes about the entity residing within the room.

Despite a surge of trepidation, the concierge eventually rose, his hand trembling slightly as he opened the door for Minto, Benjo, and Wasa to enter. Meanwhile, in adherence to the medical facility's non-intrusive protocol, Gaati remained outside the anteroom, as the heavy oak barrier door between him and Sosh's family opened into the unknown. Inside, the team found themselves alone, their hearts pounding in the chilling silence. The air was thick with anticipation, and the only sound was the shallow rasp of their breathing.

As the team entered the new room, they were struck by its magnificence. It was majestic in every sense of the word. The flickering wicks of kerosene lanterns illuminated every corner, casting a mysterious glow that made it feel like something out of a dream.

Stepping through the doorway, a gasp escaped Minto's lips. The room that greeted them was a breathtaking spectacle, a jewel unearthed from a forgotten tomb. Flickering kerosene lanterns cast an ethereal glow, illuminating intricate carvings and paintings that adorned the walls, each of them a masterpiece.

The furniture, crafted from the finest materials, was a testament to the room's opulent design. An ornate table, surrounded by luxurious divans, occupied the centre space. Minto's gaze, however, was drawn to another door, ajar at the far end. A single elephant-skin curtain, vast and imposing, partially concealed the entryway, shrouding it in a veil of mystery.

Unlike the sterile reception area, this anteroom possessed a distinct aroma. The pleasant scent of balsamic resins, smouldering in censers at the back of the room, filled the air. The inviting fragrance beckoned Minto closer, but a flicker of trepidation held her back. The unknown lay just beyond that heavy curtain, and fear kept her feet rooted to the spot.

Alone in the opulent room, the team found themselves at a loss. Just as confusion settled in, the lights abruptly went off plunging them into darkness, without a flicker of warning. A terrified scream ripped from Minto's throat as the heavy door slammed shut behind them, the sound echoing ominously in the suffocating blackness. Panic surged through her, a torrent of obscenities spewing from her lips. The rest of the team reeled, momentarily stunned. Wasa, regaining his composure first, urged them to stay together. "Hold hands," he instructed, "until we find a light or another way out."

The situation was dire. Lost in the labyrinthine palace, they were entirely dependent on each other. As if the darkness wasn't enough, a cacophony of unsettling sounds erupted. A chorus of purring and caterwauling emanated from the doorframe, merging with a loud, pulsating thrum – An unearthly sound, a pulsating thrum like a demented accordion squeezing out a nightmarish melody, blasted from the adjacent room.

Anxiety, a relentless gnawing at her sanity, had been building within Minto ever since they entered the strange building. Now, with the sudden darkness and the bizarre sounds, it reached a breaking point. Overwhelmed by the escalating terror, Minto crumpled to the floor, unconscious.

A wave of relief washed over the team as the lights flickered back to life, momentarily dispelling the overwhelming fear and desperation. Benjo, the quick-witted and curious one of the team, immediately scanned the room. A headcount after the blackout revealed a curious development: two extra sets of eyes now seemed to be observing them. Unlike before the blackout when the headcount included Wasa, Minto and Benjo, they were now four of them in the room. He nudged his father, Wasa, discreetly pointing towards a lemur monkey perched on the top door panel. The creature sported a wide, mischievous grin that seemed to mock them.

Minto, jolted awake by the either the sudden illumination or perhaps the sound of Benjo's voice, regained her senses in an instant. The presence of the lemur added an unexpected twist to their already bizarre experience. With a hint of humour in his voice, Benjo suggested that either the rightful owner of the room had chosen this inopportune moment to return, or they were looking at a rather unusual guest.

It was moments like this that Gaati's bravery and guidance were needed the most. Unfortunately, guides were not allowed into Mue's consulting rooms. Minto and the others were left on their own to navigate the unfolding situation.

As the chaos and confusion swirled around them, the elephant-skin curtain to the secret room parted, revealing a hoary-haired little old man beaming with joy. A charming smile lit up his face as he approached them with an aura of charisma that made it easy for the visitors to drop their guard and open up to him.

"Welcome, welcome, my dear children!" boomed a warm voice. The little old man beamed at them, his eyes twinkling with a kindness that seemed to emanate from deep within. "What brings such esteemed guests to my humble abode on this blessed day? Perhaps you seek guidance on a life path, a remedy for an ailment, or simply a cup of calming chamomile tea to soothe the soul? Whatever your needs may be, rest assured, you are in the presence of a friend. Speak freely, and let us see how I can be of service."

As he opened his mouth to speak, it was clear this man possessed a wealth of knowledge. He had a knack for making his visitors feel valued by asking insightful questions about their interests and hobbies, all delivered with an impressive command of advanced Kamba vocabulary. His conversational skills were truly masterful.

At first glance, the grey-haired man resembled the quintessential civil service retiree, except for a large, scarred tattoo of seven parallel lines on his right cheek, a mark that revealed his true profession – a medicine man. A closer look revealed additional peculiarities. Minto noticed freckled skin, a lipoma lump under his chin, and numerous harmless black moles scattered across his face. He even sported an extra sixth finger on both hands. These oddities certainly gave him a unique appearance.

In addition, the man's face was clean-shaven, a practice he maintained since colonial times to avoid the poll tax levied on bearded men under the penal code Act. Despite his unusual customs, his charm remained undimmed. In fact, his clean-shaven face and his unique style seemed to enhance his charisma. It was a reminder of the past interwoven with a timeless appeal.

The old man's words flowed effortlessly, a gentle stream of concern and wisdom. Yet, beneath the surface, a shrewd mind was at work. He knew more about his visitors than their initial impressions suggested but played a game of knowing less than he truly did. An intelligent report from his security team two weeks ago had painted a vivid picture – their anxieties, their hopes, and even subtle clues hinting at their inner strengths. But Mue, as he was known, preferred a more theatrical approach. He would allow them to reveal themselves bit by bit, savouring the information like a seasoned detective unravelling a mystery.

Wasa, the head of the family, responded to the medicine man's question with a trembling voice. "If you find favour in us, my Lord," he stated, "we have been sent here to seek the counsel of *muntu-wa-mue*." In Kamba, *muntu-wa-mue* means oracle. Wasa was nervous and wished someone else had spoken in his place; however, clan customs demanded that the head of the family represent them when consulting a medicine man. Admittedly, it was during moments like this one that Wasa wished he could relinquish his head-of-family status to his outspoken wife, Minto.

Meanwhile, Mue chuckled warmly, a sound that crinkled the corners of his eyes. "The family of Sosh, eh? Consider your wish granted. Please, find yourselves some comfort." He gestured to a set of sofas. "Now, about introductions." Mue's gaze swept over the group, lingering for a moment on each face. "They call me Muntu-wa-Mue," he admitted, a hint of amusement flickering in his voice. "Though, if I had my way, the introductions would be different. I wouldn't boast of being an oracle, wouldn't claim to hold the wisdom of the spirits. No," he said, leaning forward with a conspiratorial wink, "I'd simply say this: I am not the most manly of men, but at least I know a secret most men don't." A comfortable silence settled as Mue leaned back, his words hanging heavy in the air. The family of Sosh exchanged nervous glances, their curiosity piqued by this unconventional introduction. What secret could this unassuming man possibly possess? They scooted closer to the edge of their sofa seats, eager to hear more.

After a pleasant exchange, Mue pushed aside the elephant-skin curtain and emerged into the full view of his guests. He walked with a regal air across the room and took a seat on a black stool opposite Minto. Minto found it difficult to reconcile the venerated sanctuary with the diminutive figure seated before her. Furtively, she stole glances at her host, accidentally making eye contact in a moment of nervousness. Minto swiftly averted her gaze, but it was too late. The old man's bloodshot eyes, with dilated pupils and dark circles, held her own, forcing Minto to look down in embarrassment.

She pondered what kind of person Mue was: a tyrannical despot or a divine being with an awe-inspiring aura? She settled for a safer choice – charming yet unpredictable. Like a beautiful hot pepper, a charming person could be delightful, but also temperamental. However, to everyone's surprise, Mue devoted the next thirty minutes to charming them, building rapport and easing their tension. Despite this delicate balancing act of pleasing his guests while maintaining a professional demeanour, Mue found time to inquire about Sosh's whereabouts and even delivered a brief testimonial in her honour.

Despite Mue's demonstrated wit and repartee, Minto remained sceptical of his friendliness, suspecting his attempts to bond were merely a ploy, akin to a dog sniffing another for familiarity. However, Mue's resilience and sharp comments eventually overcame her doubts. To lighten the mood, Mue playfully teased Benjo about his earlier scare caused by Mue's harmless pet lemur during the power outage—a prank orchestrated by Mue himself! The blackout, it turned out, was caused by Mue's furry friend making eerie purrs to spook them. Once

Benjo discovered the truth, he burst into laughter, nearly wetting himself. Despite Benjo's previous missteps at the sacred Grotto, Mue's clever remarks had forged a strong bond with the team, easing their apprehensions.

The treatment program was scheduled to kick off with a mandatory cleansing ritual known as a *bingo* rite to purify the family. Among the Kamba people, *bingo* rites encompass various ceremonies for spiritual cleansing, some of which can be performed by qualified elders. However, the specific rite chosen for the family, on the advice of the duty diviner, was only administered by medicine men and women. The esoteric ritual itself was designed to break curses, cleanse malevolent spirits and purge witchcraft from the body through balneotherapy (a form of therapeutic bathing using special herbs) and other methods, including burning incense and offering snuff to appease the ancestral spirits. After conducting a thorough clinical assessment, the resident diviner had recommended a *bingo* ritual to purify Minto in particular. This ritual combined both spiritual and physical techniques to cleanse her of the diagnosed foreign spells and restore balance and harmony to her soul.

After the bingo ritual, the programme had a special treat in store for Mue's esteemed guests – an exquisite dinner hosted in the luxurious dining room. The guests would be treated to a delectable feast, complete with the finest wines and impeccable service. As the night progressed to slumber time, each guest would be escorted by a butler to their pre-arranged sleeping quarters within the palace. The guest sleeping wing was cosy and a comfortable haven, providing the perfect sanctuary to relax and recuperate from the arduous journey.

The morning after the bingo ritual and feast, Mue's programme would resume before dawn. Wasa and Benjo were tasked with venturing into the jungle to gather substantial fresh leaves of the tarenna, quinine bark, devil pepper, and marula roots to prepare the prescribed medication for Minto. This was a crucial task, as the medication was essential to Minto's well-being. Overall, the programme was designed to provide a unique and memorable experience for all involved, but like all good things it came with its own challenges.

After delivering his treatment programme, Mue excused himself and returned to the treatment room to prepare for the Minto's treatment. This crucial step, much like in a modern hospital, involved meticulously reviewing the patients' past medical records. However, in Mue's case, it also included examining spiritual records and seeking the approval of the gods, as requested by the ancestral spirits. If the gods did not grant permission, the medical procedure would be postponed or cancelled altogether. This process was integral to ensuring the success of the treatment and the well-being of the patients.

Before the main treatment, Mue called Minto into the treatment room and guided her through the cleansing rite. Upon entering, they found the room adorned with fragrant herbs and flickering oil lamps. A large earthen pot filled with steaming water, infused with aromatic petals and leaves, awaited at the centre of the room. As the steam swirled, Mue briefly explained the purpose of the ritual: to cleanse Minto's body and spirit of any negativity that might hinder the healing process. With gentle hands, he assisted Minto into the warm bath, murmuring prayers in a language that sounded ancient and powerful. She submerged herself completely, the warmth seeping into her muscles and the fragrant steam filling her lungs. Mue then poured a concoction of herbs over her head, the tingling liquid washing over her skin. As Minto soaked in hot steam, she closed her eyes and focused on letting go of any anxieties or fears, surrendering fully to the cleansing power of the ritual. Mue held the back of her head over the pot so she could inhale the medicinal smoke and steam. He observed keenly until she started discharging sweat, tears, and mucus as positive signs of a cure before he helped her out of the bath to a safe distance. Minto emerged feeling refreshed and renewed, both physically and spiritually, and returned to the anteroom ready for the next stage of her treatment.

Mue lingered in the treatment room, meticulously cleaning up the remnants of the bingo ritual and preparing the space for the next stage of Minto's treatment. The treatment of the foreign spell required painstaking preparation that took approximately thirty minutes before the medicine man recalled Minto into the treatment room. To enter the room, Minto was instructed to walk barefoot in a backward posture from the anteroom until her backside touched the elephant-skin curtain separating the treatment room, and then continue walking backwards until the curtain flipped over her head, blocking the door once again. It was only then that she was allowed to turn and face the treatment room. Without hesitation, Minto attempted to follow the instructions to the best of her abilities and clumsily manoeuvred her bulky body until she finally turned to face the eerie paraphernalia in the treatment arena.

As Minto entered the arena, her eyes were first caught by a magnificent carpet in the centre of the room. Composed entirely of proboscis monkey skins, it displayed a stunning array of colours – bright orange, reddish brown, yellowish brown, and even hints of brick-red. The craftsmanship was exquisite, creating a lifelike appearance with luxurious fur and distinctive bulbous noses. The golden hues shimmered in the flickering lamplight, making it a truly remarkable yet disturbing.

Minto couldn't help but wonder how these primates, native to the island of Borneo in Indonesia a staggering eight thousand kilometres away, had found their way to Banda Salama, Kenya. The possibility of an illegal smuggling operation transporting monkey skins across the vast distance between Asia and Africa seemed highly improbable, considering the immense logistical challenges involved.

Minto carefully scanned the treatment arena once more, her eyes taking in every detail. As she surveyed the scene, her gaze fell upon the raw intestines of an unknown animal, carefully arranged along the edges of the monkey-skin carpet to form a boundary. With her keen intellect, she concluded that the digestive organs were likely the jejunum of a crocodile. Despite the unsettling nature of her surroundings, Minto remained focused and determined to uncover the truth. With her sharp mind and unwavering determination, she was confident that she would be able to unravel the mysteries of this dark and foreboding place.

To commence the delicate treatment, Mue requested that Minto walk slowly and majestically, beginning with her left foot, until she reached the monkey-skin carpet. He then directed her to sit down. Meanwhile, Mue stood on the left side of the room, holding six large horns from an unidentified wild animal. Once Minto was comfortably seated, the medicine man instructed her to stretch her legs out in front of her, pointing towards the doorway. Mue then proceeded to place the horns back to back in a straight line, extending from Minto's knees to the threshold of the doorway. This ritualistic gesture symbolized the connection between Minto and the spiritual realm, allowing her to receive the healing energy of the medicine man.

Next, Mue picked up a large eland horn and painted it with irregular marks in a white powder. He then paused briefly, seemingly summoning the spirits to join the ritual. After about five minutes, Benjo was summoned into the treatment room to join Minto. Mue instructed him to seat on the carpet next to Minto, assuming the same posture as his mother. Benjo took a moment to ensure he complied with the medicine man's instructions, fearing the consequences of upsetting the ritual. Benjo's presence, as Minto's only surviving child, was symbolic, signifying victory of life over death by miscarriage.

Once Mue was content with the arrangement, he swivelled to face an alcove in the wall and began to summon the spirits. The air crackled with an electric energy, thick with the scent of burning sage. Mue's chanting filled the space, his voice rising and falling in a hypnotic rhythm.

"Hear me, Hubris the fire! I am Nemesis, the freezing water that quenches even the fiercest blaze!" Mue boomed, his voice echoing in the chamber. "You may believe repentance can extend a condemned man's life, but your situation is far beyond redemption. A desperate rat seeks refuge in fire only when the pursuing danger is far more scorching. Today, you will learn why the weaver bird builds its nest near the hornet's wrath. I offer no counsel, for your fate is sealed. Counting horns of cows, you'll be killing tomorrow is a futile exercise."

After delivering a powerful condemnation to those responsible for Minto's misfortunes, the witch doctor fell silent, taking a moment to recover from his trance. His words reverberated through the air, leaving the spectators in awe and uncertain of what would happen next. They had never witnessed such a display of power and authority before.

Shaken from his trance, Mue instructed Wasa to join his family in the treatment room. His inclusion symbolized the reunification of the family, a potent gesture against the threat of death. Fearful of any misstep, Wasa shuffled cautiously into the room, his eyes darting nervously towards the elephant-hide curtain. As he stood in wait for further instructions, a wave of trepidation washed over him.

Mue seemed oblivious to Wasa's presence, continuing to chant in an incomprehensible tongue. For five tense minutes, he moved quickly around the room, gathering ingredients or preparing the space. Wasa felt the energy in the room intensify, a tangible force building towards a climax. He braced himself, steeling his nerves for the unknown.

Mue's movements became increasingly frenetic, his chanting escalating in volume and intensity. A shiver ran down the spines of those present. The air grew heavy with anticipation, a crackling tension that seemed almost physical. Then, abruptly, Mue fell silent, his gaze locking onto Wasa. His eyes burned with an otherworldly fire, and his voice, when he spoke, echoed through the room with a power that demanded immediate attention.

Mue's voice was low and steady as he instructed Wasa to encircle the shrine seven times, his movements slow and deliberate, ensuring he avoided the sacred items scattered about. With a focus born of reverence, Wasa completed his first seven laps anti-clockwise, each step a silent testament to his respect for the ritual. Without missing a beat, he reversed direction, repeating the circuit clockwise another seven times as instructed, a dance of precision and dedication.

The air was thick with anticipation, but Wasa's careful adherence to the ritual paid off, and the ceremony proceeded flawlessly. After his careful orbits, Mue beckoned him to assist Benjo and Minto to their feet, offering them the sturdy horn of a gnu for support. The climax of the ritual was at hand: Mue, with the practised ease of a seasoned healer, blended herbal powders with honey and water, crafting a potent elixir. He offered the concoction to Minto and Benjo, who drank deeply, their expressions of bitter taste and awe at the elixir's strength. Revitalised and awash with gratitude, they knew they had been touched by the profound skill of a master healer, their spirits and bodies invigorated by the ancient treatment.

Minto, Wasa, and Benjo emerged from the treatment room, a wave of relief washing over them. The enigmatic ritual had concluded, leaving them with a newfound sense of hope. Mue's weathered face, usually unreadable, held a hint of satisfaction. With a curt nod, he signalled the end of Minto's treatment.

To their surprise, a team of Mue's personal butlers awaited them upon returning to the anteroom. These impeccably dressed figures, silent as shadows, bowed in greeting. The air crackled with an unspoken promise – a reward for their endurance. Little did they know, Mue had prepared a most unexpected indulgence for them: a lavish private dining experience, a testament to his surprising generosity.

A current of anticipation crackled through the air as the family was ushered towards the northern wing of the palace. Gaati, who had been waiting patiently outside the anteroom in accordance with protocol, was surprised when the butlers ushered him forward first. A wide grin spread across his face as he realized he wouldn't be excluded from the feast. He followed the silent guides, his heart pounding with a mixture of excitement and curiosity.

Moments later, the butlers led Minto, Wasa, and Benjo through a grand hallway. Each family member, treated like royalty, received their own assigned butler, their silent handlers radiating an aura of quiet efficiency. They glided past what appeared to be a magnificent ballroom, the promise of untold opulence tantalisingly close. Finally, the imposing doors to the dining area swung open, revealing a sight that stole their breath away.

The mahogany table groaned under the weight of an elaborate spread. Lavish dishes, unlike anything they had ever encountered before, tempted their palates. Succulent meats, the aroma of freshly baked bread, and an array of exotic fruits, vegetables, and rare wines set their mouths watering. Each bite was a symphony of flavours, a dance on their taste buds.

To add a final flourish to this extraordinary evening, Mue joined them at the table. As they savoured the exquisite meal, he regaled them with captivating stories of his life and adventures. Soothing flute music filled the background, creating a serene and magical atmosphere. It was a night unlike any other for the family of three, a perfect ending to a truly remarkable day.

As the last embers of conversation faded and the night deepened, Mue bade farewell to his guests with a courteous bow. Escorted by the silent butlers, Minto, Wasa, Gaati, and Benjo were led through a labyrinth of opulent hallways. The soft glow of oil lamps illuminated their path, casting dancing shadows on the richly decorated walls. Their journey culminated in a haven of comfort – their private sleeping quarters. Minto and Wasa found themselves in a luxuriously appointed chamber, a plush queen-sized bed beckoning them in the centre. Gaati and Benjo, equally fortunate, were presented with a room boasting twin beds, each draped in soft linens and promising a restful night's sleep. After a day filled with extraordinary experiences, they all eagerly surrendered to the embrace of their cosy accommodations, anticipation for the day to come already blossoming in their hearts.

A gentle dawn painted the sky with hues of rose and gold as Minto stirred from sleep. Disoriented for a moment, she blinked away the remnants of dreams before a wave of pleasant memories washed over her. Last night's feast replayed in her mind – the exquisite food, the captivating stories, and Mue's unexpected generosity. Suddenly, the sound of crackling fire drew her attention.

Minto emerged from her luxurious quarters to find Wasa and Benjo huddled around a crackling pit fire in the courtyard. They had already completed their early morning forest expedition, returning with a bounty of herbs clutched in their hands. Each plant, meticulously chosen for its healing properties as instructed by Mue, represented a triumph. However, closer inspection revealed the burden of their success. The two were battling to remove stubborn burr-weeds – tenacious hitchhikers from the jungle – that clung stubbornly to their clothes and skin.

The towering jungle bushes had showered Benjo with dew, leaving him drenched as if caught in a sudden downpour. The damp clothes clung uncomfortably to his small stature, and he shivered uncontrollably. It was as if the entire forest had conspired against him.

With a sigh of sympathy, Minto, all too familiar with the jungle's perils, joined them, determined to help. Minto set about removing the stubborn weeds, her nimble fingers working efficiently against the scratchy burrs. Spotting her shivering son, Minto wasted no time. "Back to your quarters, Benjo!" she instructed gently. "Change into dry clothes and wrap yourself in a warm blanket. We'll handle things here." A familiar weariness settled over her as she turned her attention to drying their damp clothes, a task she was accustomed to taking care of anyway.

The tale of Wasa and Benjo's quest for herbs held a deeper truth than initially revealed. In an attempt to shield Minto from worry, they downplayed the challenges they faced. The reality was far harsher

– hours spent navigating the dense jungle with little to show for their efforts. Wasa, ever the optimist, tried to buoy Benjo's spirits with a white lie, claiming curative herbs often became scarce when needed most.

Unbeknownst to Wasa, Benjo remained unfazed by the hunt. In fact, his sharp eyes, ever curious about the wonders of the wild, had spotted a verdant tree laden with ripe loquats. He eagerly harvested a handful, the sweet fruit offering a welcome burst of energy and a reminder of nature's bounty. If it weren't for the pesky dew clinging to his clothes, Benjo wouldn't have minded searching for herbs all day to explore the hidden treasures of the jungle.

Despite the initial difficulties, Wasa and Benjo eventually harvested the requested herbs, returning to the Fort with a sense of accomplishment. Meanwhile, Wasa proudly presented the herbs to the resident herbalist.

To Wasa's surprise, the herbalist took the fresh herbs and carefully stored away in a designated herbarium. Instead, he opted to use a selection from the older stock to prepare the medication. Wasa was initially unsettled by this practice, similar to blood donor banks in medicine, but he had no control or say in the process. He had thought the fresh harvest would be key in the mixture.

With the medication simmering away, Benjo, curious about Mue's compound, decided to explore. He wandered aimlessly until he stumbled upon the bustling recovery wards - a hive of activity serving not only as a place of healing but also as living quarters for those on the mend. Benjo's eyes widened at the sight. Hundreds of people bustled about, some tending to communal fires, others washing clothes in large wooden tubs. Laughter from children playing tag filled the air, a light-hearted counterpoint to the purposeful movements of the adults. It was clear a thriving community had formed within the ward, each section boasting its own common fireplace, cookware, cutlery, water jugs, and designated sleeping quarters. Benjo was impressed by the organization and resourcefulness of the patients.

As he ventured deeper, the tantalizing aroma of freshly cooked food filled the air, the smoke from cooking fires curling around him like playful wisps. People gathered in clusters, enjoying their morning meal. A one-eyed man smoking a raw tobacco roll in a newspaper cutting walked past him in the opposite direction. Benjo, his curiosity momentarily sated, continued on his exploration.

As Benjo continued down the path, a faint, high-pitched cry, like that of a newborn, drifted from one of the nearby huts. Disbelief flickered across his face. Could someone truly have given birth in such an environment? Curiosity gnawed at him, urging him to investigate further. With a sense of trepidation rather than eagerness, he crept closer to the hut's entrance, drawn to the unsettling sounds emanating from within.

To his surprise, a toddler wearing nothing but a tattered scrap of fabric around its neck crawled playfully towards him. Benjo's heart sank at the sight. The child's face was marred by a raw, unchecked flow of mucus extending down its chin and onto its bare chest. In an attempt to find relief, the little one instinctively licked at the discharge, its tiny body wracked with discomfort. Despite the child's outstretched arms, a silent plea for companionship, Benjo felt a pang of helplessness and continued on, his steps heavy with a newfound understanding of the hardships these people faced.

He halted in front of the fourth hut, drawn by an unsettling silence. Peering cautiously inside, he discovered a stark, single room devoid of toys or comfort. This, he realized with a jolt, was a growlery – a place where frustrated children were left to cry themselves to sleep or surrender to their fate. While Benjo found the concept barbaric, he understood the weight of circumstances beyond his control. It was a practice accepted at the facility rather than imposed by the visitors. Here, survival trumped comfort, and resources were stretched thin. Benjo, humbled by the harsh realities he had witnessed, knew his focus should remain on his mission and his family.

After his encounter with the inpatients, Benjo took a moment to reflect on the stark contrast between the comfortable life he led within the walls of Mue's Palace and the harsh realities faced by those the had just encountered. This experience left a profound impact on him, and he felt an overwhelming sense of gratitude for the privileges he had been given. He made a vow to use his position of privilege to make a positive impact on the world.

Drawn by a morbid curiosity, Benjo approached the third hut, its occupant the mentally disturbed man from the previous night's chaotic attack on the duty diviner. He cautiously peered inside. The man, still under the influence of the sleep-inducing drug administered by the security personnel, lay sprawled on a makeshift bed.

The victim's mother, recognizing Benjo as Minto's son, greeted him warmly. He remembered her from the previous evening – a kind woman he had briefly spoken with during the commotion. However, Benjo wasn't focused on pleasantries. He yearned for details about the young man's fate after the brutal altercation with Mue's security men.

Benjo edged past a hunched figure blocking the doorway – a middle-aged man with swollen legs, a clear sign of lymphedema. Finally, he gained a clear view of the young man. Still bound to a pole, he slept soundly. The sight triggered a wave of nausea as the previous night's drama flooded back into Benjo's mind, a disturbing newsreel replaying in his memory.

A wave of fear washed over Benjo as the memory of the concierge's wrath flooded back. He beat a hasty retreat, seeking the comfort of his cozy sleeping quarters within the safety of Mue's Palace walls.

Stepping back into the palace, Benjo was greeted by a stark contrast to the recovery wards. His room, adorned with exquisite French chandeliers, a shimmering pearl carpet, and plush Persian rugs, exuded opulence. Here, his family enjoyed lavish meals and refreshing drinks, a world away from the self-sufficiency practiced in the wards. While the other patients were required to bring and cook their own food in communal kitchens or pay a fee for pre-selected hot meals, the Mue Medical Foundation ensured no one went hungry, providing complimentary meals to those unable to afford them.

Benjo consulted with the herbalist and learned the medicine would take another hour and a half to prepare using the decoction method. This unexpected free time presented a delightful opportunity to indulge in the leftover feast from the previous night. The meal, an exotic spread of roasted meats, savory stews, and unique starches, was unlike anything Benjo had ever tasted.

However, Benjo's enjoyment was tempered by the presence of his roommate, Gaati. He knew Gaati, upon waking, would likely expect to share the leftovers.

With a mischievous grin, Benjo devised a plan. He crept to Gaati's bedside, ensuring he slept soundly, before tiptoeing back. Using a bedsheet, he fashioned a makeshift curtain around his bed and then savoured every bite of his exotic feast. The combination of rich flavours and unique textures left Benjo wanting more.

The team had been summoned to gather at 10:30 beneath the towering strangler fig behind the medicine man's palace for their final instructions. The air hung warm and still, except for a gentle breeze rustling through the trees, carrying with it the scent of crisp morning air. Just as Benjo prepared to head out, a sudden clatter of footsteps echoed down the hallway towards his room.

With a mischievous grin, Benjo snatched the last piece of ugali cake. In a flash, he used it to wipe clean the bottom of the empty stew bowl before shoving the cake into his mouth. He wiped his hands hastily on a damp shirt and scurried back to the dining room to return the empty dishes before joining his team at the designated meeting spot.

The source of the advancing footsteps turned out to be Benjo's roommate, Gaati, returning to gather his belongings before the meeting. However, by a stroke of luck, the two roommates managed to miss each other. Benjo had darted into the dining room through a separate entrance just as Gaati arrived at their shared quarters.

At the assembly point, a large earthen pot bubbled vigorously over a jiko stove. A thick broth, teeming with life and releasing a tantalizing aroma, filled the air. Benjo couldn't help but be amused by the lid jiggling precariously on top, seemingly defying gravity from the impact of escaping steam.

As Benjo inched closer, the potent fumes rising from the pot, a pungent blend of steaming nettle herbs, assaulted his senses. The potent fumes forced him to turn away from the light breeze, seeking refuge from the irritation.

Unlike their previous encounter, Minto noticed a shift in Mue's demeanour that morning. There was a certain domineering air about him, a subtle hint of intimidation. It was evident in the way everyone around him, staff and patients alike, seemed slightly apprehensive or even fearful in his presence. Even the gardeners and ground staff would snap to attention whenever Mue passed by.

This special hut turned out to be Mue's cash office, the heart of his financial operations. However, this was no ordinary office. Unlike the typical cash register setup Minto was accustomed to. Mue's treasury was a stark contrast with its complete lack of personnel. Minto had always pictured a cash office stocked with a cashier, cash drawers, ledgers full of financial records, and various office supplies.

Inside the treasury, one of Mue's aides, with the practiced efficiency of a seasoned butler, whipped out a pouch of raw tobacco and expertly rolled a cigar using a scrap of newspaper. With a flourish and a respectful bow, he presented the cigar to Mue, who puffed on it twice without exhaling, then placed it with exaggerated care on the edge of a low bench, ensuring the lit end wouldn't singe the wood.

In a theatrical display that mesmerized Minto and Wasa, Mue held the smoke in his lungs for a moment before inhaling again with a mighty draw, mimicking an industrial flue. He squeezed his left eye shut and exhaled a plume of smoke that billowed out of his nose and mouth, creating an elaborate dance of smoke rings that filled the air.

Amidst the swirling smoke, Mue finally turned his attention to Wasa and Minto, launching into his explanation of the treasury with a cryptic proverb: "A man who donates a cow by holding its tail is not demonstrating true sincerity in his donation." He then proceeded to list a lengthy set of terms and conditions, all of which boiled down to a single, stark warning: the Numen of Banda had zero tolerance for deceit or dishonesty. Though the cashier's office remained conspicuously unmanned, Mue's pronouncement served as a potent deterrent, instilling a sense of check and balance against anyone harbouring ideas of short-changing him.

The medicine man took a deep drag from his cigar, the smoke curling around his face as he muttered cryptic incantations. Wasa and Minto stood before him, prepared to pay the family mulct to the gods for the treatment they had received. The charges, a combination of monetary offerings and tangible items, had been predetermined and communicated to the patients well in advance.

The payment process adhered to strict protocol, with men paying first and women following. Wasa, burdened by the weight of his responsibility, stepped forward first. Cradling three plump chickens in a makeshift woven crib – a constant companion throughout their arduous journey – he carefully placed them on a flat bench in the corner of the room. However, Mue, with a wave of his hand, instructed Wasa to place the chickens under the table and deposit the monetary payment, a pouch of copper coins, into a designated black wicker basket in the opposite corner. With a nod of dismissal, Mue gestured for Wasa to step back.

Minto, filled with a quiet determination, confidently stepped forward, eager to represent the female gender. She carefully placed the exact amount of millet flour, pigeon peas, a gallon of honey, and the right measure of snuff rolled in sheaths of dry banana leaf on the table, precisely as instructed during their patient briefing. Having completed her offering, she joined Wasa and together they bowed in unison towards the payment bench, a silent gesture of gratitude for their treatment, before moving away.

Meanwhile, the medicine man's cigar, once a symbol of bravado, had dwindled to a mere ember clinging to the filter. Undeterred, Mue, with a grimace that hinted at the harshness of the final drags, squeezed two more puffs from the desiccated cigar before crushing it under his boot with a final flourish. Exhaling a plume of thick, grayish-white smoke that ascended towards the sky like a silent prayer, he rasped his thanks to the couple. "You may leave now," he rumbled, his voice heavy with pronouncements delivered.

When the couple arrived back at the assembly point, the herbalist meticulously measured out a precise dosage of medicine from the bubbling cauldron and carefully set it aside to cool before administering it to the patients. Meanwhile, Benjo's curiosity was piqued. He noticed his parents had returned from the secluded hut without the three chickens he had traded for a goatskin at the village tannery. He figured out, with a pang of guilt, that the chickens had likely been offered as payment to the medicine man. However, the reason why the birds had to be specifically red, white, and black remained a mystery. Despite his burning curiosity, Benjo kept his questions to himself, wary of the potential retribution of the Numen of Banda. After all, he knew better than to poke a sleeping bear.

The medicine man returned to the assembly point, joining the patients and staff gathered beneath the fig tree. He instructed the patients to form a semicircle formation, with everyone facing inwards, except for Gaati. Despite his exclusion from the treatment process as Sosh's agent, Gaati stood a few meters away, silently observing every detail of the proceedings. His presence served as a constant reminder of Sosh's authority and the strict adherence to the treatment protocol.

Mue carefully picked up the cooled medicine and transferred it into a calabash bowl. He then began administering it to the patients, starting with Wasa, the head of the family. Each patient received their portion and returned the bowl to Mue when finished, ensuring that the entire contents were consumed. Meanwhile, Mue meticulously measured out three equal doses of a different type of powdered medicine into wooden ladles. He then systematically administered these additional portions to the patients as well.

Suddenly, the group was interrupted by a loud outburst of shouting coming from the hut assigned to the violent patient. To quell anxieties, one of Mue's assistants rushed to the hut and returned with clarification: the same patient had emerged from his coma, demanding food with surprising urgency.

The agitated young man, having gone without solid food for what was likely an agonising long period of time, could no longer bear the pangs of hunger. As the saying goes, "a hungry belly reveals a man's character," and this young man was no exception. He craved more than just sustenance; he desperately yearned for connection and a chance to secure some food.

The medicine man, acting swiftly, dispatched an assistant to administer herbal emetic syrup to the patient before he could be fed. This syrup, a concoction of Baikal skullcap herbs and spearmint oil, was intended to induce vomiting and cleanse his intestines. While this might seem like a drastic measure, it was necessary according to Mue, to ensure the patient's body was properly prepared to receive food after such a long period of deprivation.

The burden of providing sustenance for the patient ultimately fell upon his family. Unfortunately, they didn't meet the qualifications for an exemption from the boarding fees under the Mue Medical Foundation grants. Luckily, however, the patient's relatives had come prepared, bringing enough supplies to last them for a week.

Mue completed all necessary medical procedures, his expression unreadable. Then, with a theatrical flourish, he launched into what could only be described as a cryptic pre-departure briefing. "When you show the moon to a child," he declared, his voice echoing in the hushed assembly point, "the child only sees your pointing finger and misses the heavenly glory." The trio exchanged bewildered glances. The words were undeniably profound, yet their significance remained elusive. Nevertheless, a sense of foreboding settled over them, a feeling that these were not mere platitudes.

Suddenly, Mue turned his gaze to Minto, his eyes boring into hers. "Three years from now," he intoned, his voice dropping to a low rasp, "I expect you to return to this very shrine with Benjo's younger brother. He will be dedicated to the Numen of Banda." He paused, letting the weight of his pronouncement hang heavy in the air. "Do you see those five goats grazing near the compound boundary?" Minto, unable to tear her gaze from his piercing stare, could only manage a hesitant nod. "Those," Mue continued, his lips curling into a knowing smile, "are an ex gratia payment I received three moons ago. A woman from the Kisii tribe, afflicted with a burden like yours, found solace here. I look forward to your return, in three years' time.

The counselling session marked the official conclusion of the formal medical procedures. One of Mue's assistants approached, presenting him with a flywhisk to bestow the final blessings upon the esteemed guest patients.

Mue lit a bundle of fragrant incense, the smoke curling upwards. He then requested the family to bow their heads in reverence. With a practiced grace, he swept the flywhisk in a circular motion over their heads, chanting an ancient song in a low, rhythmic monotone. The family listened intently, captivated by the ceremony's solemnity. Each word spoken held the power of protection and healing, invoking a profound sense of peace and security that settled upon them.

Meanwhile, the resident pharmacist awaited Minto, ready to dispense her take-home regimen. Before their departure, however, the medicine man had one final, but critical message. Mue stressed the absolute importance of adhering meticulously to the prescribed medication schedule, both in terms of dosage and timing. His gaze lingered on Minto with an intensity that sent shivers down her spine.

Reaching into the package he held out to Minto, Mue singled out a small, leather-sewn amulet. "This," he declared, his voice dropping to a low growl, "is of grave importance." He didn't elaborate, leaving Minto to ponder the weight of his words.

His instructions were cryptic. Upon returning home, Minto was to walk around the entire family dwelling seven times, clutching the pouch containing the amulet. This ritual, Mue emphasized, was essential for their continued lifelong protection from witches. He offered no explanation for the significance of the number seven or the purpose of the amulet itself, leaving the family to navigate a path shrouded in mystery.

The moment of farewell to the Numen of Banda had arrived. But before their departure, Mue had a surprise in store for Sosh's family. A wide grin stretched across his face as he announced, "I've secured an alternative route for your journey home! Complimentary bus tickets, courtesy of a local company that regularly extends such kindness to my esteemed VIP guests."

A collective gasp of relief erupted from Sosh's family. Used to a life off the beaten path, the prospect of battling hostile rivers and treacherous forests filled them with dread. The arduous trek through the unforgiving jungle had pushed them to their limits, both physically and mentally. Now, the promise of a comfortable journey home on a modern bus felt like a dream come true.

Mue and his team's hospitality surpassed all expectations, even for the most sceptical members of the group. Minto, a headstrong yet intelligent member of the Aimu clan, was pleasantly surprised by the warm welcome and exceptional service.

Sosh's family's delight grew when they learned Mue had gone the extra mile. He had assembled a team of security agents, led by his most trusted lieutenant and chief of security, to escort them until they boarded a bus. This detail ensured their safety and comfort throughout the journey. The watchful presence of the guards allowed the family to fully appreciate the stunning scenery as they travelled.

With a final, graceful wave of his flywhisk, Mue bid farewell to his esteemed guests. A satisfied smile played on his lips as he watched them disappear into the verdant jungle, the rustling of leaves their only farewell song. They were forever grateful for the opportunity to experience his magnanimous spirit firsthand.

Their journey culminated in the bustling town of Banda Salama, a regional shopping centre. There, they boarded the midday bus for Yatta Town, a route offering breathtaking views of the Fourteen Falls cascading down the slopes of Mount Ol Donyo Sabuk. The team departed with immense gratitude for Mue's exceptional hospitality and the security detail's unwavering protection. They surely looked forward to a potential future reunion.

Banda Salama Town thrived as an urban centre nestled in the tri-border region between Murang'a, Machakos, and Kiambu counties. This unique location fostered a diverse population of polyglots, fluent in several languages including Kamba, Kikuyu, Maasai, Swahili, and English. No wonder Mue entrusted his most trusted lieutenant, a highly skilled linguist, to oversee his guests' departure.

Indeed, Mue, a man who left nothing to chance, recognized the value of a polyglot lieutenant. Banda Salama Town was a vibrant cosmopolitan hub that embraced innovation and inclusivity. Its success stemmed in part from the leadership of esteemed figures like Mue and others. His instrumental role in driving the community's growth and development had earned him a prominent place among Banda Salama's most influential leaders.

Five

Chapter 5 – Mother is Supreme

Two weeks had passed since Sosh's family's return from Banda Salama. They brimmed with vitality and a renewed sense of purpose. Their visit to the Numen of Banda had secured intercessory protection, shielding them from a multitude of potential harm from witches. This newfound security permeated the family compound, creating a tranquil and content atmosphere so palpable, it was immediately apparent even to a first-time visitor. It is no wonder the family exuded an unwavering sense of invincibility, as if an invisible ring of protection had been cast around their home by divine forces. Their conversations buzzed with the conviction that this powerful barrier stood guard against all forms of supernatural evil. It was a testament to their unwavering faith in the Numen of Banda.

After returning from Banda Salama, Minto was pleasantly surprised to witness a remarkable transformation in Sosh's attitude and demeanour. Family meetings, once battlefields of squabbles and tension, transformed into warm and friendly gatherings around the dinner table. However, this was no ordinary gathering. Sosh, now a figure of quiet authority, took her place at one end of the long, imposing outdoor table. Her gaze, once filled with worry, now held a steely resolve.

Across the table, a curious detail caught Minto's attention. Benjo, usually content to blend into the background, found himself ceremoniously ushered to the opposite end of the table by Sosh. The distance between them wasn't just physical; it represented a bridge, a path that Sosh was paving for Benjo to walk. This deliberate positioning was not merely about a rectangular seating arrangement; it was a silent declaration. Sosh, bathed in the afterglow of the family's visit to the Numen, was symbolically unveiling Benjo as her heir apparent. Here, at the head of the table, tradition dictated that the family leader sat. Now, Benjo, once an observer, occupied a seat mirroring Sosh's – a subtle yet public indication of his newly designated role. This newfound sense of unity extended to a new family tradition of shared breakfasts each morning.

One other thing that Minto observed is that Sosh had developed an intense love and passion for her family, which was out of character. To the amazement of the family, she began the tradition of breaking fast together as a family every morning under the shade of a magnificent Dodo mango tree located behind her primary residence. This was an activity that would have been unimaginable to her just a few months earlier, but now it was becoming a treasured family tradition. Each member of the family increasingly became accustomed to the new practice and eagerly anticipated indulging in a delicious breakfast while listening to Sosh's captivating stories, which they had never heard before.

For those who were familiar with the family's history, witnessing Sosh surrounded by a collected family was a truly remarkable sight. Her outbursts of anger had subsided, and in their place was a pleasant disposition and a newfound sense of confidence. This transformation served as a testament to the restorative abilities and healing powers of the Numen of Banda.

Sosh's delightful disposition brought about some remarkable benefits. She began to open up and share previously untold stories about the family's history, breaking away from the past and revealing secrets.

This departure from her private and reticent nature allowed the family to gain a deeper understanding of their shared history.

One such insight into family history occurred when Wasa discovered from one of Sosh's tales that his maternal uncle, Mr. Makau (whose name translates to "wars" in Kamba), had been a sniper with the King's African Rifles (KAR) regiment during World War II. This revelation filled Wasa with immense pride and appreciation for both his present and past relatives. This revelation held particular significance as Sosh had refused to discuss the issue with him as a teenager.

The KAR was a British infantry force composed of African soldiers from various British colonies in Africa. Makau fought under the British East African Protectorate badge. Sosh candidly recounted how her elder brother, Makau, was mortally wounded during the Battle of the Admin Box, a bloody combat between the King's African Rifles and the Japanese Imperial Army during World War II.

Makau served as the squad's designated marksman, stationed at an observation post near the Ngakyedauk Pass in Burma. He succumbed to the injuries he sustained from enemy fire, after a Japanese scout inadvertently discovered his hiding place.

Sosh's vivid account brought to light the bravery and sacrifice of her brother Makau and other war heroes. The family also learned that Makau's remains were still interred alongside other war heroes at the Taukkyan War Cemetery, located approximately twenty-eight kilometres north of Yangon in modern-day Myanmar. His tombstone inscription reads: "In memory of Private Makau Katimbo, 1919-1944, King's African Rifles Distinguished Conduct Medal." This newfound knowledge of their family history not only brought joy to the family but also helped them connect with their past.

On this crisp Monday morning, the third week of the month, a cool breeze carried the sweet scent of wildflowers. The sky, a canvas of white and gold dappled with clouds, provided a picturesque backdrop for a vibrant green landscape. This day marked the cusp of summer, the lingering chill of spring a mere whisper on the wind.

Two weeks had passed since the family's return from Banda Salama. Sosh, radiating contentment, sat beneath the sprawling Dodo mango tree with her family. She savoured her favourite porridge — a simple yet perfect blend of fermented finger-millet-flour, sour milk, and sugar — cooked to a smooth consistency. A stark contrast to her former finicky ways, Sosh relished her simple breakfast prepared by her daughter-in-law, Minto. This newfound appreciation for life's simple pleasures embodied Sosh's journey towards reasonable and rational behaviour, edging towards self-actualization.

After finishing the first course, everyone emptied their calabash bowls, leaving them clean and their appetites sated. Just then, as Wasa was swigging the last few mouthfuls of their porridge, Minto emerged from the kitchen with a three-litre iron kettle brimming with white tea infused with ginger, cinnamon, and masala. The tea, expertly boiled over a charcoal jiko stove to meet Sosh's exacting standards, sent forth a tantalizing aroma that could draw in even the most passive passers-by.

Minto served the tea alongside boiled arrowroots and kiln-baked white yams, Sosh's favourite tubers, for breakfast. As everyone sipped their tea and savoured the delicious food, Sosh regaled them with captivating stories that kept them all spellbound.

Amidst this newfound family harmony, Sosh decided to change the subject. 'My children,' she began, her voice filled with sincerity that captured their attention. A shadow of scepticism lingered in Minto's hopeful heart, a reminder of Sosh's past negative pronouncements. However, even Benjo, usually attuned to his grandmother's moods, sensed genuine warmth in her tone.

'So, there are two essential gifts that all parents strive to give: roots and wings,' Sosh continued, pausing for emphasis. Minto remained unsure of Sosh's intentions. Was this a genuine transformation, like

Saul becoming Paul? Or was it merely a prelude to a return to the manipulative tendencies Minto knew all too well?

Despite the lingering uncertainty, Sosh's past volatility made it difficult to discern whether her current demeanor stemmed from genuine elation or something more concerning. Nevertheless, a sliver of hope emerged from her words. The very notion of "roots and wings" hinted at a potential for unity and a more optimistic future. It was a sentiment so alien to their past experiences that Minto questioned its sincerity with a furrowed brow.

The newfound family harmony, however fragile it might be, provided Sosh with a window of opportunity. Awkwardly, she tried to project a sense of her reformed self, her friendliness feeling like ill-fitting clothing after years of barbs. This unfamiliar territory caused unease to settle around the table – shifty eyes and a tense silence. Sosh recognized her earlier attempts to obliquely introduce a new topic, hinting at a change of heart, had been unsuccessful.

Circumcision, a traditional rite of passage among the Kamba people, was a concept as deeply ingrained in their culture as the whisper of the wind through the savanna grass. It marked a boy's journey into manhood, a public testament to courage and a gateway to societal acceptance. Undergoing the procedure bravely, without flinching, was highly valued; it symbolized the shedding of childhood and the emergence of a responsible adult. The process was not merely a ritual, but also served as a school for imparting societal values, beliefs, and responsibilities to young people, reinforcing cultural norms and expectations of the larger society.

Regrettably, the annual ceremony had been cancelled for the second consecutive year due to the passing of the village's long-time circumciser. As a result, Benjo's initiation had been postponed the previous summer, delaying his progression by one season. Despite the delay, Sosh was determined to see the ceremony finally come to fruition, as it was a significant event in Benjo's life. According to Kamba customs, in the absence of a certified circumciser, any qualified elder could apply to the council of elders for consideration and appointment to the role, provided they passed a rigorous vetting process.

Ensuring the highest level of safety and hygiene during circumcision is paramount. To achieve this, the council of elders conducts a rigorous vetting process for potential new circumcisers. Prospective applicants must first ensure their own children or grandchildren are eligible to participate in the same ceremony. Additionally, they must possess a minimum of three years of experience as an assistant to a certified circumciser. The successful applicant is then entrusted with the critical responsibility of performing circumcisions in accordance with Kamba customs and traditions. This is a significant role that requires a deep understanding of the cultural and religious significance of the procedure.

Sosh was pleased to announce to her family that her best friend, Mr Mwaiki, had been successfully vetted and appointed the important role of Yatta village circumciser six months ago. Interestingly, the word *mwaiki* translates to "one who circumcises" in the Kamba language. However, Mr Mwaiki's appointment was a clear sign of his qualifications and dedication to the practice, not a case of nominative determinism.

According to Kamba customary law, a new circumciser had to undergo an accreditation ceremony at least three months before the next circumcision ceremony, which typically occurred in August, coinciding with the summer school holidays.

Traditionally, the commissioning ceremony had been a sacred event that began with the pouring of libation to honour the gods. This was followed by the casting of votes by the council of elders to officially confirm Mr Mwaiki into the role of the village circumciser. The voting process served not only as a crucial step in ensuring the right person was chosen for this important role, but also doubled up as a democratic election where Mr Mwaiki received the majority vote from the council of elders. In the event of disputed election, objection, or otherwise, any new issues that arose between the appointment date and the confirmation date, which could potentially cast doubt on the appointee's integrity, could also be addressed and resolved during this stage.

Once the voting was complete, the village headman conducted a brief investiture ceremony. He adorned the new circumciser by strapping the leather bag containing the tools of the trade across his shoulder. This symbolized the trust and responsibility bestowed upon him by the community. The appointee literally carried the weight of creating the new adults on behalf of the community on his shoulders.

Interestingly, the presentation of the heirloom was a testament to Mwaiki's skills, even though he had not been formally trained in surgical incision procedures. His appointment was based solely on the strength of his observational experience gained over the years as an assistant to the previous circumciser. This highlighted the importance of tradition and the passing down of knowledge and skills from one generation to the next.

The ceremony culminated in a jubilant party, where participants drank beer and engaged in lively conversations and camaraderie. This was also an opportune moment for community leaders to come together and celebrate the significant milestone of successfully recruiting the next adult initiator, ensuring the community's continued self-sufficiency.

During the family briefing session, Sosh shared some exciting news. Two weeks prior, the village weaver had made an official announcement regarding the appointment of a new circumciser for all twelve villages, in accordance with Kamba customary law. This announcement held great significance for two reasons. Firstly, failure to adhere to the protocol of publicly announcing the appointment to all twelve villages would render it null and void. Therefore, this momentous occasion was not only a cause for celebration but also a legal requirement. Secondly, this milestone marked a new era in community leadership and progress towards long-term succession goals.

But that wasn't all. To add to the excitement, Sosh dropped an exciting surprise by announcing that the obligatory Kilumi women's dance, which precedes the teenagers' initiation ceremony, was set to occur that same evening at their family compound. Minto and Benjo went wild with excitement and broke into song and dance as if possessed. It wasn't only a wave of exhilaration and jubilation that greeted this news, but also a never-before-seen sense of pride and family unity. Hosting a Kilumi dance was not only a great honour but a rare privilege among the Kamba people.

However, not everyone shared the excitement. Wasa, burdened by his fear of crowds, became overwhelmed with dread at the thought of being surrounded by a sea of humanity. Relatives, neighbours, and even strangers would be attending the Kilumi dance, and the prospect triggered his ochlophobia Lost in their own world of pure bliss, Benjo and Minto's excitement remained effervescent, untouched by Wasa's fears. Basking in the festive anticipation, they even felt a tinge of pity for Wasa, fearing he'd miss out on the celebratory atmosphere.

The Kilumi dance, performed prior to circumcision, was a lively and colourful public celebration. It showcased a variety of dances primarily performed by middle-aged women. But beyond the vibrant displays lay a solemn and meaningful ritual. The Kilumi dance served as a conduit for divine communication between the community and the gods.

This sacred tradition had been passed down through generations, allowing people to connect with the divine and receive rare wisdom. During the ceremony, ancestral spirits revealed their essence and intentions to the community through a human mediator, often an accredited intercessor such as a diviner. This allowed the community to gain insight into the spiritual realm and bridge the gap between the physical world they live in and the spiritual realms. It was a rare opportunity for the community to gain valuable insights into their purpose in life.

While the women were the primary participants in the ceremony, the youth also donned ceremonial ornaments and performed a variety of dances specific to their age groups. The men, on the other hand, formed clusters in semi-circles, conversing and enjoying beer and wine as they observed the festivities from a distance.

As the clock struck 5 p.m., the courtyard began to fill with guests, each adorned in their dazzling ceremonial regalia, creating a display of vibrant pomp and colour. Determined not to miss a single moment, Benjo clambered up a pole along the perimeter wall of the kraal. From his elevated vantage point, he was able to take in the full beauty of the scene.

The participants were distinguished by their age-specific ceremonial attire, adorned with feathers, chains, and necklaces in a variety of colours and shapes. Their outfits were a true spectacle, adding a touch of elegance and sophistication to the event. Meanwhile, the village women bustled in, laden with copious amounts of food and refreshments to enhance the festivities. The aroma of freshly baked bread mingled with the sound of laughter, creating a warm and inviting atmosphere.

The men, meanwhile, were equally caught up in the celebratory spirit, arriving with an extraordinary amount of beer and wine. Their contributions ranged from single pints to entire kilderkins mounted on donkey packsaddles. Given that Sosh had also brewed a staggering 477 litres of wine, fermenting in the main granary, Minto suspected the alcohol supply might be excessive.

Benjo watched in awe as the ceremony reached a fever pitch, the air thick with anticipation. Villagers exchanged excited chatter, absolutely convinced of the event's significance: with Sosh's immense popularity and celebrity status, this pre-circumcision fiesta was set to be one of the most remarkable festivals the district had seen in years.

At precisely a quarter to seven, the chief compere sounded the emergency whistle, signalling the official commencement of the highly anticipated ceremony. He was a captivating sight, adorned with a dazzling garland draped around his neck, setting him apart from other participants.

The curtain-raiser was an energetic Kĩtulĩ dance performed by the first group of initiates, ten to fifteen-year-olds chosen from among those to be circumcised. The young performers electrified the audience with their vibrant display, sending a clear message that this was indeed their ceremony.

Kĩtulĩ in the Kamba language translates to "an activity so intense as to raise dust, particularly a dance performed with frenzied energy and enthusiasm by a group of people," aptly reflecting its vigorous nature. The Kĩtulĩ dance was a remarkable sight to behold. Its powerful movements, accompanied by passionate drumming and singing, created a mesmerizing spectacle. This uniquely energetic dance, often used as an entree to set the mood in Kamba festivals, left the spectators in awe and eager for more.

On this occasion, there was no better group to perform the opening dance than the enthusiastic circumcision initiates themselves. Their passionate movements filled the air with an undeniable energy, electrifying the atmosphere. Brimming with youthful enthusiasm, the performers jigged in perfect synchronization, creating a truly unforgettable experience.

The opening jig echoed across the stage and reverberated into the night air, signalling the official start of the festivities. The compound buzzed with activity as troupe leaders ensured their members were dressed in their distinct attire and lead singers perfected their cadence. Benjo watched from the sidelines, fascinated by the diverse performances. Each group's age and attire provided clear distinctions, making it easy for him to differentiate between the specific dances or musical genres.

Meanwhile, the men sat in semi-circular formations, divided by age groups. Lively discussions flowed as they enjoyed beer from calabash bowls or wine from horns, the air filled with a happy hubbub of laughter and conversation.

However, Benjo noticed one man sitting alone on a boulder outside his age group's circle. The man's isolation disturbed him, and he asked Sosh why the man wasn't partaking with the others.

Sosh explained that, according to clan traditions, a married man without children old enough for circumcision couldn't join the drinking at a Kilumi dance ceremony. Benjo found this surprising tradition somewhat reminiscent of his mother's favorited saying: poverty is a form of disability.

Sosh added that, on a similar note, a single mother wishing to have her son circumcised had to build her own hut first before her request could be accepted. If she couldn't manage on her own, she could seek help from her family. These traditions deeply troubled Benjo, who saw them as perpetuating inequality and discrimination. He resolved to learn more about the community's customs and traditions and work towards creating a more inclusive and equitable society.

A lively buzz of conversation filled the air, punctuated by the occasional burst of laughter from the semi-circular clusters of men. Divided by age groups, they enjoyed their beverages – some sipping beer from intricately carved calabashes, others raising horns brimming with ruby-red wine. The scene pulsated with a contagious energy, except for a solitary figure perched on a boulder outside the main circle. The lone man's isolation disturbed him, and he asked Sosh why the man wasn't partaking with the others.

Sosh explained that, according to clan traditions, a married man whose children are not old enough for circumcision couldn't join the drinking at a Kilumi dance ceremony. "The ceremony celebrates a boy's transition into manhood," Sosh said. "Since a man without a circumcised son isn't seen as having fulfilled his paternal obligations, he can't partake in the revelry associated with this important rite of passage." Benjo found this surprising tradition somewhat reminiscent of his mother's favourite saying: poverty is a form of disability. He likened this to how poor people are often denied opportunities simply because they are poor, observing that the man was similarly excluded from the festivities for the flimsy reason of not being married or not having children.

Continuing, Sosh noted that similarly, a single mother wishing to have her son circumcised had to build her own hut before her request would be considered. If she couldn't manage to build it on her own, she could seek help from her family. These traditions deeply troubled Benjo, who saw them as perpetuating inequality and discrimination. He resolved to learn more about the community's customs and traditions and work towards creating a more inclusive and equitable society.

As night deepened, the dance floor became a blur of frenzied movements. The teenagers, fuelled by the pulsing drumbeats, pranced and twirled with boundless energy. As one observer aptly noted, the rhythm was alive – free and infectious. Caught up in the moment, the dancers seemed oblivious to time and the crowd around them. Their exuberance felt like enough energy to power a high-horsepower engine!

On the sidelines, the Kilumi dancers grew increasingly restless. The curtain-raisers had already overrun their allotted time by two minutes, delaying the main event – the sacred Kilumi dance. This ritual served to invoke the spirit of the clan and grant permission for the circumcision ceremony to proceed. Anticipation crackled in the air, barely contained by the excited Kilumi dancers. The lead singers, eager to take the stage and showcase their skills in honour of the ancestral spirits, playfully urged them on with lunges towards the dancing arena.

The Kilumi dance was a versatile traditional ceremony that held great significance in the community. It was adaptable and therefore performed on various occasions, including appeasing the spirits during times of need and expressing gratitude to God for blessings such as a bountiful harvest. However, the Kilumi dance performed before a circumcision ceremony was the most solemn, intense, and dramatic of

all Kilumi dances. It served as both a cleansing and thanksgiving ceremony, bringing together both men and women to celebrate a defining
moment.

During this ceremony, participants were limited to wearing only
three distinct colours – red, white, and black – each holding deep
symbolic meaning. White symbolized the desired state of good health
in the community. Red represented the power and life of the society
perpetuated in the young initiates. Black symbolized the impurities,
suffering, and misfortune that the community presented to the gods
to be cleansed. These colours were imbued with the hopes and fears of
the community as they embarked on their initiation journey.

The Kilumi dance was a powerful display of unity and strength. It
brought together members of the community to celebrate a defining
moment. Although both men and women participated jointly, the
men's role was limited to providing rare skills such as expert drumming or virtuoso lead singing. This dance served as a reminder of
the community's troubled past, invoking the clan's deity to help them
transition into a state of purity, healing, and prosperity.

Finally, the chief compere blew a herald's trumpet to signal the
end of the Kītulī dance and the start of the evening's main event. The
Kilumi dancers, who had been waiting patiently, breathed a sigh of relief. The sable antelope's horn trumpet echoed through the compound,
bringing the chaotic soundscape of Sosh's homestead to an abrupt
halt.

As the Kītulī dancers exited the stage, the Kilumi drummers
stepped forward to tune their Miase drums. Crafted from African
teak wood and adorned with intricate designs reflecting the beauty of
Kamba culture, the Miase drums are used exclusively for Kilumi ceremonies. They are considered the finest drums among the Kamba people.

At the sound of the trumpet, all participants surged forward towards the performance area and formed a single large semicircle

around the dance floor. Anticipation crackled in the air, and everyone eagerly awaited the start of the event. The excitement was palpable.

The Kilumi ritual was a time for the community to introspect, reflecting on their collective consciousness and expressing their hopes, fears, thoughts, and beliefs before the clan spirit. For this reason, everyone followed the countdown with profound attention.

The drummers worked meticulously, carefully tightening the leather tension cords. Next, they warmed the drumheads using an amber-wood fire, then tested them with a slow and steady adagio tempo. With expert precision, they adjusted the drums once more, eliciting unique and powerful deep bass tones that filled the air with a sense of magic.

As the flames danced across the drumheads, the tightened surfaces produced percussive sounds that echoed down to the valley and back. The drums were ready. In response, the dancers glided gracefully onto the dance floor, their hips swaying in a synchronized, silent frolic. They formed two lines in the centre of the arena, one for the men and one for the women, facing each other. This inclusion of male dancers, after years of gender separation in the performance, was a promising sign for a successful event. The decision was made to honour Sosh's celebrity status within the community, as many of the male dancers shared a history with him in the Mau Mau war.

A sudden, sharp whistle blast from the lead soloist pierced the air, signalling the drummers to launch into the performance. It was the official start of the festivities. All the female dancers, except two at either end of the line, gracefully knelt. Their synchronized shimmies moved in perfect harmony with the rising drumbeat, their vibrant jewellery twinkling in the light as they swayed. The pulsating rhythm of the drums reverberated through the air, captivating the audience with its hypnotic melody.

As the performance intensified, the purpose of the two remaining women became clear. When the high-pitched ring of the ride cymbal, a small, suspended cymbal struck with a drumstick, joined the powerful snare and bass drums to create a driving groove, the women at the end of each line began their rhythmic counterpoint. With tambourines securely fastened to their ankles, they stomped their feet in unison, the percussive *chac-chac* adding a melodic descant to the music. The crescendo that followed was a harmonious and captivating blend, transporting listeners to a state of pure bliss.

The crowd, energized by the performance's brilliance, erupted in waves and applause. But the spectacle was far from over. In a blink, the drummers transformed the beat into a rhapsodic flow, and the male dancers responded with a dazzling exhibition of synchronized acrobatic backflips. They launched themselves high into the air, defying gravity with pinpoint precision as they landed back in the exact spot they'd started from. The audience roared their approval, completely mesmerized by this incredible display of skill and artistry.

The Kilumi Festival has a long history of launching the careers of entertainment stars, village idols, and community heroes. It serves as a crucial platform for showcasing new talent in dance, drumming, solo performances, and lead singing. Indeed, this year's festival was unlike any other. Living up to its reputation as a talent launchpad, the event at Sosh's compound crackled with an even more vibrant energy, hinting at the potential for uncovering new stars. The event vibrated with exhilarating joy, more akin to a raucous rave than a solemn ritual. The postponement from the previous year had left participants restless, creating a tense and unsettled atmosphere of anticipation. If the overwhelming hubbub of the crowd, caused by people chatting and catching up, was anything to go by, Sosh worried this festive fervour might overshadow the sacred purpose of the night.

Undeterred, the bold chief compere took charge. With a flick of his wrist, a prearranged signal, the lanterns were extinguished, plunging the venue into darkness. This sudden blackout wasn't a mishap, but a calculated move to startle the crowd and restore order. So masterful was the chief compere that the audience remained oblivious, unaware of the extinguished lanterns.

The unexpected darkness caused the crowd to fall silent, much to the chief compere's satisfaction. He maintained the blackout for a moment, allowing the disorientation to settle in. Finally, when he deemed the moment ripe, he began chanting, intending to evoke fear and reverence in anticipation of the clan spirit's manifestation.

Without warning, an eerie whistle pierced the air from the chief compere, followed by a flicker of light that brought the lanterns back to life. A collective sigh of relief rippled through the crowd, many of whom were now undeniably afraid of imaginary ghosts. Despite the momentary chaos, the chief compere continued officiating the rite with the unwavering confidence of a seasoned priest boasting over three decades of experience. Like a conductor leading his orchestra to a crescendo, he raised his hand in a flourish, signalling an increase in intensity for both the dance and the chanting.

As the arena flooded back with light, a shocking sight greeted the participants. One of the drummers lay writhing on the ground, his body contorting in a manner that resembled a seizure. First-time participants, unsure of what had caused this reaction or how to respond, watched in horror. Whispers rippled through the crowd, with some speculating that the drummer might have offended the spirits, while others feared a medical emergency. Whatever the cause, it was clear something was terribly wrong with the drummer.

In stark contrast to the panicked newcomers, the sight of the fallen drummer seemed to hold little concern for the chief compere or the older participants. Supernatural occurrences during Kilumi rituals, often attributed to disgruntled spirits, were not uncommon. According to Kamba beliefs, clan spirits sometimes manifested by possessing a human vessel, a medium, to communicate their messages or intentions to the community.

The talk of malevolent spirits during Kilumi rituals prompted Minto's neighbour, Koki, to share her own unsettling experience. Two years ago, at the last Kilumi ritual held at Mr Mwaiki's home, Koki became the victim of a terrifying spiritual attack. She described the experience as akin to being pulled into a swirling vortex, surrounded by a horde of strange, otherworldly beings. Confiding in Minto, Koki revealed the details of her one-and-a-half-hour ordeal. It began with a feeling of being deluded, followed by numbness to her surroundings; a hypaesthesia of some sort and hallucinations of strange smells, similar to symptoms of dissociative psychosis—a mental health condition characterized by a detachment from reality. Disoriented and paralysed, she felt an overwhelming sensation of being stretched in all directions by unseen forces. It was surreal!

As Koki recounted her ordeal, two women dancers emerged, clad in striking black and white attire, to assist the fallen drummer. They moved gracefully around him in a seemingly desperate dance. After what felt like an agonizingly long time, the legs of the fallen drummer jolted upwards, as if in a defiant response to the taunting chants of the singers. To Minto and Koki's astonishment, the drummer slowly began to regain consciousness.

As the chief compere's incantation reached its climax, the polyphonic blend of drums, whistles, and tambourines swelled to a crescendo. Participants, no longer holding back, surrendered themselves to the emotional intensity of the moment. The chief compere, gliding to the centre of the stage, belted out an ancient shamanic song from his core. He came to a halt, facing south, and implored the ancestral spirits to manifest before their devoted descendants. The gods did not disappoint.

A deafening explosion erupted above the arena, shattering the air with a sound akin to a powerful crack of thunder. Half the participants dove for cover, but a few brave men, particularly the professional hunters, remained standing, seemingly unfazed. Majority of the people from the crowd, awed by the hunters' unwavering stance, offered applause for their courage. Others, however, voiced their disapproval, criticizing them for what they termed recklessness, disrespect to the gods, and risking their lives.

The bizarre sound continued, a haunting cry that seemed to defy explanation. Its source remained hidden within the dense canopy of the fig tree, casting an unsettling shadow over the arena. Confusion and panic rippled through the crowd as they searched for the source of the unearthly blast. Only Benjo appeared unconcerned. A faint chuckle escaping his lips, a hint of amusement playing on his face. Did he possess some secret knowledge about the source of the unsettling cry? The suspense hung heavy in the air, threatening to break at any moment.

Once the commotion subsided, the crowd gazed in awe at the source of the unsettling noise. Perched on the fig tree was an African shoebill, a fascinating creature known for its distinctive appearance and unique vocalizations. Its enormous, shoe-shaped bill, perfectly adapted for catching fish and other aquatic prey, made it a formidable predator in its natural habitat. However, when disturbed or threatened, the shoebill could unleash a loud and intimidating squawk that could startle even the bravest onlookers.

Unsurprisingly, the experienced hunters remained calm amidst the bird's shrill cry. Well-versed in animal sounds, they could easily distinguish between the shoebill's call and gunfire. The whale-headed creatures, as some called them, were no strangers to the big-game hunters. These birds possessed the fascinating ability to produce a surreal sound by clapping their lower jaw against their upper jaw, creating a distinctly hollow boom like a gunshot sound.

One experienced hunter took the opportunity to educate the younger crowd. He explained that African shoebills are known to emit an uncanny, repetitive sound, remarkably similar to a machine-gun blast, when threatened or agitated.

Despite the expert's detailed explanation, some in the crowd remained convinced of a supernatural element. However, the truth was far more fascinating than any ghost story - a bird simply defending its territory from perceived intruders. Ultimately, the interpretation of the event was subjective, shaped by personal beliefs and convictions.

Unlike the hunters, Benjo's composure stemmed from a prior encounter with the very same bird. Two weeks earlier, on a dark and eerie night, Benjo was tasked with collecting firewood from the family stockpile. Out of sheer curiosity, he impulsively shot his slingshot skyward, accidentally striking the shoebill's nest. The enraged bird responded with a deafening, gunshot-like squawk, sending Benjo fleeing in terror. He trembled uncontrollably, almost wetting himself out of fear. It was no wonder Benjo found it amusing to see the locals experience the same unsettling treatment by the territorial bird.

Seizing the opportunity presented by the chaos, the chief compere announced the arrival of the ancestral spirit. With utmost respect, he prostrated himself and offered a prayer of welcome, inviting the spirit's blessings and guidance upon the community. After the prayer, he poured libations to the gods and offered them food at the family shrine.

The ancestral spirits graciously accepted the community's invitation and bestowed their blessings. The chief compere acted as a conduit, communicating the unseen message transmitted through actions by the spirits to the community. Through the chief compere, the ancestral spirits also granted absolution to the community for their sins, impurities, suffering, and misfortune before officially commissioning the forthcoming circumcision ceremony.

Following the absolution, the chief compere blew a large bullhorn made from a Sanga cow, signalling the toastmaster to officially open the banquet. A sumptuous feast of mouth-watering delicacies and exquisite wine awaited the guests, catering to every palate. However, embarrassingly yet unsurprisingly, some guests overindulged, becoming intoxicated and exhibiting boorish behaviour. Minto was disgusted by a couple who, having drunk too much wine, intermittently vomited, and passed gas. Nevertheless, even though such behaviour is frowned upon and discouraged among the Kamba people, it unfortunately remains not uncommon during public festivals.

With their mission complete, the ancestral spirits departed, leaving a lingering sense of their presence behind. The families, drained from the demanding day filled with strenuous activities, required a rest to recuperate. Tuesday, a much-needed respite, provided time for most families and their boys to prepare for the upcoming circumcision ceremony.

Despite the break, the festivities had taken their toll. Most men nursed splitting headaches, while dust-mite allergies plagued some women and children. Minto, however, was one of the lucky few unscathed.

Wasa, on the other hand, wasn't so fortunate. A debilitating hangover kept him glued to the bed. Minto tried to persuade him to help round up the cows for milking, but her attempts fell on deaf ears. After her fourth try, she conceded defeat and left him to sleep.

Minto slumped in her chair, the frustration tightening her jaw. She'd attempted tethering and milking the cows alone, but the task felt insurmountable. Breakfast for the family depended on that milk, yet without help, it seemed impossible. She blamed the morning's mishaps on Wasa's excessive drinking, which left him lethargic and unable to assist her. As she lay helplessly on the wooden bench, she began to ponder why alcohol had such a paralysing effect on its victims.

Drawing from her high school biology class, Minto recalled that alcohol, with its ethanol molecules binding to brain inhibitors, slowed response to stimuli. This, as her teacher Lucy had explained, was why Wasa couldn't help. The hangover was his body struggling to metabolize the alcohol, a process that could take up to six hours depending on how much he drank. Clearly, waking him up wouldn't solve anything.

A sliver of a star student in high school biology flickered back in Minto's mind, her memories a testament to her once-keen intellect. Years of marriage and motherhood hadn't dimmed the embers of her once-bright curiosity. It was a stark reminder of the day her own education was brutally extinguished. Two clan elders, accompanied by her stunned aunt and a pair of imposing warriors, had descended upon her father's compound during a school break. Their mission was clear: to enforce a preordained marriage upon her, a union with a complete stranger whose claim had been secured by a dowry, not her consent. The most agonizing memory remained etched in her mind – her father's helpless silence as the warriors tore her away from the only life she'd ever known. This barbaric custom, dictated by ancient laws beyond her parents' control, had snatched away her dreams and confined her to a future she hadn't chosen.

During Tuesday's break, a sense of apprehension hung heavy in the air as families prepared their sons for the upcoming circumcision ceremony. Benjo, like many of the boys, felt a knot of fear tighten in his stomach. Stories from older boys at school painted a conflicting picture of the traditional procedure.

On one hand, Peter, an upper primary student whose family had converted to Christianity, no longer participated in the tradition. He had become a constant source of worry for Benjo, regaling him with harrowing tales of the "barbaric ritual." Peter believed the circumcision served as a harsh reminder that boys belonged to the community, not themselves. He had also tried to sway Benjo by boasting about the painless modern circumcision performed in government hospitals under Christianity.

On the other hand, there was Ngeta, the schoolyard bully with the fitting nickname ngeta means Chokehold in Kamba. He revelled in Benjo's fear. His descriptions of the circumcision as a violent, painful, and brutal act were graphic and brutal, designed to inflict maximum terror. Sadly, it was this conflicting information, along with the constant taunts echoing around the schoolyard, that had poisoned Benjo's perspective on the traditional practice.

Sosh noticed Benjo's anxiety and stepped in to boost his morale. She launched into a series of heroic folktales from the Aombe clan's tradition, aiming to strengthen his resolve. Her most captivating story was about a legendary warrior nicknamed Yunga wa Muamba, which translates to "tree trunk, son of the rock."

The tale described Yunga wa Muamba as a young boy who displayed remarkable bravery during his circumcision, enduring the rite without a single tear. He grew up to become the most decorated field marshal in Kamba history, renowned for his courage and strength. His legacy continued to inspire generations.

Legend had it that Yunga wa Muamba became a towering figure, standing two metres tall. His strength was so immense that when he missed an opponent with his spear during close combat, the weapon flew fifty meters and lodged itself entirely through a massive palm tree. Some versions even claimed the spear remained there to this day, a testament to his power.

Sosh's storytelling was captivating. By the time she finished, Benjo was filled with excitement, a stark contrast to his earlier anxiety. Her approach was both practical and engaging. Using age-old folklore, she had effectively neutralized his fear of circumcision in a way that was both creative and enjoyable for Benjo.

Sosh's love for Benjo was evident in everything she did. She had defied tradition by declaring him her heir, a bold move that placed him above her own son, Wasa, in the line of succession. This unconventional decision went against the grain of Kamba customary law, but Sosh was a force to be reckoned with. Her unwavering commitment to Benjo's well-being was a testament to the depth of her affection.

Sosh's love for Benjo was fierce. In a moment of desperation, she might have even considered enduring the circumcision herself to shield him from the ordeal. However, the absurdity of the notion soon dawned on her. It was akin to offering to swallow bitter medicine for a friend – an impossible solution.

Benjo, meanwhile, wasn't oblivious to his grandmother's worry. He began to understand the depth of her anxiety. Inspired by the Kamba proverb, "no matter how tall your grandmother is, you must do your own growing up," Benjo felt a surge of determination. He decided to face his fears head-on, approaching the circumciser's knife with courage and bravery. This decision wasn't just about calming his grandmother; it was also a powerful symbol of his own journey into manhood.

Throughout the ordeal, Sosh remained by his side, offering words of encouragement and allegorical stories filled with hidden meanings to keep his spirits high. Despite the challenges, their bond remained unbreakable, a testament to the enduring power of love and family.

During Sosh and Benjo's therapy sessions, they received an unannounced, though mandatory, visit from Benjo's godfather. The godfather's role, one of great responsibility and pride, is to mentor, encourage, and guide young initiates through the significance of this rite of passage. He serves as a role model, demonstrating to his godsons how to live up to the expectations of the community. This relationship of guidance and support extends beyond the ceremony, ensuring the candidate not only successfully transitions but also assumes and maintains his new responsibilities as a reliable member of society.

While many in the community saw a godfather as beneficial, Sosh, a member of the Clan Council of Elders (the equivalent of a modern-day parliament that reviews and makes laws), held a dissenting view. She believed unsolicited advice, like wet cement, could leave lasting, unwanted impressions on a child's character. She was determined to be Benjo's sole guiding force, unapologetic about her stance.

However, recognizing this as the most significant rite of passage for Benjo, Sosh embarked on a period of introspection to reassess the importance of a godfather. She wanted to ensure she was making the best decision for his future, considering all the potential benefits. In her reflection, Sosh not only recognized her position as a respected member of the law-making body but also her role as a custodian of customary law. She then recalled a powerful clan proverb: "Adults with one ear do not advise children." This proverb doesn't literally mean having one physical ear, but rather criticizes adults who are poor listeners, insular, and don't respect other opinions. This triggered a shift in her perspective. She began to appreciate the importance of listening to the wisdom of those who had come before her, rather than solely relying on personal experience.

Meanwhile, the godfather arrived and without a word presented Sosh with a checklist. It outlined the non-negotiable prerequisites that Benjo had to follow from 6 p.m. that evening until the circumcision. The godfather explained these provisos, including avoiding sugary drinks and sugarcane to minimize bleeding. He also reminded Benjo, in a stern voice, that crying during the ceremony would be not only disgraceful but also an abomination to the ancestors. Sosh absorbed this information silently, her jaw clenched.

The godfather, perhaps sensing Sosh's inner turmoil, broke the ice with a proverb: "He who slices a calabash into three pieces must drink water with the middle slice." His choice of words was deliberate, a reminder to Sosh that raising a child was a community effort. Overly possessive parents, the proverb implied, shouldn't prevent their children from being shaped by the wider community.

The godfather's well-chosen proverb struck a chord with Sosh. Even her well-known rigidity softened a touch in the face of his wisdom. With a sigh, she finally released Benjo into his godfather's care. As she watched the pair head towards the shade of a nearby mango tree, Sosh couldn't help but reflect. Another proverb crossed her mind: 'A bird uses the feathers of other birds to build its own nest.' This one emphasized the importance of community, of cooperation and shared knowledge in achieving a goal.

Reflecting on the godfather's epigram punctuated with proverbs, Sosh began to understand the community's emphasis on patience. The final proverb in particular, 'Without patience, one will never know the taste of a good beer,' resonated deeply. It was a powerful lesson she wouldn't soon forget.

This newfound understanding filled Sosh with a warmth she hadn't felt before. Her hostility towards the godfather melted away, replaced by a newfound respect. As the counselling session ended, Sosh approached Benjo's godfather with respect. 'It is easier to build strong children than to repair broken men,' she stated with one more proverb of her own, her voice firm yet kind.

Her words broke the ice. A genuine smile spread across the godfather's face. 'Thank you, your Eminence,' he replied, his voice filled with gratitude.

The godfather presented Sosh and Benjo with a solemn oath, outlining the consequences of failing the circumcision test. The oath declared: "If a candidate cries during the incision or withdraws their consent to be circumcised without a valid medical reason, they will become an outcast and live with a stigma for the rest of their life." The godfather fixed his gaze on Benjo and asked, "Can you afford to bring such shame upon your family?" Benjo confidently replied, "No."

The godfather then cautioned them that the circumcision day comes only once in a lifetime, urging them to approach it with courage. According to Kamba customary law, those who cry during the circumcision are never allowed to marry anyone other than a fellow outcast who has also failed the test. Additionally, male candidates who fail are barred for life from representing their clan in war or hunting. They become potential targets to be offered as restitution during post-war dispute resolution or ransom payment for prisoner-of-war exchanges. In some extreme but rare cases, a circumcision outcast may even be offered as a human sacrifice for the common good of the clan or community, such as during a period of prolonged drought and famine. These consequences, though harsh, are deeply ingrained in Kamba culture and serve as a reminder of the importance of bravery and resilience in the face of adversity, the godfather concluded.

The godfather paused to ensure his message had been fully understood by Benjo and his grandmother before collecting his leather bag and departing. He had no time to waste, as he had several more homes to visit with the same message before midnight. It was no doubt going to be a long night for Benjo and Sosh.

The highly anticipated appointment with the surgeon's knife had finally arrived. For the 46 candidates, it was a moment of truth, a date with destiny. At precisely 03:30 a.m., all the initiates were scheduled to assemble for a roll call at Mr. Mwaiki's compound, the designated location for the start of the circumcision ceremony. This pre-dawn gathering was deliberately chosen to elude the covetous eyes of envious sorcerers. It was ostensibly believed among the Kamba people that envious barren women, sometimes through hired witches, sought to undermine the success of the upcoming generation largely to take revenge on successful mothers who looked down upon them. To ensure the utmost secrecy of the event, only the key organizers and members of the Clan Council of Elders were privy to the details.

Unfortunately, Sosh, one of those invited, fell ill with a sudden fever and whooping cough the night before the ceremony. She had been exposed to dust and cold winds during the Kilumi ritual. Unable to attend, she appointed her son, Wasa, to stand in for her.

The circumciser, Mr Mwaiki, surprised everyone with an unexpected change of plans. The previously communicated schedule, with a 3:30 am roll call, was abruptly scrapped. Instead, a hush fell over the courtyard as Mr Mwaiki called the boys forward not at dawn's first light, but under the cloak of a deep midnight sky. Confusion flickered across the godfathers' faces, a silent question hanging in the air. Nevertheless, the circumciser is granted carte blanche powers by the clan council of elders to do as he pleases in the interest of the community to ensure the event's success.

One by one, the nervous initiates were ushered before Mr Mwaiki and his two assistants for a meticulous examination. This detailed inspection, a crucial step to ensure each boy's well-being, took a painstaking three hours to complete. Under the watchful gaze of the godfathers, Mr Mwaiki meticulously checked each candidate's physical condition, ensuring they were healthy and strong enough to endure the upcoming ordeal.

With the well-being of the boys confirmed, Mr Mwaiki turned his attention to the ancestral spirits. Solemnity filled the air as he poured a libation, a gesture of deep gratitude. The first offering, a draught of pure, unblemished lamb's blood, symbolized purity and a fresh start for the initiates. In the second libation, Mr Mwaiki poured a potent sugarcane wine, drawn from drums reserved for aged wine. This offering signified not only the attainment of manhood but also the accomplishment that awaited them.

As the first rays of dawn began to paint the eastern sky with streaks of gold, a new order crackled through the air. At precisely 3:40 am, Mr Mwaiki barked a sharp command. The initiates scrambled into a single file, their bare feet padding softly on the dusty earth. Their destination: a towering fig tree standing sentinel at the banks of the Thika River, several kilometres away from the village.

The stark naked figures of the boys resembled statues sculpted from ebony, their small frames trembling under the relentless assault of the frigid.

Before the circumcision, a team of skilled assistants emerged, equipped with the necessary tools and preparations for the boys. In a unique tradition, a key step involved numbing the area with a natural anaesthetic. Each boy would have their genitals submerged in ice-cold water for at least fifteen minutes before the procedure. This timetested method, passed down for generations, served as a natural alternative to modern anaesthetics.

To ensure its effectiveness, the water was carefully prepared the night before. Earthen pots were filled with river water and then buried deep in the cool mud along the banks of the Thika River. The overnight chill created a natural numbing agent, a cost-effective solution that utilized readily available resources.

The chilled water was then transferred to calabash containers for the procedure. Two trusted assistants, chosen from among the godfathers, would help each boy through this step. Once numbed, the boys would wait patiently, their godfathers by their side, until their names were called.

Tradition dictated that the circumcisions be performed in a temporary operating area built near a sycamore or fig tree. The Kamba people believed that constructing the structure too far in advance could attract malevolent forces with ill intentions to harm the initiates. However, sycamore and fig trees were seen as sacred, believed to be homes to ancestral spirits and conduits for prayers reaching the heavens.

The circumcision room is a place of intense activity and concentration, where every movement is amplified by the palpable tension in the air. It is therefore common for initiates to feel a sense of dread as they await their turn to enter the room. Their minds are focused on two things: overcoming the fear of the knife and getting through the process without screaming or shedding tears.

The air in the circumcision room hung heavy with a mixture of anticipation and trepidation, a place of intense activity and hushed concentration, with every movement amplified by the palpable tension that crackled through the air. Here, young initiates awaited their turn, their minds a battlefield of emotions. On one hand, the fear of the surgeon's blade loomed large, a menacing spectre threatening their childhood innocence. Meanwhile, a determination akin to a 'come death before surrender' belief was anchored in the custom of not letting one's clan down by failing the circumcision test. Yet, woven into this tapestry of fear was a fierce determination to overcome this challenge, a silent vow not to succumb to pain by whimpering or shedding tears, for in this culture, stoicism was the ultimate badge of honour.

As soon as each candidate entered the surgeon's room, they were greeted by their assigned godfather, who introduced them to the circumciser and the two assistants. The mere mention of the circumciser's name was enough to send chills down the spine of each initiate. However, the godfather exercised every trick in the book to bolster their confidence before guiding them to take a standing position at the centre of the room. The success of godfathers was measured by the number of candidates they had successfully led through the rite of passage. A successful godfather was not only highly regarded in the community but also feted with gifts and titles.

The initiate was asked to stand with their legs spread apart and both hands raised parallel to the ground. The godfather then moved to stand right behind his candidate for two reasons. One was to provide a sense of security and reassurance by the godfather's calming presence. The second was to ensure safety by preventing the patient from jerking in response to pain, potentially injuring themselves or the circumciser.

The initiate had to remain completely still, like a statue, until the operation was successfully completed. Once the circumciser had removed the foreskin, one of the assistants, usually a trained herbalist, applied an anti-bacterial herbal ointment containing lysine to the wound before the boy was escorted out of the surgery into the adjoining recovery room.

The rite-of-passage ceremony held significance for both boys and girls. However, the practices differed significantly. While the boys underwent circumcision, a more public ceremony, girls traditionally underwent a separate and controversial procedure known as Female Genital Mutilation (FGM). This practice is not endorsed by the medical community and is recognized internationally as a violation of human rights. In fact, the ceremony taking place downstream marked a significant moment for the Kamba community, as it represented the last such event for girls. The Kenyan government has permanently banned FGM, prioritizing the health and well-being of its citizens. While this practice was widespread in pre-colonial Kenya, the influence of modern Christianity, parliamentary government, and evolving societal views have led to its decline.

The new circumciser's procedure was a flawless triumph, exceeding all expectations. Remarkably, for the first time in a decade, no candidate failed or withdrew due to unforeseen circumstances. The emergency wards and counselling rooms, reserved for failed candidates, remained unused.

A wave of pride and honour washed over both the initiates and their supervisors. With the belief that a strong start brings a successful finish, they were determined to make the most of this opportunity. As they marched towards the recovery rooms, songs of triumph and victory filled the air, their spirits soaring with each note.

According to Kamba traditions, circumcision initiates remain under close supervision by the resident herbalist and circumciser for the first two days of their seven-day recovery in the rooms. Here, they receive the necessary care and medication to ensure infection-free healing.

While the recovery rooms for boys and girls are separate, both benefit from the shared expertise of the same physicians and herbalists. This allows all initiates to access the collective knowledge of the medical professionals. However, the counsellors are gender-specific: a male counsellor for the boys and a senior female matron for the girls. This ensures effective communication and support for the specific needs of each gender. The well-ventilated wards are furnished with animal-hide mats for beds and African kanga sheets, providing comfort and protection from the cold and insect bites.

During the initial three days of recovery, a team of expert counsellors closely monitored each patient for signs of anxiety or withdrawal. Their primary focus was to keep each initiate on track for a smooth recovery. They provided counselling services, but also referred cases requiring herbal remedies to the duty herbalist when necessary. They also employed the power of storytelling, using oral narratives and folk tales to calm the novices and prevent negative psychological developments like depression.

Much like nurses in a post-operative care unit, the herbalists played a crucial role in the recovery process. Their primary duty involved conducting regular clinical assessments of the patients and administering essential herbs as needed. On the first evening, for instance, the herbalists applied a mixture of finely ground earth and powdered reed roots to all the patients' wounds to aid drying. They also conducted individual assessments, identifying only one case of bleeding. This patient was transferred to the treatment room, where the wound was cleaned with fresh antiseptic sap from a green sisal leaf, followed by tranexamic acid extracted from the African custard-apple tree to stop the bleeding.

The third day of recovery holds special significance for the novices, marking the day they participate in a significant event called Kwī-vana. This traditional Kamba practice involves a charged verbal exchange of bawdy taunts between pairs of initiates. It is a unique opportunity that allows initiates to demonstrate courage, emotional intelligence, and strength of character, while also fostering bonds with their peers.

During the Kwīvana ceremony, participants trade ribald jokes and compose impromptu vulgar songs, aiming to outdo each other with insults. While primarily a verbal contest, the event serves to instil a sense of tolerance among these new adults. This ritual signifies a powerful transition from childhood innocence to adulthood and holds a cherished place in their culture. It teaches the young adults the virtue of patience and the skill of keeping one's nerves under provocation.

Through play-acting and observing others, novices learn that discussing sensitive topics with peers shouldn't be shameful or embarrassing. However, counsellors are nearby to remind them that everyday life requires them to be more cautious and maintain a certain level of modesty when addressing such topics in public. This fosters a respectful and tolerant society.

In this ritual, Benjo saw an opportunity to settle a score in a long-standing feud with his classmate Rachel, a blue-eyed girl who had previously insulted him. Despite his previous attempts at revenge being thwarted by the school's strict disciplinary measures, Benjo was determined to get even. He believed that boys were often unfairly judged as being in the wrong, even when they were the victims of bullying by girls. The Kwīvana event presented the perfect opportunity for Benjo to exact his revenge.

Without hesitation, Benjo began to hurl unprintable obscenities at the poor girl, while pretending to engage in the permissible lascivious exchange. Most of the personal verbal attacks were drowned out by the noise of other participants, and the supervisors remained outside the enclosure, seemingly unconcerned by the words being exchanged. Although they were not allowed to interfere directly with the exercise, their lack of intervention allowed Benjo to viciously continue deconstructing the character of his classmate until she began to cry.

For Benjo, this was supposed to be sweet revenge. Yet, his act of bullying breached the protocol of the ceremony, intended to foster tolerance among peers. Rachel's tears were a stark reminder of the emotional toll such cruelty can inflict. Yet, Rachel rose above Benjo's intimidation. As they say, revenge is best served cold.

A proud daughter of the Asoka clan, renowned for their tenacity, Rachel was not one to back down easily. The intensity and vulgarity of their exchange went far beyond the usual banter, and unexpectedly caused other participants to halt the exercise to cheer the two verbal combatants. The cheering crowd's reaction, a rare occurrence during the Kwĩvana, further bolstered Rachel's confidence. She rose to the occasion and matched Benjo's taunts with her own fierce wit, captivating the audience with her verbal dexterity. Astonishingly, Rachel the underdog surprised everyone by sustaining the challenge to match Benjo's taunts eyeball for eyeball until the exercise was called off.

On the fourth day of the event, a group of respected elders from the village visited the novices. These wise individuals shared their knowledge and valuable insights about life in the community. Speakers from various fields, including hunters, beekeepers, blacksmiths, woodcarvers, warriors, and legal experts, took turns at the podium. Their speeches were captivating, filled with humour and spontaneous wisdom that left the audience enthralled.

After each presentation, the moderator opened the floor for questions, which the elders answered definitively. The novices were taught the importance of respecting their elders and avoiding relationships with married adults, who now saw them as young adults. This was just one of many lessons designed to help them transition smoothly into adulthood.

Following the presentations, the elders showered the graduates with a variety of valuable gifts. Their generosity and warm hospitality not only added to the joyful atmosphere but also taught a valuable lesson about giving back to the community. Witnessing the wisdom and knowledge of these revered individuals was a truly humbling experience. The newly minted adults left the event feeling enriched and empowered.

The elders' visit is a cherished tradition that takes place on the fourth day of all circumcision ceremonies. It undoubtedly served as a highlight of the event, leaving a lasting impression on the novice initiates.

The fourth day marked the deadline for settling the circumciser's fees in full, which were determined by the number of children registered in each household. The council of elders determined the prices and periodically adjusted the base prices depending on the prevailing barter trade prices of livestock and a basket of grains such as maize and beans.

A special basket, the *kyondo*, is used as the standard unit for pricing grain. It is approximately twenty kilograms in size. During a typical circumcision season, a fully grown billy-goat could be exchanged for five *kyondos* of bean grains or ten *kyondos* of white maize grains. Failure to pay the fees in full by the deadline could result in the exclusion of the child from ascending into a junior warrior, the first rank of clan leadership in the Kamba community. It was therefore crucial to make timely payments to avoid any inconvenience.

On the fifth day, the physical activities intensified. The boys were sent out with mock bows and arrows to hunt for small game, such as lizards and grasshoppers. These creatures symbolized the wild beasts and malevolent enemies that could potentially threaten the villages, emphasizing the need for strong, capable men to defend their communities. This symbolic event served to prepare the boys mentally for their future role as warriors, the first step on the path to leadership in Kamba society. The hierarchy progresses from junior warrior to warrior, then to junior elder, elder, and finally, a venerated member of the clan council of elders.

Meanwhile, girls in groups of five to ten were dispatched to gather resources. With their hands, they snapped small twigs, and using sickles, harvested tussocks of grass, binding them into sheaves for transport back to the courtyard. Their activity mirrored two of the most essential daily occupations for women in the village: gathering firewood for meals and harvesting grass for thatching huts. This task emphasized the importance of teamwork and instilled a sense of collective community responsibility in the girls.

After successfully completing their assigned tasks, the apprentices were bestowed with blessings from the eldest elder, with assistance from the circumciser. This sacred ritual involved the sprinkling of beer over the bodies of the newly initiated adults using a calabash container and a flywhisk. It served as a wish for good health and prosperity, marking the end of the circumciser's official role in the ceremony and allowing him to return home.

Although technically ready to return home after the benediction, the graduates were required to attend a mandatory counselling session on the sixth day. This crucial session prepared them for the challenges of transitioning into adulthood. They were scheduled to return home on the seventh day, allowing them one more day to reflect on their journey and savour their accomplishments. The blessings and counselling served as a powerful reminder that they were not alone and had the unwavering support of their community.

On the sixth day of their initiation, the initiates were awoken at dawn to begin their daily chores. These tasks were designed to instil responsibility, decision-making skills, and the ability to implement plans—essential life skills for their future endeavours. Despite the shared excitement of returning home to a celebration of songs, dances, and gifts, Benjo woke with a gnawing sense of foreboding. He kept this disquiet buried deep, unwilling to share the unease that had settled in his gut with his mates.

Meanwhile, the village delivery women, a group of middle-aged mothers, arrived promptly to deliver food supplies. For the seven-day recovery period, a considerable number of women from the twelve participating villages volunteered to provide food and refreshments. A steady stream of food flowed to the initiates, courtesy of volunteer women from their home villages. To ensure a smooth and sustainable supply throughout the recovery period, Mr Mwaiki's senior wife co-ordinated a rotating schedule among these generous women. Offering services to incoming adults was considered a great honour, and often, volunteers outnumbered the need. In most cases, those exceeding the required number were politely turned away on a first-come, first-served basis.

At 4:45 a.m., the cow horn signalled the start of the day's work. This cue prompted the initiates, armed with brooms made from African broom grass, to descend upon Mwaiki's courtyard like a swarm of locusts. As the sun rose, they energetically swept the expansive courtyard, starting from the gate and working inwards towards the inner court. Their efforts culminated at the animal byre, located at the far end of the compound near the rubbish landfill.

In Kamba culture, sweeping the family compound is a ritual with specific procedures. Sweeping always begins at the gate and moves inwards, never the other way around. Sweeping livestock droppings outwards is believed to bring bad luck to the family's wealth, symbolising driving away resources and inviting poverty.

The Kamba people hold a symbolic belief that every element of their livestock—fur, dung, and goat pellets—is valuable and contributes to the family's wealth. Sweeping manure out of the main gate is akin to leaving the door open to let in poverty. Livestock is seen not only as a source of income but also as a symbol of security and stability for families. This belief is deeply ingrained in their traditions.

In some divorce cases, if a bride's family cannot refund the dowry due to poverty, the clan council of elders might intervene, requesting that payment be made symbolically in goat droppings, with the number symbolising the original dowry goats.

The initiates diligently swept, collecting animal droppings and other solid waste to deposit in a composting pit adjacent to the cattle pen. This waste is then combined with green waste and weeds to create nutrient-rich compost used on the farm's crops to promote healthy growth and increase yield.

After finishing, the team gathered near the animal kraal, waiting for further instructions. Suddenly, a commotion erupted from the main gate. Benjo looked up to see the village crier lifting the acacia bough blocking the entrance, accompanied by two clan warriors in impressive war regalia. The unexpected arrival of strangers sent a wave of unease through the novices.

In Kamba culture, the arrival of the village crier accompanied by warriors in war regalia signified either a declaration of war or the passing of a revered elder. Benjo's stomach lurched with dread. He recalled a terrifying dream from the previous night, where he had plummeted into a bottomless void, only to wake in a cold sweat, relieved it wasn't real.

Rationally, Benjo dismissed the possibility of war. His clan hadn't been involved in one during his father's lifetime, let alone his own. Yet, the village crier's presence made him uneasy. He watched intently as the group approached Mwaiki's compound.

Benjo's mind raced, desperately seeking an explanation for the early morning visit. The Aombe clan had been peaceful for generations, rendering the warriors' display of power baffling. His only exposure to war came from his uncle Kineene's war stories about precolonial cattle raids against the Maasai tribe in competition for pasture. Uncle Kineene's tales were so captivating that Benjo felt transported to the battlefield itself, but that is as close as he came to war, as far as he was concerned.

Despite his efforts, Benjo couldn't understand the reason behind the unannounced visit. He wasn't aware of any recent deaths among the clan elders. Unlike Benjo, the other novices were oblivious, caught up in the day's excitement. They assumed the crier's visit was a customary part of the ritual, nothing to worry about.

The village crier and his warriors entered the compound with purpose, the bough gate slamming shut behind them with a heavy thud. They marched towards the main house, where the crier delivered a seemingly urgent message into Mwaiki's ear in hushed tones. Mwaiki promptly rose and beckoned two senior elders to follow him outside.

Under the shade of a towering Egyptian balsam tree, the six men huddled, their voices laced with urgency. A dark, foreboding sky loomed overhead, and a chilly wind rustled through the leaves. An unsettling feeling hung heavy in the air; this wasn't going to be a good day.

Meanwhile, inside the house, Benjo was called to the breakfast room alone. A solitary plate awaited him – a stark contrast to the usual communal meal shared by the circumcised graduates. The communal experience, meant to forge lifelong bonds among the initiates through shared hardship, was now strangely being breached. Unease gnawed at Benjo. His gaze darted from the untouched plate to the shadowed figures huddled beneath the balsam tree. A yearning to rejoin his comrades, to share their anxieties and camaraderie, welled up within him. Little did he know, the day's events would forever alter the course of his life.

Nevertheless, the message of a village crier is unquestioned. He enjoys enormous, delegated authority from the clan council of elders. He is the face of clan authority, his pronouncements carrying the weight of the elders' wisdom and decisions. As such, when the village crier and the two warriors appeared on the threshold, their expressions impassive, a jolt of unease ran through Benjo. A yearning to rejoin his comrades, to share their anxieties and camaraderie, welled up within him. Little did he know, the day's events would forever alter the course of his life.

The emissaries, shadows against the rising sun, whisked Benjo away from Mwaiki's compound to an unknown destination—at least, unknown to the initiates. The emissary and his bodyguards vanished through the main gate, leaving the graduates in bewildered silence. The air crackled with unspoken questions. What did it all mean? Was it something serious? ·

Mwaiki emerged from the secret meeting under the balsam tree; his face feigned confidence to demonstrate leadership, yet his furrowed brow, mirroring the unease spreading through the group, gave him away. He stood in the middle of the courtyard and blew a shrill note on his carina which, usually a herald of celebration, felt ominous today. It summoned the graduates to an impromptu meeting at the assembly point.

A hush fell over the gathering, heavier than the morning mist clinging to the nearby hills. Even the usually boisterous graduates were subdued. A senior member of the invited esteemed guest elders, his weathered face a map of past hardships, stepped forward.

"Mwacha,◈ he greeted them, good morning. "Aa," we are good the initiates replied in unison, their harmonised response reverberating into the Yatta plateau. "My name is Munyambu wa Weu,◈ he introduced himself with a firm voice. *Munyambu wa Weu*, which in Kamba means the lion of the wilderness, is a name that resonated with a low murmur of recognition among the crowd. As the murmurs grew, Munyambu raised his hand, calling for silence. The initiates knew him well as a highly respected beekeeper.

"This morning," he began, his voice heavy, "we awoke to a breathtaking view of the mountains. A gift from the Divine One, wouldn't you agree?" Munyambu digressed to break the ice. Heads bobbed nervously; the question felt oddly placed, a jarring note in the tense atmosphere. "Let us be grateful," Munyambu continued, ignoring their uneasiness, his voice dropping to a sombre tone, "for life is a fleeting flame."

"It is with a heavy heart that I share news delivered this morning by the village crier," he paused, letting the silence stretch, thick with anticipation, "Yatta Plateau's most beloved fig tree has fallen." The announcement hung in the air, a cryptic message that sent a jolt through the graduates.

In Kamba tradition, a falling fig tree isn't just about agriculture; it's a coded whisper of death, a euphemism for the passing of someone revered. But who? Their minds raced, piecing together the unsettling events: the interrupted ceremony, Benjo's disappearance, the unsettling absence of his respected grandmother at the event. A wave of shock and sorrow washed over them as the truth dawned: the beloved fig tree that had fallen was none other than Benjo's grandmother, a pillar of their community.

Disbelief and sorrow hung heavy in the air as news of Sosh's passing spread. Murmurs of shock and denial rippled through the audience. Sosh had been a constant presence in their lives, a pillar of strength and leadership. Her absence felt like a chasm opening at their feet.

Mr Munyambu, a respected lawmaker, a member of the clan council of elders, and guest of honour, allowed a moment of solemn silence to settle. He wanted them to truly understand the gravity of the situation – the loss of Yatta district's most decorated living freedom fighter.

Then, with a heavy heart, Munyambu revealed the fallen fig tree, the symbolic announcement of Sosh's passing. Sosh, a woman of immense virtue and a cherished daughter of the Aombe clan, was one of the greatest warriors Yatta had ever known. She had never lost a battle in her illustrious military career. Until now. Sadly, Sosh succumbed the previous night after a protracted battle with pneumonia. The relentless infection ultimately caused complications that led to kidney, liver, and heart] failure.

The silence that followed wasn't just one of mourning, but also a stark reminder. Death, a universal truth, could touch anyone, regardless of social standing or past victories. Even the most decorated heroes were not invincible.

The news hit them like a physical blow. Rachel, Benjo's classmate and fierce competitor during the Kwīvana challenge, crumbled to the ground, overcome with grief and faintness. A counsellor rushed to her side, swiftly transporting her to the recovery quarters for first aid.

Munyambu, his voice tinged with sadness, began with a Kamba proverb: "Death leaves a scar in the heart no one can heal, but love leaves us memories no one can steal." A somber understanding settled over the audience. Even Yatta's most formidable warrior couldn't escape this universal truth. Sosh, despite a lifetime of victories, was defeated in the shortest battle of her life.

Sosh's passing was a heavy blow, but Munyambu's words also offered solace. He reminded them of her remarkable legacy: the Sosh Educational Foundation, which had transformed countless lives. Many disadvantaged young men and women, thanks to Sosh's vision, had received a quality education, paving the way for successful careers. Countless girls bore her name, a testament to her heroism and widespread fame. Sosh's memory wouldn't simply endure; her spirit would inspire generations to come.

Despite the jarring intrusion of the clan emissary who stormed into Mr Mwaiki's compound earlier, Benjo found himself escorted home by a man transformed. The emissary, now the picture of politeness, was the most courteous human being Benjo had ever encountered. He kept Benjo engaged with a constant stream of frivolous banter, a transparent attempt to distract the young graduate from dwelling on the growing unease and unanswered questions swirling in his mind.

When Benjo finally arrived home, a knot of apprehension tightened in his stomach. His grandmother's courtyard overflowed with people, their faces etched with solemnity, a sight that honestly unsettled him, but did little to surprise him given the series of unsettling events since morning. A whirlwind of emotions – confusion, fear, and a gnawing worry – swirled within him. He felt numb, as if in a dream, adrift in a sea of uncertainty.

Looking back, Benjo would understand this experience as a state of shock, a period where his body moved on autopilot while his mind grappled with the unanswered questions swirling around him. He began to appreciate, in retrospect, the calming effect of the emissary's badinage on their way home. The lighthearted banter, though seemingly out of place, had unknowingly provided a temporary distraction from the growing turmoil within him.

As Benjo reached his mother's house, he was greeted with open arms by his beloved Aunt Tei, Minto's elder sister, whose name, meaning "one who is exceedingly kind," perfectly reflected her nature. Under the circumstances, there couldn't have been a better person to welcome him.

Overcome with emotion, Minto sat on her bed within the small, curtained area. However, as the saying goes, one loyal friend is worth ten thousand relatives. Minto was fortunate to have two of her closest friends by her side. Benjo's arrival was another boost to her spirits, helping her navigate her grief.

It had been exactly one week since Benjo's hasty departure from home in the dead of night, accompanied by his father and godfather for the mandatory circumcision ceremony. Despite the unceremonial departure from the circumcision event, Benjo felt a wave of relief wash over him as he returned to the familiar comfort of his mother's home and the embrace of his family. However, nothing had prepared him to face the confronting sombre funeral dirges that greeted him upon his arrival.

The abrupt end of Benjo's rite of passage due to his grandmother's passing left him in a strange limbo. Though back in the familiar embrace of his mother's compound, Kamba customs presented a new hurdle. Newly circumcised young men like Benjo were forbidden physical contact with their mothers, aunties, sister and female cousins, a stark contrast to the playful wrestling they shared just a week prior during the harvest feast. A simple hug, once freely offered and received, was now off-limits. Society recognized Benjo's new status as an adult, and the customary greeting of a silent bow replaced the warmth of physical touch. Despite the discomfort, the presence of familiar faces, including his mother's relatives and confidantes, offered a sense of solace during this grim time.

If it weren't for his grandmother's passing, Benjo would have returned a hero. The circumcision ceremony, a crucial rite of passage marking the transition to adulthood, would have culminated in a grand homecoming party. Elegantly celebrated, it was every young man's dream to return with pride – a rapturous reception, wild celebrations, and personal gifts from family, symbolizing their new status. But this once-in-a-lifetime event, impossible to replicate, was stolen by circumstance.

Grief clouded Benjo's judgment. In his youthful disappointment, he placed the blame on Sosh for the lost celebration. He naively believed she could have held out longer. Sadly, Sosh was nowhere to explain the situation, for as the saying goes, "dead people tell no tales".

Traditionally, in Benjo's clan, an elite troupe of dancers would meet a returning graduate more than two kilometres away from their home village. This troupe would put on a display of pomp, song, and dance to ceremoniously welcome the newly graduated adult back to their father's compound. The graduate, adorned in ceremonial regalia, symbolized their successful transition into adulthood. As they journeyed home, they would be showered with gifts ranging from tools and weapons to live animals and ornaments. They were the village knight, resplendent in shining armour.

Sadly, Benjo's homecoming was a stark contrast to the usual celebratory tradition. Having travelled back from the circumcision ceremony in a neighbouring village, he encountered a deafeningly sombre mood back home. The atmosphere was heavy with grimness, punctuated by a keening cacophony of hopelessness. It was as if some angels of disquiet had disrupted his return. Disappointed and let down by the absence of the customary celebrations, Benjo resigned himself to the situation, accepting that it was what it was.

Benjo's aunts, hesitant to break the news, tiptoed around the subject of Sosh's passing, hoping to prepare him for the grieving process with tact and sensitivity. However, no amount of foot-dragging was going to remove the burden of breaking the news to Benjo. Eventually, Aunt Tei, known for her gentle wisdom, gathered enough courage and took it upon herself to reveal the full story of Sosh's tragic demise.

Like an espionage agent debriefing their boss, Tei skirted around the key message and began by recounting the night before the pre-circumcision Kilumi dance. She narrated how Sosh, their beloved grandmother, had suddenly fallen ill with pneumonia. She described Sosh's brave fight against the relentless coughing, fever, chills, and difficulty breathing, and spoke of the village medics' valiant efforts to save her life, before sadly noting that Sosh had succumbed to respiratory distress two days ago.

The news slammed into Benjo's young soul like a tidal wave. Devastated, he found his mind reeling and his limbs numb. This was the first time since the suspicious events of Sosh's demise started milling around that Benjo completely unravelled emotionally. He felt as though he had been struck by a blunt object, sending him into a coma, only to wake up with a blank mind.

As Benjo wrestled with the loss of his beloved Grandma Sosh, his aunts offered unwavering support—an emotional first aid of sorts. They had been patient listeners all along, offering words of comfort and wisdom as Benjo grappled with his fears and anxieties. Aunt Tei, a pillar of strength, provided a healing sanctuary for him. With her calm demeanour, akin to the serenity of a millpond, and the unwavering patience of a dove, she allowed Benjo to express his feelings and ask questions without judging his intentions. Like a professional counsellor, Tei knew that the most important help you can offer is a willing ear, allowing the bereaved person to talk and express their grief in whatever way they need. This may include crying, angry outbursts, screaming, laughing, expressions of guilt or regret, or engaging in activities that reduce their stress, such as walking or gardening.

Sometimes things get worse before they get better. As minutes passed into hours, Benjo began to grapple with the unresolvable truth of his grandmother's passing. Aunt Tei, a gifted, if not natural, mind reader, saw the unanswered questions in Benjo's young mind about where people go when they die. Without being asked, she explained to Benjo and those present the concept of Zamani, a heavenly abode where Sosh would ascend to continue watching over them. A heavy silence descended upon the room as Benjo processed this new reality. Death, he concluded, was an inevitable part of life, irreversible and final. The crushing realization hit him like a ton of bricks. A hot lump rose in his throat, choking him with unshed tears. He remembered the first tenet from a recent lesson at his circumcision initiation ceremony: a man doesn't cry. Stifling his emotions, he forced a stoic facade.

After a long, heavy silence, Aunt Tei, her voice laced with compassion, finally spoke. 'Death,' she said gently, 'is not something to be feared, but a natural part of the cycle of life. It reminds us to cherish every moment with our loved ones, for one day they will be gone.' Her words resonated deeply with everyone present, leaving an imprint on their hearts and minds. Benjo felt a gradual sense of peace wash over him as he contemplated her message. Death wasn't something to fear, but a reminder to embrace life fully and appreciate each precious moment.

Aunt Tei further explained that nobody leaves this world alive; in which case, human death is not a tragedy but a rite of passage into a better life. From that point on, Benjo's journey through grief, while marked by initial shock and stoicism, revealed an underlying strength that surprised even the adults. He found solace in Aunt Tei's unwavering support and wise words. Her guidance and comfort proved invaluable during this challenging time.

To escape the suffocating silence within the house, Benjo decided to wander the courtyard. The murmur of conversations offered a welcome distraction, a chance to lose himself in the world outside his grief. He drifted towards a group of men huddled under the shade of a sprawling acacia tree.

As he neared, the deep, resonating voice of a wise, grey-haired old man filled his ears. The man spoke of premonitions, a sixth sense gifted to some elders, allowing them to foresee their own passing. These wise souls ensured their affairs were settled well in advance, making their wishes known on matters of inheritance and burial.

A jolt ran through Benjo. The elder's words echoed Aunt Tei's explanation of Zamani. According to Kamba beliefs, Zamani is a place of peace and rest for ancestral spirits. He inched closer to listen, feigning nonchalance as the man continued.

"Sosh," the elder proclaimed, his voice carrying the weight of experience, "was one such soul. She embraced the inevitable with grace, uttering these very words before her passing: 'Having fulfilled my purpose on earth, I graciously accept the invitation to join my ancestors in the realm of eternity."

Benjo's breath hitched. Sosh's voice, strong and resolute, echoed in his mind. He envied the old man who had the rare opportunity to hear the last words uttered by Sosh. He wished he had the chance to talk to Sosh one more time. He could have asked her to postpone dying until he completed his initiation honours, which he deserved.

The old man continued to weave tales steeped in Kamba tradition, a treasure trove of wisdom waiting to be unearthed. Benjo felt a pang of shame – how much about his heritage did he truly understand? And the lost opportunities now that Sosh was dead. However, a newfound determination sparked within him. He resolved to tap into this wellspring of knowledge, to seek out the elders, and learn from their stories.

Benjo navigated the bustling crowd, his ears pricked for snippets of conversation. A gaggle of elderly women huddled around a sprightly old crone, their faces lit with amusement. Intrigued, Benjo sidled closer, catching the tail end of a folktale about the burial customs for unmarried individuals in Kamba society. Apparently, they were laid to rest at the fringes of the homestead, a tradition believed to ward off misfortune from the living, especially those seen as the community's driving force—the unmarried youth.

The tale concluded with the old woman effusively praising Sosh, declaring her the greatest matriarch to ever grace not just the Yatta district, but all of Kenya. Benjo, careful not to betray his presence, averted his gaze and moved on.

Further ahead, he stumbled upon another gathering, a circle of middle-aged men engaged in a lively discussion. The topic, as Benjo inched closer, piqued his interest: mistaken identities during wartime burials. Feigning the need to adjust his shoelace, he crouched low, eavesdropping intently. His deliberate efforts to stay out of sight were a strategy to listen to stories from the mature age group, which would otherwise be put on hold temporarily if the adults noticed a child's presence in their midst.

The speaker, a man with a weathered face etched with experience, explained the intricate procedures followed if a fallen warrior's body was mistakenly buried elsewhere. The elders would assemble a team to exhume the misplaced corpse, replacing it with a live sheep or a banana stem if a sheep was not locally available. Additionally, the rightful family would be required to perform a ng'ondu ritual—a cleansing ceremony—to purify their kin's spirit before the proper reburial.

Another elder chimed in, adding that these meticulous customs were deeply rooted in the community's belief system. They ensured respect and protection for the departed warriors' spirits. The ng'ondu ritual, he emphasized, served as a powerful symbol of the community's reverence for their ancestors and their commitment to maintaining a harmonious balance with the spirit world.

After enduring a series of unsettling tales, Benjo sought solace within his grandmother's house, a place that now felt strangely unfamiliar without her presence. As he approached, the hushed murmur of voices alerted him to a gathering. Peeking inside, he saw the clan council of elders and family representatives engrossed in planning Sosh's burial.

One agenda item particularly piqued his curiosity: Sosh's attire. The chair of the council announced that Sosh would be buried in a full business suit and tie. A stifled chuckle escaped Benjo's lips. The image of Sosh, who had always loathed formal wear, in a suit did seem rather comical. Yet, the custom held a grain of truth: tradition often dictates attire in death, regardless of personal preference. Another council elder proposed that Sosh be buried in full military combat gear, but the idea was overruled by the council because the Kenya Land and Freedom Army predated the post-independence Kenya Defence Forces and therefore it was illegal to do so. The proposal by the chair carried the day.

Traditionally, young men like Benjo would not be allowed at such meetings, especially for a prominent figure like Sosh. However, Sosh, recognising Benjo's potential, had granted him a rare exemption. She had appointed him as an apprentice on the council while she was still alive, and even designated him as her official heir on her deathbed. In any case, Sosh was known to circumvent common norms with impunity.

Sosh's choice of Benjo as her heir apparent stemmed from her deep disappointment with her son Wasa. She viewed Wasa as unreliable and out of touch with reality, unfit to carry on her legacy. She often spoke of him with a heavy heart, once even remarking that a strong daughter-in-law could replace a disappointing son. According to Kamba customs, such utterances by an elder of Sosh's status amounted to a formal curse, and many people believed that many of Wasa's problems in life were a result of this curse.

In contrast, Benjo was a prodigy. His astute wisdom and remarkable memory impressed even the most seasoned elders. Sosh saw in him a reflection of herself, a kindred spirit with the potential to lead.

Despite his young age, Sosh was confident he would carry her torch with the same dedication and passion she had displayed throughout her life. Choosing her successor wasn't a decision Sosh took lightly. She understood the weight of her legacy and the impact it would have on her family's future. In Benjo, she had found the ideal candidate to ensure her vision would endure.

The dignified proceedings surrounding Sosh's burial unfolded seamlessly. The outpouring of honour and respect humbled Benjo, leaving him with a newfound reverence for life. The clan council declared a week of mourning, punctuated by a grand ceremony befitting a leader. The sheer number of volunteers offering to cover the costs overwhelmed the committee chairperson, who reluctantly declined some offers amidst heartfelt protests. To illustrate, over one thousand heads of cows were donated for the feast, well above the land carrying capacity of Sosh's property, thus forcing the chairperson to reduce the number of donated animals to a manageable number. The committee used a formula of 'first come, first served' to accept the donations, with a bias towards higher social rankings in society. A donation of fifty bulls by the clan leaders from Banda Salama was accepted due to their high social ranking in the community, even though the pledge came later than others.

According to Kamba traditions, a person of Sosh's standing in society deserved celebration, not just mourning. She was the epitome of a life well-lived and therefore a role model to be emulated. Honouring a hero's life, the Kamba people believed, would bring blessings not just to those attending, but to the entire community, ensuring longevity. This grand burial served not only as a tribute to Sosh but as an investment in the future prosperity of the living.

The guest list for the funeral was a prestigious one, a veritable who's who of the Yatta district, perhaps even Kenya. Dignitaries from all walks of life received invitations - government officials rubbed shoulders with religious leaders, and trade unionists mingled with military personnel. The Yatta District Commissioner himself served as the master of ceremonies, ably assisted by the chairperson of the National Ex-Freedom Fighters Organisation.

Exhausted from the long day, Benjo retreated to his quarters, yearning for sleep. Yet, his mind churned with the devastating loss of Sosh, leaving him utterly spent. Despite his fatigue, the chilling prospect of nightmares filled with echoing sounds kept him awake.

Memories of Sosh flooded his mind like a vivid film reel, bitter-sweet and painful. He felt like a detached observer in his own life. How could someone so strong, so indomitable as Sosh, be snatched away by fate's cruel hand? The once vibrant homestead now seemed to reflect his own turmoil. The previously clear blue sky was now ob-scured by oppressive grey clouds, the sun a distant memory. A suf-focating emptiness hung in the air, mirroring the gaping hole left by Sosh's absence. As the sole grandchild burdened with her passing, a deep, aching sadness welled up within him. Why did it have to be him?

Then, Sosh's wise words echoed in his mind: "A sweet tree doesn't yield many fruits, and a large family often disintegrates after the loss of its patriarch." It was a simple yet profound explanation for his po-sition as Sosh's only grandchild. He clung to this knowledge, finding solace in the fact that he was the cherished fruit of a sweet tree, loved by his grandmother until her very last breath.

A solemn vow formed in Benjo's heart. He wouldn't let Sosh's legacy crumble under his watch. After much reflection, he found peace in the acceptance that life wasn't always a bed of roses. He re-called a Kamba proverb: "When a fig tree falls, it leaves behind the sycamore tree." This resonated deeply. It spoke of his inherent respon-sibility to step up as Sosh's rightful successor. He became resolute in his determination to uphold her legacy, ensuring his family's contin-ued prosperity and unity in the face of any challenge.

Progressively, Benjo began to hear voices in his head. "We all love the beginning of a story, but nobody wants to know how it ends. In-stinctively, we look away when the moment arrives." Benjo thought he was losing his mind and wiped his eyes to confirm he was okay.

But his eyes were heavy and sore with double vision. The voice in his head continued, "I love the end when it all comes a cropper and the ensuing hopelessness of inertia. Rest in peace, champion." Exhausted, Benjo dozed off.

www.ingramcontent.com/pod-product-compliance
Lightning Source LLC
Chambersburg PA
CBHW020507120726
47904CB00003B/730